JK COOPER

Summary: The bond is broken. Ascension is coming. The Advent is rising. And the enemy is winning.

An ill-prepared world crumbles before the power of the Alpha Prime and his ascending Summer Omega daughter. Presidents and kings bow before Mareus as Advent pack numbers grow. In the wake of their severed bond, Kale and Shelby struggle to find meaning in their changed relationship—but it takes more than love to repair it. The keys of Ascension are held by the magical races that have found refuge on Earth, and the third key has been identified—but it is held by a mistrusting and often devious race. In order to claim it, Shelby and Athena race against each other on a journey that brings them face to face with a darkness never anticipated, the very darkness that destroyed Alsvoira.

Long held prophecies and beliefs are shattered as the true meaning of the Advent begins to take shape. Earth may always have been a temporary refuge.

Paperback Edition

ISBN-13: 978-1-939993-82-3
ISBN-10: 1-939993-82-2

DEDICATION

To Bauer, our massive Akita,
who keeps our feet warm while we dream up new stories.

THE SUMMER OMEGA SERIES
ADVENT

PROLOGUE

A thena watched the Feral pace back and forth inside the silver-coated steel cage as the sun set on Copeland Manor. The pack had taken to calling the manor Advent Estates. *A little much*, Athena thought, but she couldn't squash their enthusiasm. They had salvaged everything useful from the mansion, the grounds, and the Hunter helicopter, including three small cages meant to hold individual Lycans in cramped, painful quarters during transport.

Athena had forced several captive humans to combine the cages into one larger enclosure in the Copeland gym at Mareus's request, wrapping bars together with silver wire. She let three of those humans run free, or as free as the walled-in grounds allowed. A poor excuse for sport, but it was all she had to work with. *Difficult to enjoy that type of hunt.*

She'd been loping after a particularly fast woman with several of the recently turned in tow—teasing her prey, really—when her father's Feral guest arrived. It was anxious, angry, and eager to get out, though that eagerness had spiked twenty minutes earlier when it began beating itself repeatedly against the one side of the cage.

Athena wrinkled her nose at the acrid scent the accursed metal always left in the air when it touched Lycan flesh, somewhere between burnt hair, smelting steel, and wet dog.

"Stop that!" Athena punched one of the bars, ignoring the shock of pain as her skin hit silver along with her own unique tang of burnt wolf that she added to his.

It snarled at her and resumed trying to crack its skull open on the silver-treated bars, sending an almost gong-like tone reverberating down the marbled corridors of the manor. Athena stared hard at the creature, admiring the dark gray coat that lightened to white at the tips and letting feelings flow through her as she brought her double-bladed scythe in and out of existence. The snath came and went from reality with a small humming pop that only she could hear due to her Lycan-enhanced senses. The dark wood of the handle—the color of black ash—vibrated at a molecular level, tickling her palm as it crawled with warmth and life. Locking her eyes with the Feral's, she began to peer into its mind, peeling away its layers of defense.

She recoiled at the madness she found below the surface of the Feral's mind just as she felt her father's arrival next to her. "I thought you said he was your friend?"

Mareus growled. "He was . . . is." Athena could sense him conversing with Viersin, getting memories and facts straight as he spoke. She could also sense his pain and frustration at his hand that wasn't healing as fast as it should. "But Ptyas wasn't the most stable wolf to begin with. He was a Mystic. Seeing so much of the future makes it hard to remain sane, I am told."

"No kidding. I've listened to you read from your old book plenty. Ramblings and riddles. The Mystics were off their rockers and then some." Athena smiled sweetly at her father, but secretly enjoyed the jab of anger that went through him at the mention of the *Isluxua*, which Otto failed to recover from Sadie. Athena couldn't say she felt any sorrow for the loss of her father's lieutenant.

"Do not speak of the sacred text so lightly, Daughter. It has proven accurate and helped you unlock the first key." His tone felt cold and dangerous. Mareus turned back to the Feral.

"What is wrong with him?" Athena asked, still staring at the Feral. "I sense . . . derangement."

"Ptyas chose a comatose madwoman as his bond."

"You let him choose such weakness?" Athena ran one of her magical blades along the bars, setting off a spray of purple sparks that managed to get the Feral's attention, sending it to one corner where it glared at her with suspicious eyes.

"Careful, Daughter. It sounds very much like you're questioning my decisions." He rubbed at the curled fingers of his left hand that refused to fully extend, even as the scars healed. Athena felt her father's cold anger flare hotter.

She held the scythe up to her eyes, let it vanish, and bowed. "Only curious."

Mareus sighed. "Kieren served as Ptyas's scribe for decades. She was damaged, mentally and physically, during one of the early conflicts. He loved her, wanted to heal her. I allowed it because it suited my needs, but he was not the same after. I sent him through the crystal portal not long after. The Advent on Alsvoira had been lost by that time, and I knew I would need Ptyas's knowledge again. As it turns out, I need both his knowledge *and* him, and so do you."

Athena turned back to the mad Feral. "He doesn't seem to remember you." She dug deeper into him. "He's torn apart inside. His human scribe never gave him autonomy. Kieren is deep, broken, lost." *How would that be, both of them bystanders in this body?* "Any semblance of control Ptyas has is mostly instinct, and what he managed to force through to the surface." *Impressive.* She looked up, eyes wide. "Okay, he's stronger than he looks. It's a miracle he's managed to keep them both alive."

"I choose my followers wisely, Daughter. The second key lies with him."

"But how do we get consent from that schism of a Lycan? Neither can give it. Can't we find another Feral?"

Mareus shook his head. "The *Isluxua* was clear."

She rolled her eyes with a short laugh, summoned her scythe again, and ran the blades across another bar, letting the metal ring like vibrating crystal.

He looked at her. "As clear as it gets."

She smiled and said nothing.

"You need a Feral Mystic willing to give you consent. I brought only one Mystic to my side on Alsvoira. I do not know how many Mystics made it through the gate. I doubt many went Feral. He must be yoked to you. You must make him whole, if you wish to unlock the second key."

Athena suddenly understood. "You want me to break the bond between human and Immortal Wolf? Is that even possible?"

"I wouldn't have thought so once, but I feel nothing left of the union between my parents or their latest incarnations. You did well severing that link." Mareus rapped one of the bars, like one would a fish bowl. His knuckles singed at the contact, but Athena barely felt him flinch from the pain through the pack link. "Do not fear, Ptyas," Mareus said. "We will bring you back to us." He crossed his arms. "Do it, Athena."

"Here goes . . . something." She dismissed her scythe and reached out with her senses to the ley lines beneath Copeland Manor. They still oozed magic from the wounds she'd made in them a week earlier. Much like a leech that leaves behind chemicals that prevent coagulation, Athena had left a mark in them that gave her easy access. She would need the extra strength.

She poured her Omega magic into the Feral, infusing it into the slackened bond she felt inside him. He resisted. She poured ease into his mind. *We will take care of your Kieren, Ptyas. Let her go.*

The bond flexed, but it was no fragile thing. It bounced back. Athena pushed again, and it bent further, but snapped back with a jolt that rocked her with pain. Apparently, this union was not one the Goddess intended to be broken. Athena gritted her teeth, unwilling to spend weeks working on this bond like she had with Shelby and Kale. "I need to be closer to him. Open the door."

"Are you sure?" Mareus held a protective hand out in front of her, three fingers curled inward. "He can be unpredictable."

"I can take care of myself." Athena glanced down at his hand. He tucked it back beneath his arm.

Reluctantly, Mareus slid the bolt free from the lock and the cage swung open. Athena stepped into the center of the opening, daring the Feral to go through her for its escape. She closed her eyes and tapped deeper into the magic beneath them, pulling more than she could hold. Her scythe reappeared in her hand, purple light flaring from it. When she opened her eyes once more, they also glowed a deep violet, reflecting back at her from a dozen silver bars, wisps of the color floating from them like tinted smoke.

The Feral cowered away from her.

"It's time to let go, Ptyas." She lifted her scythe above her head and swung it at the broken creature.

"Athena, no!" Mareus growled behind her, his tone pushing into her and demanding obedience.

She ignored his Call, despite how much her body wanted to obey. *This must be done.* The dual blades of her scythe burned through air, fur, flesh, and bonds. She could feel her father shift, come crashing through the cage to stop her, but she stepped to the side to let him see the result of her attack. He stopped.

In the corner of the cage sat one Immortal Wolf and one thin, wild-eyed woman with matted and soiled hair. The woman began sobbing. Ptyas stood over Kieren, protective, but also bowed to Viersin, immediately joining the pack link. He looked down at the woman who clung to his fur and spoke to Mareus and Athena through the pack link. *You will get her the help she needs?*

Yes, old friend, I will, Mareus replied.

Viersin must swear it to me, Ptyas said.

Athena felt the presence of Viersin rise in the pack link as her father allowed his Immortal Wolf to surface briefly.

Kieren will be seen to, Ptyas, Viersin growled. *You need not doubt us.*

Ptyas lowered his massive head at the slight rebuke. *Then I consent.* He lunged forward and bit Athena on the thigh before she could react.

She screamed in rage and swung her scythe through the beast's neck, but the wolf was dead before her blades struck. Ptyas crumbled to the ground without a drop of blood falling from the gash, like an empty shell, the husk of a wolf that curled inward on itself much like Mareus's fingers.

"What?" But Athena fell to her knees as fire raced through her, remaking her from the inside out. It felt similar to the first time she'd shifted, but different, stronger, more violent. "What's happening?"

Mareus shifted, his face pale as he caught her in his arms. "Ptyas bonded with you. Five Rivers! I don't know what that will do to a Lycan. He was not an Omega. I . . . I do not know what this will do to you, Daughter."

She shuddered. "Will I keep the first key?"

Mareus blinked, then set his jaw. "You *must!*"

Athena felt the command of her Alpha in the growl of his last words, but also his trepidation, and then her link to him and the pack broke. The fire within her burned hotter as she screamed, but it turned into a howl as her body shifted without her control. She could taste her father's fear, not for her, but for the possible loss of her druid powers, the key, all the progress they had made. Her wolf felt larger, stronger, heavier than she was used to. Lethality. It coursed through her.

She looked up at her father through wolf eyes that saw the world in bright swaths of colors. The link to his pack reformed, but it felt different. Everything felt strange and new. She needed to see what Ptyas had done to her, *for* her, but Mareus blocked her escape from the cage.

"Wait," he said.

She dodged to the side and slashed at the bars. The thick metal shredded under her massive claws, her flesh sizzling on the silver. She pushed through the opening, wincing at the pain, but determined. Once free, she darted toward the far side of the gym. Her father bounded behind her in his wolf.

Stop, Daughter, go back to the cage until we know what this has done to you, Mareus said through the pack link.

I have to see for myself.

Very well, but do not attempt to leave the gym.

Keeping her thoughts to herself, she wondered, *Does he think I've gone mad? Or Feral? Have I?*

She slid to a halt in front of one of the massive mirrors that lined the wall, her claws destroying rubber and the tile beneath them. She gasped. She was far larger than she had ever been as a wolf, nearly matching her father's massive frame. Her wolf's aspect that she had been born with and Ptyas had blended, her black coat touched with streaks of gray and white, but the unique pattern on her side remained.

She shifted slowly, watching the transition in the mirror as muscle and bone snapped in and out of alignment to reconfigure into the human face and body she recognized. *That's a blessing. I half thought I'd have a beard or something.*

That isn't how it works. I do not have a human side, so only I, as an Immortal Wolf, become a part of you. It was the voice of Ptyas. *Speak the words to gain consent.*

"Um, he's talking in my head."

"You'll get used to the voice of another in your mind with time." Mareus half shifted at her side. "Mostly." He took a deep breath, stared at her hard, and voiced his fears. "Do you remain an Omega? Is the key intact?"

Athena closed her eyes, poured ease and acceptance into her father. She felt him calm at her mental touch. *That's still there.* She opened her eyes, lifted a hand, and summoned her new weapon. She smiled as the wicked scythe appeared. "Yes, to both."

He sighed in relief. "You are another First. The first Lycan to bond with an Immortal Wolf. There is power in a First."

The words came to her. "I, Athena-mit-Ptyas, petition the second key from you, Ptyas, Mystic of the Goddess, Keeper of the Scrolls."

I consent.

Her smile turned to a grin as a golden glow surrounded them. "And I have the second key." Her mouth opened wide as a thrill rushed through her, and she shuddered, this time in exquisite delight. "I . . . I can feel it." The glow softened to leave behind sleek jet-black armor that fit her human frame perfectly.

Her gaze slid along the armor, inky metal far lighter than it looked. She found no hammer marks, welds, or creases, each piece beyond smooth. Crimson lines pulsed with a soft light, like lava beneath the surface. These lines met at the center of her breastplate, where they coalesced into the side profile of a wolf clad in a helm with goat horns. Athena admired the sharp spikes that protruded from the pauldrons over her shoulders and from the gauntlets at her knuckles. Her helm hugged her face and scalp and indeed had two twisted goat horns on each side.

She brought her scythe into existence and laughed at the demonic presence she emanated in her black and red armor.

"Your eyes no longer burn amber, my daughter," Mareus said, "but a haunting violet, like lightning."

"It is the storm inside me you see, Father."

Looking to Mareus, Athena noted that he wore similar armor. His molded to him perfectly as well, even though he was still half-human and half-wolf.

She shifted, watching the armor morph with her in the mirror, feeling it match her form throughout the process from human to wolf. *Oh, this is going to be fun.*

I'm glad the Fae armor pleases you, Ptyas said.

On the other hand, having a voice in my head, besides my own, is going to take some getting used to.

Theophinus stood deep in the tunnels of Underhill before a shimmering gash in reality, one of the four demon gates that had appeared after the death of the Goddess closed her crystal portal forever. Three linked back to Alsvoira, while the last, and most recent, came from a world the demon king had conquered before Alsvoira's fall. The Fae guarded these gates and prepared for the next attempt to overtake Earth. This tear in reality hovered a foot above the damp cavern floor deep beneath a section of China, but linked to Underhill by powerful magic. The edges of the rift sparking with electricity that helped illuminate delicate, lace-like stalactites.

The portal Theo guarded was known as The Blood Gate, partly for the crimson color along its edge, partly for the coppery smell it leaked into the cavern, and partly for the nature of the creatures on that far side: blood-red parasites.

He coated his side of the portal with entropy magic that would disrupt molecular bonds, even though Theo wasn't sure demons existed. *Bedtime stories to scare young Fae halflings into subservience.* He'd guarded this gate for a hundred years and had never seen a demon. "I'm bored. Do you think we could get Netflix down here?"

His companion guard grunted in annoyance. Alecsion had been born without a sense of humor and with an intense loyalty to the fairer half of his race. Despite being his twin brother, Alec was Theo's opposite in every way, other than appearance.

Theo ran a finger over the pointed tip of one ear. Sometimes he wished he had qualified for the Changeling Program, but infants placed in human homes had to appear entirely human. *Can't glamour as a baby. My eyes and ears gave me away.* With a thought, the point rounded, feeling human beneath his fingertip as the magic took hold, warm against his skin. He'd learned to control illusions when he was thirteen, two years before his brother.

Not that that means much. I'm still a halfling in a Fae world, stuck guarding a gateway we should have abandoned two centuries ago. "Hey, Alec, do you think there are any left over there? Or did we kill them all as they tried to come through one by one? Are we guarding what amounts to an empty hole?"

His twin stood at attention on the far side, a fuzzy mirror image of himself through the shimmering light. He didn't answer, just stared intently ahead, focused on the endless mission.

"We're like bookends or one weird sandwich, with a magical gateway to nowhere as the bologna in the middle." Theo poked at the portal with the titanium tip of an arrow, setting off blood-red sparks. "There's seriously some good things on Netflix right now, brother. What say you?"

But Alec didn't get a chance to answer as a massive hand shot out of the portal to grasp Theo's arrow. Instinct and decades of training kicked in.

Theo dropped the arrow, took a step back, pulled another arrow from his quiver, and sent it flying in one smooth motion. Titanium sunk through the middle of the hand. The first arrow clattered to the stone ground as the hand retreated behind the shimmering portal.

"Did you see that? My magic did nothing to stop it."

Alec nodded, his own bow at the ready with an arrow nocked. "It will try again."

Theo's heart raced. "I don't know. I think I taught it a less—"

But a twisted face forced its way through the portal on Alec's side while three hands emerged on Theo's, one still impaled by his arrow. More Fae arrows flew, the metal, wood, and fletching treated with magic to make them true and lethal. The arrowheads themselves were forged in the sentient fires of Mount Estorathi, giving the titanium an ability to intuit Theo's will as he fired, but the bony black spines that dotted the thick crimson skin of the demons sent half of Theo's arrows bouncing off the emerging arms like rocks skipping across water.

Through the fuzzy light of the portal, Theo could see Alec fared better. One small demon, the size of a well-fed cat, fell dead at his feet.

The face that followed would haunt Theo's nightmares for as long as his half-immortal life would last. He took another step back and nocked another arrow, speaking the words he had been taught in the guttural tongue.

"Hesska thrughahuta nes tofkaa fesk net!" He'd been told it was a warning in the demon tongue to return to its own world or face death. Theo wasn't sure if he'd pronounced it right or if the demon just didn't care. It grinned with black teeth that oozed a green liquid and slid farther into Earth's plane of existence, then stopped as three bulky shoulders nudged the edges of the portal, blocking Theo's view of his brother.

Theo laughed and let his arrow dip. "You're too fat. Did someone eat too much nasty green honey before trying to invade another dimension? Who's a chubby wittle devil? You are!"

"Don't taunt the demon," Alec scolded him as more of his arrows whistled into the breach on his side.

"What? It's not like it understands me."

The demon growled a thunderous noise that shattered irreplaceable stalactites, pelting Theo with bits of stone.

"Sounds like it does," Alec yelled.

Theo grimaced and began shooting arrows at the beast's eyes, trying to end this while the creature remained trapped by its own girth. He learned the hard way that demon eyes are made of some kind of stone. His arrows chipped one, but the demon simply rolled the damage away to fix perfectly smooth smoldering black crystals on him once more.

"These things are tough."

"And so many. I'm running out of arrows."

"What?" Theo took a fraction of a second to glance below the portal. The view was blocked by half a dozen tiny red bodies. A swarm of demons. "I'll come help. Mine's still stuck."

Alec grunted in agreement, which concerned Theo who had expected his twin to command him to remain at his post. He planned to ignore that command anyway, so he began sidestepping around the gate, an arrow trained on the fat demon.

The demon grinned again, put its three hands on the sparking edge of the portal, and pushed with a bellow that cracked more precious stone. The portal widened.

"Living fire!" Theo swore.

"Language."

"Sorry, but my help will have to wait. You good?"

A positive grunt.

Theo slipped back around to his side of the Blood Gate as the demon forced its way into their world—rhino thick skin, black boney protrusions, impossible muscles, and all. He sent arrow after arrow into the same spot on the demon's chest, hoping an actual heart was beating beneath its well-armored rib cage. Titanium bounced off with sparks, wood splintered, but a few slipped through.

The demon screamed.

Theo had to put his hands over his ears at the sound, the rumble shaking the floor and messing with his footing. He staggered to a wall, leaned against it, and managed to nock another arrow. He trained his aim on a hole that belched spurts of fire where his last arrow had found its way through.

"Please," he whispered, sending his desires into the sentient arrowhead. When he could see nothing else but the target he desired, he let the arrow fly. Titanium slipped through flames. Something detonated inside the demon. Light burned through arteries and veins, illuminating crimson skin in streaks of orange. The monster collapsed, its head cracking the stone floor as it slammed onto the ground. Ugh, the stench the thing released as it died made him dry heave. Theo ran forward, collecting as many undamaged arrows as he could from the floor as he made his way around to the other side. For a brief moment, he wondered how he could sell this epic battle to Fortnite. It would make for a great season of the video game.

Alec waded in a nightmare of roiling bodies, some dying, some clawing their way over the corpses of the fallen. Claws, twisted faces, shredded black wings, and snarling tusks.

"Living fire! I thought mine was ugly."

Alec chuckled, which wasn't a great sign. He only did that when he was nervous or scared. Theo let loose a string of arrows as he eyed his twin. Orange blood mingled with the black and crimson viscera that clung to his body. *He's hurt.*

Theo sprinted along the edge of demon bodies, putting an arrow through anything that moved. He jumped over a stack of demon corpses to land next to Alec.

Theo pulled one of his last arrows and sent it flying at the silver bell high above them. It chimed and a string of chimes followed throughout the tunnels of Underhill. "Help is on its way, Brother."

Alec eyed the piles of demons. "I think . . ." His voice was weak. "I think that's all of them." His bow sagged, and he leaned into Theo, revealing the gash on his neck where one of the creatures had bitten through muscle, tendon, and major arteries. The veins had gone black around the wound.

Theo clutched his brother. "How are you still standing?"

Alec grunted. "Duty." More orange blood pumped out at the movement of his vocal cords. He slumped.

Theo helped him lay down, resting his head on the bloated and deformed body of a demon. "Shhh, don't talk." He tore a strip of silken cloth from his sleeve and pushed it against the wound.

Alec's eyes shot around violently. He coughed, splattering Theo with orange. His hand scrambled blindly for his bow. "Another. Duty."

Theo looked up. Sure enough, one demon pushed its way out of a pile, injured but not dead. It dragged itself toward a wall where water dribbled down gray stone, streaking bubbled lumps of sparkling material. "I don't care."

"Duty." Alec coughed again. His hand found an arrow, its fletching torn on one side. He lifted it to Theo.

Theo shook his head. "No. I'm not leaving you."

Alec pressed the arrow into Theo's hand. "Now."

Theo swore as he let go of his brother, slid the notch in the arrow against string, and pulled. The bowstring felt taut against his cheek and nose as he sighted in the escaping demon. "You and your stupid duty."

The arrow flew, but it curved to the left, bouncing off the stone curtain. The demon dodged right, its body vibrating as it lifted a talon to the wall. Theo cursed and found another arrow. In a flash, he poured his fury and will into the titanium forged arrowhead, nocked, pulled the string back until he heard the yew wood splinter slightly, and loosed the arrow. It flew true but slammed into the wall, lodging deep into the stone. Theo felt his forehead scrunch as he stared at where his target had only been seconds ago. The demon had vibrated through the stone to escape.

"Diffuser!" He gritted his teeth. "Fires, I should have known." Theo's hands shook as he lowered to his haunches, his sweaty head in the bloody palm of his hand. "I missed, Brother."

But Alec didn't answer, not even a grunt. Theo turned toward him, knowing what he would see before he saw it. His brother's eyes stared where the demon had vanished, but they saw nothing. Alec was gone.

Theophinus walked on a lush carpet of hand-stitched gold and scarlet leaves beneath an impossibly ornate roof, the illuminated paintings nearly lost in shadows several hundred feet above the living molten lights embedded in delicate pillars that didn't appear like they could support the air above them.

Theo always thought they resembled frozen spider silk or the finest lace. They even flowed and shifted in the gentle air currents of the room, but they also held the weight of an entire city, as the entropy that would have sent stone and earth crashing down, was shifted elsewhere. That's how much of Fae magic worked, increasing or decreasing entropy, but it had a cost in reverse somewhere else in the world. Consequence, the bane of magic. *Somewhere a bridge is eroding away faster than any engineer predicted, just to keep up our pretenses,* Theo sneered the thought.

He took the last few steps toward the queen of Seely Court, letting the sneer turn into a smile. Even with the bonds on his wrists he could still manage some mischief. Theo lifted his hands to his face and pulled a thread on his forearm, releasing the tiny moths and butterflies that made up his formal silver and green slacks, crisp shirt, and jacket. At the same time, he sent a new glamour over his skin, enjoying the tingling warmth of his magic taking hold.

His outfit dissolved, sending a cloud of tiny insects into the crowd, while jeans and a t-shirt with a human expletive implied in the emoji graphics took its place. Those Fae who weren't batting away butterflies gasped at the audacity of his attire, murmuring and swearing amongst themselves. He waved with his bound hands as the morning glory vines of his restraints kissed his wrists with soft, dewy, lazy petals.

I've never been all that popular anyway, especially with these snobs. Might as well give them what they expect. A ripple went through his last cloud of winged insects. The butterflies and moths lined up into a dazzling geometric pattern in the air, shimmering like a flag caught in sunlight. *That didn't last as long as I hoped.*

Queen Silphinaera stood next to her crystalline throne atop its golden dais with one slender hand held out. Did her every pose have to appear so sickeningly graceful? The living butterfly banner floated to the ceiling, broke into smaller, well-ordered groups and flew off to distant corners.

The room fell silent at this small display of her power. At least a hundred of upper-crust Fae bowed slightly toward the dais in deference as their queen sat with an effortless grace few Fae could mimic, and even fewer humans. Theo did not bow. Instead, he created an eyebrow piercing and a facial tattoo of morning glories to match his shackles, adding these to the illusion coating his body, his glamour.

Each Fae family was represented by a flower. Every nobleman and noblewoman in the room had some form of that flower on or near their person. Intricately stitched flowers graced silken pennants that hung from silver poles held by servants. Expensive recreations of flowers done in rare gemstones hung from silver threads around thin necks. A few of the actual flowers were braided into hair.

Theo tried to make note of the last ones. He liked the elegant simplicity. *Maybe they aren't all snobs.* One of those few was the queen herself, a morning glory peeking out of her hair above one pointed alabaster ear.

He placed a finger on his cheek, pulling down on the illusionary facial tattoo as he confronted the queen about the not-so-subtle use of their family flower as his handcuffs. "Is this really necessary?"

"Silence!" An officer of the court, a stiff elven woman in crisp fall colors sporting a sneezeweed on her collar, called him to order. She touched a bit of glass that dangled from her own wrist, and his bonds tightened.

The queen leaned forward on her crystalline throne as Will-o'-the-Wisps danced around her. She was a perfect nymph, all angular beauty, flawless skin, and green eyes two times larger than any human. She blinked at him. "You allowed a demon entry into this world when it was your duty to prevent just such occurrences."

All the rebellious bravado drained from Theo. "My brother was injured. I had to help him."

She nodded, a hint of loss in her eyes. "Was it your duty to help him?"

Fae rarely sweat, but the back of Theo's neck prickled with the idea of it. Fae were all about rules, even if the rules made no sense. "No."

"Did tending to his wounds aid in dispelling any demons?"

"No."

"Did he die anyway?"

Theo swallowed. "Yes."

"So, you neglected your duties to attempt something fruitless that put the world in danger?"

Theo swallowed his budding anger. "Yes."

"What do you have to say for your defense?"

"It was a small demon. And injured."

One edge of her lips quirked up, but one of her sons was dead. It wasn't the time for jokes.

Theo apologized. "Forgive me the levity. It is how I handle grief."

She waved a hand. "Forgiven." But she locked a hard look on

him. "For the levity only, mind you. Show us your crime." One of her wisps floated toward him, the fuzzy blue light hovering in front of his face with inhuman patience, a fragment of sentient fire from a world long lost.

He had feared she might do this, make him relive it. He resisted.

The officer touched the glass charm at her wrist again, without a verbal warning this time. The morning glory vines sprouted thorns as they tightened, magically enhanced to sear Fae skin.

Theo grunted, gave the woman from Sneezeweed a glare, and took hold of the wisp, grasping it between his bound hands and pulling it close like one would a lover before a kiss. He whispered the words that would give it access to his memories and let go. The room exploded in a flash of dazzling light.

The wisp played out the scene for all to see, projecting the cavern and all that transpired there into the air above their heads. Theo didn't watch, just listened to the court's reactions, gasping at his disrespect of the portal. Gasping louder when the demons appeared. Gasping loudest when he said he did not care about the escaping demon.

There was silence as the wisp drew back in the display and hovered to the queen's side. Theo hung his head in resignation.

The queen took a long breath before she continued. "Your crimes are many. Do you really not care about your duties or our laws?"

Theo lifted his bound hands and rubbed between his eyes with one. "Well . . . I do care most of the time, even though you change the laws often to integrate human vices or to suit your mood."

She nodded, a hint of pride in her eyes at his understanding of the law. "And have I changed *these* laws? Have I altered your duties?"

"No, but it doesn't matter." Again gasps. "I'd do it again." Theo tried hard not to roll his eyes as more gasps rolled through the crowd. *This is why I spend all my free time in the human world. The Fae are so over-the-top.* But he had to spend part of his life in Underhill, serving his duty guarding the gate and renewing his mark. All Fae had a birthmark in the shape of their house flower that faded each day away from their homeland on Earth. They had to touch Underhill soil or risk unpleasant consequences. *Nothing like a little madness, physical deformities, and pain to keep your subjects in line.* "My brother deserved someone with him in the end."

"So, you admit your neglect?" The queen's question sounded sad.

He shrugged. "I guess so. What will the punishment be this time, Mom?"

The officer shoved a silverwood staff into his gut. "There is no familiarity in the court!"

Theo fell to his knees as the wind rushed out of him. *What did I ever do to the Sneezeweeds?*

"You are only half Fae, so the punishment will be half as strict." The queen cocked her head to the side in an unnatural way. "Banishment."

Theo gasped with the rest of the court this time as he staggered back to his feet. That was not a normal punishment for any crime. "You call that *half* as strict?"

She gave a single, slow nod. "It is death to neglect duty. You know this. Did you think my blood in your veins could prevent that?"

Theo shook his head, even though he had thought exactly that. The Fae hadn't put anyone to death in his lifetime.

She gave him a half-smile. "I suppose I could send you to clean the ballywog tanks for a hundred years. Would you prefer that?"

Theo considered it, but knew he never could. He had an irrational fear of mud, one of his Fae inheritances. The thought of working with it for a hundred years, the filth spotting his clothes, touching his skin, or getting in his mouth, made him gag violently.

"How long will my banishment be?"

"For *all* time."

No one gasped. The room had gone dead silent. You could hear breathing and nothing more. She had just pronounced the worst possible judgement that could be passed upon their kind. Everyone stared at the queen, Fae faces a mix of horror and delight.

"What? Mom?" Theo dodged another strike from the staff. "That's insane!"

She smiled wider. "I know. It is, isn't it? So deliciously insane." She leaned forward again. "But I am also generous."

A few Fae sighed in relief. She would have stipulations attached to the banishment that could lighten the sentence.

"The world is in turmoil, but there are those who can heal it. I think you may be such a soul. You have never been good at being a Fae, but you may still serve your kind. Bring me the girl with green eyes that are sometimes gold and sometimes red without the aid of glamour. She will undo your banishment." The queen tented her long fingers. "Go. Your punishment is law."

Theo opened his mouth to argue, but it fell shut. He felt the wave of change roll through him and the other Fae of Seely Court as her voiced law took effect. There would be no changing her mind. There would be no help from other Fae. It was *law*.

The officer dug sharp nails into his arm and dragged him out of the courtroom, past the elven nymphs and pixies who looked on him with adoration, pity, and hints of love. Many Fae were drawn to impossible romances with tragic endings, which is what he appeared to be at the moment.

The officer shoved him through a glowing doorway. He stumbled into a restroom in an upscale restaurant, still wearing his less than appropriate glamour of a graphic t-shirt and torn jeans, but it did at least hide his pointed ears and lavender hued eyes. He didn't want to know what punishment he might get for being seen in his natural form while banished. He exited the restroom and entered the restaurant's main dining area. Smooth jazz assaulted his ears along with the stale scent of old cigar smoke beneath a thick deodorizer.

A man in a pinstriped suit looked at him with contempt and raised an eyebrow. "Do they let just anyone in here now? Hasn't the world gone mad enough with wolves and tanks roaming the streets?" he asked a woman half his age next to him in a scarlet dress that hugged her body.

Her glance lingered on Theo a moment too long, then she shrugged and buttered a roll.

Theo stepped back into the restroom, which was no longer a portal to Underhill. He looked in the mirror. He had applied his DJ persona glamour, which was almost exactly his true self, minus a few features. He applied another, one he hated, letting the illusion sink in and take hold well before he exited the restroom again, dressed in a black suit that smoldered with wealth and taste. He cinched up the tie, raised his chin, and strode back into the dining area. He gave the man at the table a sneer and conjured the snobbiest British accent he could muster.

"Seems they seat the riffraff near the washrooms." To the woman, he said, "If you use less butter, you'll resemble the substance less." He turned on an expensive heel and beat a path toward the exit.

It was raining. Theo stood just before the revolving door, eyeing the puddles for mud. Seeing only water, he stepped out. He glanced at his watch, a Rolex sprinkled with rainwater. It shifted to a Timex as he rounded the corner, his clothes taking on a more mundane appearance. Someone—a woman—ran past, carrying a shotgun in the open.

Theo watched the woman as she kept running, glancing over her shoulder occasionally. *That's weird.* He'd been on demon duty for the past two weeks and hadn't been topside. *What's going on? Hopefully it doesn't get in my way. I have a month to find this girl, before the pain starts and madness creeps in. Three months before disfigurement starts. Five before those are permanent. Living fires, did mom need to lose both her sons?*

He walked past a store that had a broken front window that had been covered in plywood. *Looting? Here? Maybe just a break in. Turmoil indeed.* He caught his reflection in the next window that had been left intact. His heart hurt to see it. *Sorry Alec. I failed you in more than one way. Duty. I'll find this girl. I'll also find that demon for you.*

S helby stared at the star-studded sky from her spot on the roof of the abandoned rest area, unable to sleep. She couldn't stop worrying as the warm wind brought hints of smoke from the west her way. She worried about the slow-growing pack. She worried about the Hunters who were preparing to head out in the morning. She worried about her father who they wanted to go with them. She worried about the Feral who had been gathering in clumps in the forest around them, but not coming closer than that. Mostly, she worried about Kale.

The lost bond ached. It was a hole that couldn't be filled. She knew he still loved her. He'd told her so a hundred times, but it wasn't the same. He was sleeping just feet from her, but might as well be a hundred miles away. *I miss feeling home.*

I miss it too, Eira added. *Skotha feels so distant.*

Here I thought you might call me petulant again.

The wolf shook her head. *No, it is not petulance to love deep and true. It is not childish to mourn the loss of something so rare.*

Shelby hugged her chest as her heart tightened. *We agree on that.* She swallowed the tears that warred beneath her eyes.

Sleep, Thyra. There is much to do tomorrow. And worry is wasteful. You suffer unnecessarily if things go well and twice if things go poorly. Stop.

She stifled a laugh. Most of the rest of the camp was asleep, and she felt manic. She thought she might never stop if she let herself fall into laughter. *Stop? Easier said than done.*

Eira smiled back. *I know. Try.*

Shelby laid back down and rolled to her side but shot back up as a shadow stood at the edge of the roof. Another stood next to it. She recognized the shape of her father and calmed slightly, but anxious to see what caught her father's attention.

A large wolf bounded onto the roof. Grant's shadow tensed and then relaxed. It sat down, and the smaller shadow joined it. Shelby thought that it might be Bryanne. The two had taken to watching each other's back, a professional courtesy.

The wolf picked its way through sleeping forms, gently and silently. Iorna stepped to Shelby's side. The Mystic of the dead Goddess stared at her for a long moment. Shelby felt her concern and realized the Feral might be trying to talk to her. Shelby shifted beneath the thin blanket. Her clothes were tatters anyway.

Sorry, but I noticed you do not sleep, Iorna said.

That does seem to be the popular topic tonight.

I do not understand.

Just been discussing my lack of sleep with myself and the wolf that lives inside me. Why are you up?

Iorna sniffed the wind and looked skyward. *I have been thinking about the Feral. You may want to move us north.*

Shelby stretched her wolf body out, enjoying the warmth of fur. *I should have done this earlier,* her mind moaned to herself. Then she responded to Iorna. *Why?*

Most of us stick to the northern reaches of this world, where game is plentiful and humans few. The Feral will cross continents to meet you, but it would be a kindness for you to meet them halfway. It would also put space between us and our enemies. The Mystic locked her amber eyes on Shelby's. *At least until we are ready, until you are ready.*

Shelby dipped her head to show acceptance of Iorna's wisdom. *Where would you suggest? Bryanne said Wyoming was full of Advent. Idaho? Montana? The Dakotas?* That made Shelby start. Her heart still ached for the loss of their pack elder.

Iorna rubbed a paw at her nose. *You should consult the Isluxua.*

But didn't you write it? Can't you just say?

Iorna managed to roll her amber wolf eyes. *I only wrote a part of it, with the help of my scribe. I saw much that cannot be described and much I do not remember.*

Shelby frowned at that. *I thought Immortal Wolves remembered everything?*

We do, Eira replied.

Iorna nodded and repeated the words of Shelby's wolf. *We do, but the Mystics watched shifting visions of time. Events changed. Memories changed with them. I have pieces of a thousand futures, fragments of what might have been overlapping inside me. I do not fully trust my memories, for not all of them are memories but glimpses of potential futures. The Isluxua narrows those down.*

Shelby blinked. *That actually makes sense.*

Iorna barked a quiet laugh. *Then you are truly lost. Sleep. We will consult the book in the morning.*

It wasn't much of a plan, but it was more than she had a moment before. It was enough. She padded the few feet of distance to Kale and curled up next to him, relishing the scent of manly decisiveness and responsibility on him, even if those were taking his time away from her.

That scent mingled with a magical tang of oiled metal that somehow had undertones of autumn leaves. He had taken to wearing the armor rather than clothing. It was more comfortable than it looked, and she admitted it was nice not to end up randomly naked. She could tell he was half awake.

That responsibility is a heavy burden. I may not feel you, but you are still mine, Kale. I will help you carry it. She yawned and fell asleep with her muzzle on his armored chest.

Kale woke in the middle of the night. It was a common occurrence for him since taking over the pack. He had to remind himself to sleep more than he liked. He found blue-tinted fur on his chest, keeping him mildly warm. He rubbed between his eyes with a thumb while he felt the pack link, checking for any more losses and noting the addition of more than a dozen new Feral.

He checked on Genn. His mother's thread in the pack link was safe and secure. He worried about her. He couldn't sense her grief like Shelby, but he had plenty of his own, so he could guess her state.

She is strong, a survivor, Skotha spoke to his mind.

I know. I just wish she didn't have to be. Surviving a loved one is a horrible thing.

Skotha nodded. *It is at first, but then you see that a part of that person lives on in you. You keep them alive. It is better that you and your mother did not perish. You keep Elias alive.*

There was an eagerness and anger in Skotha as he spoke. Kale thought he understood.

You want to finish what you started. You want me to give you control again, so you can hunt down Viersin.

Skotha calmed. *I do miss autonomy at times. I live through another. I am lucky that your love and my love are one. And revenge belongs to both of us. Elias, countless Immortal Wolves . . . Viersin and Mareus must pay for those lives.*

Agreed. He will, I swear. And I'll give you your freedom more often. Perhaps we can agree on an hour a day to start and see from there?

Skotha nodded. Kale could feel his desire for more, but also a deep patience.

Kale checked the pack link once more. Sensing no danger, he focused on Shelby.

"Glad you finally fell asleep, love."

He shifted, let the armor go with more reluctance than he liked, and curled into her.

He didn't sleep long before another body pressed into his, pulling him from a dream that wasn't pleasant. Kale started to growl but stopped himself. He didn't have to open his eyes to recognize Bubba, who smelled like protein bars and MREs. Much of their meager rations had gone toward restoring DeShawn after the battle. Their resident PK hadn't put on all his weight, but he no longer looked like death's malnourished cousin.

"Share some of that delicious fur with a brother. Not fair you wolf types have them built-in blankies." Bubba muttered something more about fleas, but it was mostly incoherent as he fell back asleep.

Amanda and Chelsea rolled closer too. Sean seemed to have created a spell to keep him comfortable. Either that or he slept too soundly to note the dropping temperature. He snored softly.

Kale smiled and let his friend snuggle against him. *I've made a weird pack. Dad would've liked it, I think.* The smile faded. Despite the warmth and closeness of the two people he loved most in the world, Kale found himself shivering. The only thing that kept him from getting up and pacing the perimeter of their camp was an unwillingness to wake them. It took him hours to fall asleep again.

ryanne leaned over the *Isluxua* with Gennesaret across from her on the rotting picnic table as the sun rose over the trees. They'd found an abandoned rest area off the old highway somewhere in northern Colorado, forgotten when new interstates took over and exits closed. It had served as a base for a couple days, most of them sleeping on the roof of the bathrooms. The inside had proven overwhelming for the Lycan sense of smell, so the Hunters claimed that.

Bryanne still dripped from the quick makeshift shower she'd taken earlier, her clothes sticking to her. She leaned back, careful to keep her lack of towel from damaging the book. The bathrooms didn't work, but there was a manual water pump on one end of the overgrown rest area that worked. It had felt a luxury to splash clean water on her skin in the moonlight, rubbing away the dust of travel and dried blood that may or may not have been hers.

Genn and Bryanne had spent hours under the one pavilion still standing, pouring through the tome. The flashlight they'd been using died last night, so Bryanne took advantage of the break to clean up, but returned to the task with the sunlight. She was one of only four in the pack who could read it.

"Through the demon gate to the pool of light." Bryanne paused. "That's not great. Demons are bad news."

"Wait, Demons are real?" Genn asked. "I suspected, with how often they appear in ancient texts, but had hoped my suspicions were unfounded."

"Unfortunately, they are very real. Nasty creatures that eat magic, but they rarely make it to Earth. They are also the reason Alsvoira fell."

Genn pursed her lips. "I thought that was Mareus."

Bryanne nodded. "Him too."

"First things first, the key. Go back a bit," Genn prodded.

Bryanne heard and felt movement. She glanced up to watch Grant walk past, leading a group of Hunters on their perimeter check.

Genn cleared her throat.

Bryanne blushed and read the passage to Gennesaret again, rushing a bit as she tried to hide blusher embarrassment. "Royal blood shall unlock the third. Stars in the desert, powdered with white. Signs in the mountains, roses will bloom. Bring key and lock to where palace meets brine." The Bandruí looked up from the *Isluxua* and took in the expression of concentration on her Lycan friend. "That means something to you?"

Genn rubbed her temples. "Royal blood must refer to Fae royalty, right? They have that?"

Bryanne nodded. "Yes, they have a queen and king. It's not as straightforward as human royalty, but it fits. They aren't the only race with a structure that resembles royalty, but," she rubbed the bow and arrow symbol at the top of the page, "this represents the Fae for sure. They are partial to that weapon."

"Were you there?" Genn squinted at her. The Lycan had long known what Bryanne was but did not know everything "On Alsvoira?"

Bryanne laughed. "How old do you think I am, woman? My grandmother was. She told me stories. They were like fairy tales to me at first. I wouldn't meet one of the fair-folk until I joined the agency."

"That makes you more of an expert than anyone else here. We'll need you. As for the rest of the passage," Genn paused for a long time as she considered her conclusions, "that's either Hollywood or Salt Lake City."

"What? How sure are you?"

Genn shrugged. "Maybe eighty percent sure it's one of those. The puzzle works for either. Stars in the desert may refer to actual stars, the crystals left behind in the sand by the Great Salt Lake, or actors and actresses. Powdered with white is either the makeup of pampered Hollywood elite or the salt residue left as the lake evaporates. The middle part escapes me, but the last part is pretty clear. Palace meets brine. So, we look for a fancy building on the ocean or tucked up against the salty lake."

"They are both quite a way in different directions."

"Salt Lake it is," Kale spoke up from the edge of the pavilion where he leaned against a post. Shelby was at his side. Both wore their armor.

Bryanne had felt them coming, the bending of grass blades, the movement of insects and nematodes at their footsteps. She did not jump. Genn didn't either. Bryanne didn't question him. It made sense. They had been moving slowly north anyway. It would also be difficult to hide the pack in the middle of Los Angeles.

He explained his decision despite no one asking. "Shelby and Iorna feel like north is the best route to take. We'll meet up with more of the Feral on the way." He looked off into the distance. "We need to find a faster way to travel."

"I've taken care of that." This time Bryanne jumped. She had not sensed Grant's arrival. He stood on the crumbling concrete to her left.

He must have doubled back and avoided setting off any of her natural triggers. How did the man do that? She glanced his way. *And how does he look that good after marching through alternating woods and desert for weeks?* He stared back at her, a soft smile on his lips as though he knew what she was thinking. She became very aware of her matted wet hair and sticky clothing. She coughed. "How?"

"I had the Hunter network buy us a couple buses."

Getting the Feral onto a bus is like herding six-year-olds away from a carnival. It took all of Shelby's Omega influence and much of Kale's Alpha prodding to convince a third of them to get on board. Iorna promised she would lead the rest of them their way through the wilder parts. They were still drawn to Shelby, so it was just a matter of time.

Time we may not have, Shelby thought bitterly.

What did I say about worry? Eira prompted.

Wasteful?

That is correct. Stop.

Most of her worry that morning had little to do with getting her pack on three charter buses that smelled like gym socks and stale crackers. The Hunters were leaving, most of them anyway. Only a handful were staying, mainly to keep tabs on the new pack and report any progress against the Advent. Her father hadn't decided what he was doing.

He has decided. He just hasn't told me yet.

Her Omega skills were growing. She could sense the Wiccans and even the Hunters in her group. She could influence their feelings. She could touch upon their memories. Her father was no exception.

Grant was leaving her. He'd packed a backpack, talked to Gennesaret about his plan, and even told Kale. Shelby had felt it all, but she also knew he hadn't told her yet as a protective, fatherly thing, not to hurt her. He thought delaying the hurt made it sting less. It didn't.

Bubba lumbered up to the bus, wearing an overstuffed tactical vest. They had more food and supplies, courtesy of the Hunters, but Bubba hadn't packed on quite the weight he normally carried. Kale didn't trust the food not to be laced with silver, but so far it had proven safe.

Shelby blinked at Bubba. "What is that?"

"Multitasking, that's what it is." He tugged on some Velcro and stuffed a carbo-load bar into a pocket.

"Multitasking?"

"It's bulletproof, just in case I let one by. Can't be snatching 'em out of the air all the time. And then all the calories a growing Playa Killa could ever need. Ask me what I call it?"

"Do I dare?"

"Don't be mean now, girl. Ask."

"What do you call it?"

"Bubba's Super Fly Snack Pack, patent pending, of course." Bubba wiped his nose with the back of a hand and looked off toward the south. "Mr. Copeland was gonna help me set patents and such up."

Shelby looked down.

Bubba randomly leaned forward to hug her, his grip vise-like as he crushed chips and other goodies stuffed into a dozen pockets. "Wasn't your fault, girl. You remember that. Elias was a big wolf. He made his own decisions."

She sniffed and nodded. "I know."

"Your boy Kale better be good at business though. After I help you two beat the big bad wolf, I expect some restitution."

"Deal."

She wiped her own nose as he stepped onto the bus and Grant stepped off the other one, his backpack slung over his shoulders, straps tight against his chest. The sight of him like that made Shelby miss Sadie. The fiery girl would have had something to say about how hot he looked in a tight backpack or something.

"You're going with them." It wasn't a question.

He caught her tone. "Yes. I have to."

"Do you, though?" Shelby tried to keep any hint of petulance out of her voice. *Thanks, Eira.* She felt much like a child, selfishly wanting her daddy to stay with her and not go off to work.

He sighed. "They are rudderless. Jack never made it out. I thought knocking him out was a kindness. Now I'm not so sure." Apparently, while Shelby had been enthralled by the *Isluxua* and unlocking the first key of Ascension, Jack Wilstead had put the barrel of his gun to her head. Grant summarily had taken care of Jack's wayward intensions, leaving the Master Prelate of the Hunter Order unconscious on the shore of the muddy creek bed. Grant looked off to where several Hunters loaded into a van. One saluted his way. He saluted back, stiff and sad. "Jack's probably dead. We didn't see eye to eye, but he wasn't the monster you think."

"I'm beginning to realize Hunters are people, doing what they think is right, even if it's horrible." She shook her head.

Grant swiped at an eye. "My little girl is growing up too fast. If I don't convince new leadership to work with you, things will go back to horrible. You know the world has gone mad when I'm going back to the Hunters."

She swallowed hard and nodded. "Totally mad."

He wrapped a hard arm around her and pulled her close, squeezing the air out of her. "Stick to the side roads. Avoid the bigger cities. Mareus has been busy. Nowhere is safe."

Shelby stared at a pillar of smoke in the distance that punctuated his point. There was a matching one in the other direction. War had broken out across the United States while they had been hiding, healing, and deciding their next moves. "You better call every night, Grant. I'm more worried about you than you are about me."

He kissed her forehead. "I will." And then he turned, strode to the van, and vanished behind a sliding door. She felt him though, even as the van turned down a dirt road trailing dust, even as the buses carried her in another direction.

thena relished the opportunity to explore the capabilities of her new armor and the body of her Immortal Wolf. She had an *Immortal Wolf!* She led a group of Lycans through one of the suburbs of San Antonio. In her wolf, she loped at speeds she'd never been capable of before. She crashed through the metal doors of a Hunter strong hold and tore the men inside to ribbons before they could reach their guns.

She snuffed out the multiple pockets of resistance, one by one, circling inward toward the town hall, where a few of the community leaders had barricaded themselves inside against the rapidly decaying fabric of their fragile law and order. Everyone in Texas had a gun and a plan, but few were prepared for werewolves. It wasn't part of any end-of-the-world plans to deal with giant wolves who heal faster than most can shoot. *Too much time wasted playing zombie video games.*

She shifted and stepped into the beam of one of the spotlights they'd set up on the rooftop, letting the armor cover her naked skin just as she crossed the threshold of light. *I'm the worst tease.* "This will be far easier if you just surrender your little town to the Advent. Everyone else has. Even San Antonio and Dallas have already given in."

"Never!" someone shouted from inside.

"Perhaps a little more motivation?" She motioned to one of her group in human form who pushed a woman to the forefront.

Is that necessary? Ptyas asked.

This is war. We do what we must to gain control. Now shut up. Athena was not used to a separate voice in her head. She'd longed to have an Immortal Wolf of her own, but she wondered how any of the Lycans with them stayed sane.

Maybe they don't. Athena wasn't sure whose thought that was.

She growled and grabbed the woman by the arm with her half-shifted hand, her claws digging into the woman's flesh. Athena dragged her into the light. Someone swore inside the building, loud enough to hear even without wolf ears.

"Charlie Higgins is the mayor, correct?" Silence answered Athena. "You recognize his wife, I think. You do not want to see what happens to her if you refuse."

A bullet pinged off her armor, right above her heart. The ricocheted round slammed into one of the wolves lurking in the shadows at her command. The Lycan whined as silver sizzled through flesh. She glanced down at the shiny metal protecting her. *Not even a scratch. This stuff is cool.* Her scythe appeared in her hand and found the woman's neck, just touching skin. "Someone in there has a better zombie plan than most, but you never planned on me. Surrender now and she lives."

"Don't you do it, Chuck!" the woman screamed and slammed the back of her head into Athena's nose. Bone cracked.

Athena gritted her teeth as her broken nose snapped back into place and began healing. "That was stupid."

"Go to Hell!" The woman tried to elbow her in the side, but the blow slid off her sleek armor like water off oil. "I'd rather die."

"Have it your way." Athena partially shifted and bit into the woman's neck. She let the woman slump to the ground as a spray of bullets came from the building. The bullets bounced off her armor as she walked languidly toward the building with her grinning wolf visage held firm. A ricochet grazed an exposed cheek. It began to heal a split second later.

Athena raised her scythe. The dual blades flashed purple as it flew the remaining thirty feet, slicing through glass, a thick conference table, and a filing cabinet that had been used to block a window. A man grunted inside as the symbol of death cut through skull bone. The double blades reappeared in Athena's hand a second later. *That's convenient.*

The shots stopped. "We surrender." Someone waved a handkerchief out a broken window. "Chuck's dead."

It is over. You won, Ptyas said.

Athena growled. "No, they had their chance." She fully shifted. Her massive wolf broke through the front doors, blowing the ancient wood off hinges and scattering office furniture in all directions. She poured fear and despair out of her as she towered over the men cowering inside. They died whimpering and soiling themselves.

The campground had been vacated in a hurry. There were dying coals in some of the firepits, a few tents standing, several ice chests left behind, and one fifth wheel parked beneath a tree.

Shelby sniffed, smelling the coppery tang of blood. She knew that was a couple days old. Lycans had passed through here but had not stayed long after driving the humans out. *I hope they weren't Feral, looking for me. I'd hate to think I made this happen.*

Eira cocked her head to the side inside her. *No. The Feral know how to avoid people. You've seen that. This was the Advent.*

Shelby made her way from the bus to the fifth wheel camper. She knew what she would find there, but she had to be certain. She could smell death before she opened the door, but it overwhelmed her when she cracked the seal.

The man slumped against the bathroom door, still clutching the shotgun, his eyes glossed over as they stared at Shelby without a hint of life. His throat was gone. She stepped inside, slowly stepping over his feet and the puddle of blood. She closed his eyes. "I'm sorry this happened to you."

Then she heard the heartbeat, faint, but beating faster at her words. The smell of fear mingled with hope and human waste in the air.

Kale put a hand on her shoulder.

Shelby looked back, still missing the bond that would have told him everything she was feeling and thinking. "Someone's alive in here. He protected her."

They found the older woman in the shower, covered in her own filth. She'd done it to mask her scent. Her husband had told her to do it, helped her do it, before he closed the door and loaded the shotgun.

Shelby shrank back at the full force of the smell. Kale ignored it. He reached down, lifted her up, and carried her out, covering her eyes as he stepped over her husband's body. He set her gently down on a blanket with Genn and Bryanne.

"Take care of her." He then turned to his small pack. "Check the woods for others. Scavenge food and supplies from the trailer, tents, and ice chests. Fill every container we have with water. The Hunters left us well-stocked, but we don't know how long we'll be out here." He looked back at the fifth wheel. "And someone please bury that brave man."

"George, his name was George." The old woman coughed and then burst into tears.

"We'll put George under that big tree on the hill." Kale's voice was flat, hard. "We'll say our goodbyes to him tonight before we move on."

The funeral took place after everyone had used the camp showers. Kale felt it appropriate that they were all clean for the funeral, but the flowery scents of shampoo and soap—the scents of the living— seemed to thicken his already heavy thoughts at the solemn event. *So much death,* he thought, lamenting the loss of his pack mates and father.

More death will follow, Skotha told him, and Kale's vision darkened at the edges as he heard Skotha's words. He felt their truth.

They huddled around the four freshly turned graves where they'd buried the three bodies found in the woods alongside George. A few others had attempted escape too late. The Wiccans and Bryanne had used spells to carve out the burial plots. Chelsea had personally picked out four large rocks to place at the head of each grave. She and Amanda used their magic to sear the name of each soul into stone beneath vine and flower designs. Kale admitted it was a nice touch.

He took charge as Shelby and Genn led the survivor, sweet Clare, up the small hill, hiding his shaking hands as he stepped behind the graves to face his pack. *How did my father always make it look so easy? To be calm, sure, and decisive in the face of everything?*

He had many years to master those traits. You will get there. Do not be afraid to lean on those who support you. Skotha's wisdom sometimes annoyed Kale, but proved a comfort as the sun began to set behind the trees.

"Thank you all for coming and for your help putting these souls to rest. I just wish we had arrived earlier to do something to prevent the tragedy." He stepped next to the stone marked Cori.

"Cori was thirty-five. Her hiking boots were well-worn. She loved the outdoors as much as any of us." He took a step to the side, coming to stand at the head of the next grave. "Tyler had a picture of three kids in his pocket. He had people who cared for him, who will miss him. I believe he gave them a chance to get away."

Kale looked up to see his best friend, Bubba, pulling a handkerchief out of his tactical snack vest and handing it to Amanda. The poor girl had lost her friend not long ago too. Kale noticed a small wiener dog at Bubba's feet. The dog chewed on some beef jerky. Bubba caught his look and shrugged.

Kale shook his head at his friend but then gave Amanda a small nod to acknowledge her pain as he took another step to the side. "Kathy had a new manicure, her nails painted in bright paisley designs. She held a hatchet in those manicured hands when we found her. There was blood on the blade. She fought bravely against terrible odds. We can do the same."

Kale paused after he stepped to the side, staring down at the stone that had been marked with George. The vines wrapped around a shotgun and the words "Husband, Father, Warrior" had been etched beneath it. He glanced up at Chelsea and nodded, not even trying to hide his shaking hands. *Let them see my anger and grief.*

"George served in the Marines. He leaves behind his lovely wife Clare, four daughters in Arkansas, and six grandchildren. He would not back down when certain death came, bravely sacrificing himself. And his bravery saved a life. He will not be forgotten. The Advent will see a reckoning for every life they have taken." He knelt and touched the headstone. "Goodbye, George. I wish I could have known you."

Kale stood, stepped to the side, and asked Clare if she would like to say a few words. The woman shook her head and embraced Kale, her tears wetting his shoulder. Genn came up beside her and wrapped her thin arms around them both. Shelby joined them, and Kale could feel the waves of comfort flowing from her. *She's getting better at that. It still isn't the same as our bond was, though.*

Kale cleared his throat inside the cocoon of embraces. "It's time we go. The sun is almost down."

Each of the women peeled off slowly. Genn took his hand and they walked down the hill together. He glanced back to see Shelby holding Clare. The sun burned red behind them, an effect of the smoke.

"Leave them, dear." Genn tugged him toward the buses. "Let Shelby do her job after you've so marvelously done yours."

Kale could feel the comfort and love blaze behind him. It almost felt like their bond renewing for a moment, but it was just Shelby doing all she could for the grieving widow.

Bubba sat on the bus steps, the wiener dog curled up on his lap.

Kale raised an eyebrow. "Where did the dog come from?"

"Just showed up during the funeral. Must've smelled my Super Fly Snack Pack."

Kale rubbed his forehead. "Another terrible name. You can't keep it."

"The name? Why you always hatin' on my dope names?"

Kale managed a chuckle. "The dog. You can't have a dog in a Lycan pack."

The dog backed away from Kale, ears and tail low, as if it could sense the predator inside.

"Hey now," Bubba said. "Ya'll carry your spirit animals inside you. I get to have one now too . . . on the outside of this fine body." Bubba stroked the dog behind the ears and it nuzzled into him. "Besides, I ain't leaving it out here to get eaten after its owner probably was. Are Lycans heartless now?"

Kale sighed. "Fine, but keep it out of the way and don't blame me when it freaks out around all the wolves."

"Sweet." The dog hovered off Bubba's lap and up the stairs. "Come on, Oscar, I've got some Vienna sausages just for you."

Kale laughed. "Did you name your wiener dog after a hot dog?"

Bubba shrugged. "What, you gonna hate on that now too?"

adie slipped past the Lycan sentries that wove among the pines at the edge of the east Texan estate easily enough, covered by a moonless night, her coat inky black. *Not that copulating hard when you're near invisible and smell as fresh as a summer daisy.* She smiled at the thought. She'd been experimenting with natural scents since she left Kale and Shelby's pack. Sometimes it came in handy to smell like something rather than nothing. She could imitate juniper, pine, cedar, honeysuckle, and fresh cut grass. She was still working on petrichor.

She'd been watching this pack for a week. They weren't Advent . . . yet. Francis, the Alpha, had been approached by a couple of Mareus's lackeys, but they had been rebuffed. *Who names a boy Francis?* Sadie knew she took a risk coming here, but she didn't want to see a resistant pack die. That's what was about to happen. It was join-or-die time for them. She'd known that would be the outcome for a

47

couple days but had finally scraped together the courage to do something about it. *I hope I'm not too late.*

She'd also been experimenting with connecting to pack links in more subtle ways than she had with Athena and Mareus. *I was clumsy, inexperienced.* She'd been able to reconnect with the Advent pack and with Kale's undetected. The trick was to piggyback on someone else's link, so she didn't appear like a new member.

I spent enough time with Shelby and Athena to tune into their frequencies. She'd been tapping into their pack links a few times a day to check in. It had started as an experiment, but it became a way to keep tabs on both factions in this war. Athena's link had suddenly shifted two nights earlier, making the link less reliable and fuzzy, but the kill order on this small pack had been clear enough.

She slipped around the edge of a farmhouse, avoiding the traps. They had taller grass and were easy to spot, if she took her time. A wolf or a human on the run wouldn't be so lucky. She stepped up the front stairs and connected to the pack, not in a subtle way. The reply was immediate.

Who is this? His Alpha voice demanded an answer. *How did you do this?*

A friend with a warning. We don't have the time for me to explain it all. The Advent is coming, now.

The Alpha growled. *We sent them away, tails between their legs.*

Sadie groaned inwardly. *Feculence, Alphas are stubborn.* That made her miss Elias. Through the link she was more diplomatic. *No, you sent away the initial offer. Mareus is sending a small army with sterner terms. Join or die, that's what they're saying.*

How do you know this?

Because I'm a copulating venatrix who's been spying on them for my pack! Open the front door and I can prove it!

The door swung open. A man donned a robe in the backlit doorway while two large black wolves snarled at her from either side. She admired his large build, square jaw, and Ewan McGregor-esque looks. He'd slicked back his dark brown hair in a fifties style that suited him.

Trying to explain the name, Frankie, with a front that you're older than you look? Grant is way hotter, she mused to herself. She'd dug into his past. He was just twenty, taking control of the pack when his father died in an oil rig accident a few months back. Some things a Lycan can't heal from. *But heavenly feculence does he smell good. What is that? Like pine and sandalwood had a musky baby.*

She let her coat change colors several times, let out an array of scents, and then sent a spike through the pack link, much like radio feedback. The wolves whined and took a step back. She shifted to her human form, covering herself as best she could with her arms, but more annoyed at the necessity than embarrassed. "See, I am what I say I am."

Francis eyed her with suspicion. "How do I know you're not an Advent spy?"

Sadie groaned audibly this time. "Because, *Frankie,* Marcus is a giant pair of buttocks, personality-wise, but he isn't an idiot. He would never send someone like me alone to your door where you could tear my throat out and rid him of such a tool. He would never let me reveal myself. I'm risking everything only because they're coming tonight. You have maybe half an hour to prepare. And I can help."

Francis sent out a Call for the pack to come to him. Most of them were there already, but some were in the nearest town. Sadie was still connected. She wasn't surprised when the two black wolves shifted and grabbed her wrists.

"Huh, twins? That's cool. Careful with the merchandise, boys." She spoke to the Alpha as they dragged her inside and past him. "Being cautious is great and all. I applaud it most days. Not tonight."

The Alpha glanced at the twins who held her. They nodded.

Two minutes later, Sadie rocked back and forth in a chair. "I can't copulating believe you tied me up!" They had given her a robe, at least, beforehand. *They're the kinder sort of kidnappers.*

Francis growled. "Considering a gag too."

"Rude."

He set a chair in front of her and sat down. "But before I shut you up, tell me something useful."

Sadie smiled. "Finally, someone's seeing the light." She took a deep breath. "Okay, the Advent doesn't handle rejection well, much like a friend of mine. He's a PK. That's a whole other story. Anyway, they sent in the next level enforcers. You've lost three members of your pack."

Francis shook his head. "No, I haven't."

Sadie rolled her eyes. "They haven't left yet, duh, but they're sitting in a barn a few miles from here, waiting to join the Advent after whatever goes down here is done. You'll see. Three of your pack won't show."

He ran a hand over the stubble of his beard. "Is that all?"

"Nope. Those three gave away your defenses. I didn't catch all of it, but enough to help me slip in. The Advent will have an easier time dodging your booby traps than I did, and it was really no trouble for me at all."

The man swore. Obviously, he had been planning on those defenses leveling the playing field. *So, he has been expecting the Advent to come back. Not as dumb as he looks.*

The man gave her an annoyed look. For a second, she thought she might have sent that through the pack link, but she was human, so she couldn't have. Only Alphas, and for some reason, Shelby could use the pack link in human form. Totally unfair. He must have just gotten some information from one of his pack in a direct message.

"Three of my pack are unaccounted for."

She nodded. "Yeah." Sadie bit back the *I told you so* that wanted to bubble out of her mouth, but the way she had let her answer drawl out probably communicated that anyway. "It's time to trust me."

He pulled a knife out of his boot and held out the gleaming silver blade, protected by the antler handle. "I don't like it." He slid the blade between her wrists, cutting away the rope. "But I don't want to lose anyone else. What help are you offering?"

"Somewhere to go. People who think like you do."

He snarled. "You want us to run? Like cowards?"

She nodded. "Hades yes I do! Run, and run hard and fast. My pack tried the direct resistance path. We lost half, including our Alpha."

That made the man think. "You lost your Alpha and remained a pack? How?"

"Our Alpha's son stepped up. We also have the Summer Omega to hold us together."

He twirled the knife. "You lie."

"Often, but not about that. Mareus himself came for our pack, the rumored Alpha Prime, because he knew she was there." Sadie let go of his pack link and sought out the fuzzy connection that was Athena. She reconnected. "We don't have time to argue about it. They're here, just outside your estate. Condemn it, I waited too long."

A howl came from one of the sentries. The Alpha looked up, speaking to his pack, giving commands.

"They'll come from the north and south, surround you. They will ask one last time for you to surrender yourself to the Advent. They plan to kill you no matter what you decide. Mareus wants your pack, but he doesn't want someone who resists him like you have." Sadie held up a hand. "You seem like a smart man. If we run east now, we might make it. I set up a few booby traps of my own, just in case."

"What types of traps?"

She smiled coolly. "C4 strapped to a bundle of miscellaneous silverware and coins."

He gave her a quizzical look. "That's what I have."

Her smile transformed into a grin. "I know. I may have moved half of yours over the last two nights, but I wired them to burner phones that should have enough juice left in them, if we act fast. I hid a cell phone preprogrammed with all the numbers just on the other side of your duck pond."

He grinned back at her. "Okay, I like you. Well, you only live once. If I'm going out tonight, let's make it fun."

He shifted and raced out the back door, dark brown fur marked with streaks of black. Smaller than she expected from an Alpha, but still larger than her and commanding in his own right. *Now I know what Lycan McGregor would look like. It's not bad.* She shifted and followed close behind, flanked by the twins. The rest of the pack waited just outside a granary. They ran east, skirting the pond. Sadie led the Alpha to a log where a cell phone waited in a freezer bag. She shifted and lifted the bag up. "You want to do the honors? Just hold down one first."

He shifted, took it, swiped the screen and held down the button. Explosions lit up the night, sending dirt, silver, and wolves flying. The man whooped in delight.

Sadie laughed. "Wait for them to regroup and move around the pond. When they hit the midpoint, hold down two and then three right after."

"You, my venatrix friend, can crash my pack anytime."

Pain ripped through every cell of Gultor's body as the demon passed through stone, metal, and blacktop that bubbled at his touch. Diffusing through matter was one of the most painful things he could do, but it was also the reason his kind had been sent through the gate. Molecules pulled past one another, screaming in protest, as his will dragged them along. He flopped onto the surface, demon blood mingling with the boiling asphalt.

Some metallic beast squealed at his arrival, slowing as it passed over him. Instinct drove Gultor up and into the creature, his intent to tear it apart from the inside and absorb any magic it might offer.

Instead, he found himself reforming in warm darkness, surrounded by fabrics that melted against his skin and wings. He was inside a carriage of some sort, in a storage area near the tail end of it. A hint of magic drew him to one side of the compartment. He sucked up the tiny spell placed on the metal frame of the vehicle, half healing the wound in his shoulder with it, but sending the majority back to his master.

Gultor flexed his muscles, setting the melted fabric on his skin aflame with the release of energy. He would need to find more magic to finish healing, but he could feel tiny bits of it moving around him in all directions. He also felt a huge reservoir of it in one direction, northeast. That would be his goal.

The vehicle made a sputtering noise, like a geyser about to blow. It shuddered, slowed, and stopped.

Gultor phased through the floor and jumped to another metal carriage. He missed the storage area, the ashen scales of his body reforming around his molten core next to the human conducting the vessel. The man screamed as flames rose from synthetic fabrics to lick bulging red muscles over onyx bones and spines. Gultor unfurled his bat-like wings and slashed at the human with claws and talons, ending the pitiful screams. The vehicle slammed into another.

Gultor phased through metal and rolled into another vessel and then another, hiding himself within the metal without fully forming. The spell in this carriage healed his shoulder. The vehicle died shortly after.

Three vehicles later, Gultor realized the spell in each carriage helped keep the mechanisms that drove them intact, pushing back entropy, at least for a time. Gultor waited beneath the tarry roadway for one that would take him in the right direction. He leaped into the back compartment, rolling into the melting fabric to settle in, licking at the spell in the metal, but leaving it intact.

Greater magic awaited.

Shelby moved to the front of the bus as they slowed. One of the Hunters that stayed behind drove this one and she could feel his tension building. "What's happening?"

He sucked on his teeth. "Looks like there's a small line for gas is all." He grinned and winked at her.

She stared out the window at the good mile of cars in front of them that curved toward the gas station. There was a similar line coming from the other direction, half lost behind trees. "Why so many?'"

"People fleeing the cities as the Advent takes over or the military rolls in. It ain't pretty out there, sweetheart."

She bristled at the familiarity in his words and tone but calmed herself. *He essentially joined our pack too, Lycan or not, Hunter or not. We're all on the same side now.* "Do you think they'll have any left by the time we get up there?"

He shrugged but pulled out a pair of binoculars from his vest. He peered out the window with them while continuing to suck his teeth loudly. "Hmmm, looks like the owner has bumped up the prices by a few dollars. That'll push some people out of filling all the way up. Only accepting cash. That will make it hard on a few too." He folded the small pair of binoculars and slipped them back into a pocket. "I'd say we have a good chance of getting what we need."

Shelby wanted to strangle the man ten minutes later as they limped closer to the station. He never stopped sucking his teeth. *Starting to think they left him with us just for that reason.*

Patience, Thyra. He's not the most obnoxious human I've encountered. Maybe top five.

Shelby laughed out loud, which had the blessing of making the Hunter jump and stop his nervous habit for a few precious seconds. He eyed her questioningly.

"Sorry, just thought of a joke. Looks like we're next."

He shook his head. "Nah, we're zippering it, so the other line gets to go first, then us."

"That's what I meant. We're next for our side." But a spike in the anger and tension in the vicinity made Shelby stand up and look around the bus. *It's coming from outside.* "Open the door, please."

The man pushed a button and the door hissed open on hydraulics. "Potty break?"

"Something more urgent." She jumped the stairs and half sprinted toward the pumps, where a man in a way-too-tight blue Polo shirt was arguing with the station owner about the cash rule.

"You still have power," blue Polo said. "You can take credit cards."

"But how long will that last?" the owner answered. "I gotta watch out for me and mine here."

"Like you aren't doing that plenty, gouging us with these insane prices. You know that's illegal in disaster situations?"

"Yeah," the owner spat in the dust, "and who's gonna enforce it?"

"You're seriously going to turn us away? Our house was on fire when we left. No firefighters anywhere. We won't make it to our cabin without this gas."

"Not my problem."

Blue Polo stepped up to the owner, his nose only a hair's breadth apart from the owner's. "It will be. I waited in that line for an hour. I'm getting gas."

"Not without cash, you ain't."

The man looked to his wife and kids in the car then back at the owner. He took a step back and reached for the back of his waist. A handgun came back with his hand, shaking as he pointed it at the gas station owner. "Yes, I am! Fill er up, Ed."

The owner's hand twitched. He had a bulge in his overalls that hinted at a handgun of his own.

This is going south fast. Shelby stepped between them, pouring all the patience, compassion, and calm she could out into the two men, and everyone else in the area for good measure. "Okay, gentlemen, let's work this out."

"Get out of the way!" Blue Polo shook the gun at her, his finger dangerously on the trigger while he did so. "I have no problems with you."

"Thomas, put it away," the woman yelled from the car. "This isn't the way."

"Listen to your wife, Tommy. She's smarter than you." The owner had to make a dig, his hand slipping inside his overalls.

"Shut up, both of you." Shelby had had enough. "You're being children. Children with guns, which is a terrible combo. You're really going to shoot each other in front of children over a couple gallons of gas?" She gave up on patience and compassion and went with pure compliance. "Here's what's going to happen. Thomas, you put down the gun. Ed, you pull your hand away from your gun. I pay for his gas. You get your money. We all live. How does that sound?"

The gun dipped slightly, but not enough. The owner's hand didn't inch farther inside his overalls, but it didn't come out either.

Both men's eyes widened slightly as she summoned more power and pushed again. It wasn't enough.

Shelby pushed with all her might, tapping into ley lines. "That's what's happening. Accept it." *Comply, you stupid, stubborn men!*

The gun fell to the ground, and Thomas burst into tears. "I just want to get them somewhere safe. I'm sorry."

The owner softened. "I'll take the credit card, just this once, but don't tell nobody. I can't do it for everyone."

Shelby sighed in relief, but then noticed she was wearing the armor, scythe and wheat in gauntleted hand. *That has to be the weirdest sight. No wonder they looked surprised earlier.* But the men didn't seem to care any longer. Her push for compliance had them accepting her as she was. *That's good. This would be very hard to explain.*

It's going to go viral, Eira pointed out. *Look at the cars.*

Sure enough, half the people had cell phones out, filming and taking pictures of the confrontation and her resolution of it.

How do you even know that term?

I pay attention.

Shelby shook her head, frustrated with her need to play peacekeeper. *Just what we needed too, me broadcasting our location to the*

Advent. She let the armor vanish, banishing the scythe and wheat as well. She pulled out her cell phone, leaving the men to finish paying and pumping gas. *No signal. That's a blessing. It will take some time before those videos get uploaded.*

Someone clapped and cheered as she walked past their car. Her husband and kids joining in. One of the kids mouthed "Wonder Woman" at her through the glass.

"I am not a superhero" she replied back.

Maybe you are, Eira countered.

Nope, just your typical werewolf with Fae armor, a Druid's scythe, a magical being in my head, and a bad attitude. Pretty much every teenage girl ever. Now let's pay a few hundred dollars to fill up my buses full of wolves and Wiccans.

Shelby was grateful for the gas an hour later. They passed five stations with Sold Out signs hanging on the awnings, two that had been burned to ashes, and three that had tanks parked in front of them, men in camo sending civilians away.

"It's getting real bad out there, ain't it?" Frank's teeth sucking didn't bother Shelby any longer. It was kind of soothing after a while. She missed Kale. He was on the bus behind them with most of the original pack. Shelby was needed on the Feral bus to keep the wolves used to the wild from going crazy in such a confined, unnatural space.

She nodded. "And it will probably get worse before it gets better. The Advent doesn't seem like the most benevolent of rulers."

The man chuckled. "Who woulda thought I'd be riding along

with a wolf, talking about how much worse other wolves are? Weird world."

She laughed too. "Weird world indeed. Look out!"

Three men were pushing a car into the middle of the highway. Frank swerved, clipping the car and sending the men flying. Another car was rolling out as they passed.

The Hunter grabbed the radio, clicked a button, and yelled into it for the other driver. "Do not stop. I repeat, do not stop."

He checked the mirrors, foot hovering over the brake, but relaxed as the other bus made it past the rolling cars.

Shelby shook as she took her seat again. "What was that?"

"Ambush most likely. They stop the cars with a roadblock, take gas, take food, and maybe let you live." He whistled. "Thought it would take longer before stuff like that started happening. Not a good sign."

Shelby looked ahead. "We're going to have to abandon the buses at some point."

He nodded and tapped the dash. "We'll run outta gas in a few more hours. Doubt we'll find another station with it, unless we're lucky, or we move farther away from populated areas."

Shelby half shifted, keeping her clothes from shredding. She reached out to Kale along the pack link. Another thing that made their lost bond hurt. She never had to shift to speak to him before. *You think we should go farther off the highways? It will take longer to get to Salt Lake, but we're more likely to find gas and supplies.*

He mulled it over. She could feel his uncertainty. She gave him courage and bolstered his ego. *We need you to be strong and decisive, love. Sometimes you'll make the wrong decision. We all do. We'll still follow you.*

He absorbed her words and emotions. *Yes, let's move away from the cities. I didn't like that near confrontation. We would have destroyed them, but I don't really want to attack humans who are just trying to survive if we don't have to.* He then sent something similar through the pack link to everyone.

Shelby conveyed it to the bus driver and asked him to make the announcement on the speaker system, so the humans, Wiccans, Druids, and PK could be informed.

That reminds me, she said just to him. *There have been whispers of what we will do with the humans we come in contact with. I overheard a few of your pack discussing at the last rest stop whether we turn Clare.*

Kale growled. *We aren't turning humans. We're not the Advent. We won't recruit that way.*

What if Clare asks to be turned?

Silence for a moment. *Has she?*

No, but it is a possibility. We may run into those who want this, those who want to stand a chance in this changing world, who want to fight the monsters who took loved ones from them.

Kale sounded surprised when he replied. *I didn't expect you to be the one arguing for this. I thought you were horrified when Rachel was talking about it, thinking about it.*

Shelby missed the bond. He knew most of this because he had been so connected to her at the time. He was surprised now because that connection was gone. *I have to get it back. I can't keep feeling lost and homeless.* To him, she said, *I was and still am horrified by not giving people a choice, forcing it on them, or manipulating them into it, but we're going to need allies and more in our ranks before this is all over. Just keep it in mind.*

I will. I've been thinking about it too, and what we do when we encounter other packs. I'm not going to be like Mareus. I don't want to kill other Alphas to get ahead.

Oh, love, you are nothing like Mareus. We'll find better ways. I promise. She sent him warmth and comfort, her equivalent of an Omega hug. She then sent him a kiss, which was hotter and more urgent.

She could feel his smile as he spoke again. *What you did today . . . we may need more of that.*

Anything for my Alpha.

Grant stepped from the third van he'd seen the inside of in two days, with a helicopter ride between the last. He eyed the gray doors of the warehouse. *Not someplace I thought I'd ever come back to . . . willingly anyway.*

Inside he held more than a little trepidation over returning to the North American Hunter HQ. It mingled with concern for his daughter and an odd sensation of missing Bryanne's company and conversation. Outside he was true to his Hunter call sign: Iron Ice. *Can't let them see I'm worried.*

Instead he stretched and cracked his back. "Too many hours sitting. It's not the Hunter way."

"No, sir," the gawky teen who had been his latest chauffeur, squeaked out as he slid out of the front seat.

Is his voice still changing? "How old are you, son?" The patch on his chest said Collins.

"Seventeen, sir, but I'm top of my class."

"I have no doubt." Hunters begin young, but Grant didn't expect one to be trusted with his retrieval, not as an enemy or an ally. *What's happening to the Hunters?*

Collins beamed at the praise. "Ninety-seven percent accuracy with my handgun."

Grant whistled. "Not bad." He sniffed and wrinkled his nose. "Huh, Indianapolis still smells like Indianapolis. Exhaust, sewage, hints of hay, and is that kettle corn?"

"There's no place like home."

Grant chuckled. "That phrase usually refers to Kansas."

The boy smirked. "I'm actually a transplant from Topeka, so I'm allowed to use it anywhere. You ready, sir?" He saluted awkwardly and motioned toward the doors of the squat, ugly building that blended into the cityscape, which was exactly what the Hunters wanted it to do.

"Lead me in," Grant said.

The chaos on the other side of the doors stood in stark contrast to the calm exterior of the building. Men and women ran past carrying reports. Someone tripped as Grant went through a full body scanner, scattering papers. The man snatched up only a few and ran down a hallway, leaving a trail. The guards who waited on the far side of the scanners gave him a salute, both teenage girls.

"Huh, things have changed. Some for the better, but . . ." Grant trailed off.

"Yeah," Collins said, wiping his nose, "there have been a few setbacks this week. Changes had to be made."

They stepped over the discarded papers to take the painted cinder block hallway to the left that led to the HQ control room.

Pipes and bundles of wire ran along the exposed corrugated steel ceiling. Grant glanced down at lists of Lycan sightings, graphs of increased demonic activity, and maps splashed in red. Black streaks crossed out many cities.

"The Advent is winning." Grant kicked a paper.

Collins looked down at the mess, his shoulders slumping. "Yes, sir." When he looked up again, there were tears forming in the corner of his eyes. "My best friend was killed yesterday in Chicago. Chicago! We thought we had that city locked down."

Grant put a hand on the boy's shoulder. "There are no words that can undo what happened to your friend. You have to carry that pain, but you also carry his memory, which is a gift to him for as long as you hold breath. You keep fighting as long as you can, as hard as you can, so that memory never dies. You got that, soldier?"

Collins sniffed. "That sounds like experience talking, sir. Who did you lose?"

Grant looked up at the dirty ceiling tiles. "The love of my life and more soldiers than I can list in the time we have."

"I'm beginning to know the feeling." Collins sniffed again but stood taller. "We're here."

"I know." Grant pulled the door open and stepped into the real madness. Men and women shouting at one another, gesturing at the display that lined one wall. Red wolf skulls floated over most major cities and hundreds of smaller cities and towns. Most of the same cities had been dotted with green castles, the mark of Hunter strongholds. New skulls appeared as he watched. "That many?"

"Probably more. We don't have the best intel. Our communication with those in the field is deteriorating." Collins stepped past Grant and cleared his throat. No one paid him any attention. He tried again. Nothing.

Grant put two fingers in his mouth and whistled, the sound loud enough to cut through the din of despair in the room. Silence fell as all eyes turned to him. "Who's in charge here?"

A young man rushed forward and hugged Grant. "Thank God you're here, sir."

Grant stiffened, then patted the man on the back. "Not the usual protocol, but times are weird."

"Sorry, Iron Ice, sir." The young man pulled himself away, his patch showing Thompson. "I'm just glad someone with experience showed up when we needed it. The proverbial fan is well-coated, sir."

"I can see that." Grant eyed the display boards again. "What do we know, Thompson?"

The man gulped, audibly. "We've lost every major Hunter stronghold other than the southeastern states, Indianapolis, New York, Boston, Charleston, Salt Lake, and San Antonio."

"How did they find them all?" Grant snatched a report from someone, glanced at the contents and passed it back. "Get that in the system now and have the survivors pull back to the secondary Seattle location. We'll get them out." Grant gaged Thompson's reaction to his orders.

The young man nodded to the soldier with an air of relief. He then answered Grant's question. "We think someone is talking, someone with a lot more knowledge of our inner workings than most. Do you think Jack . . ." Thompson couldn't finish the sentence.

Grant grimaced. "I'd hate to think so, but it's possible. Torture makes us all weak in the end. Might be my fault he was captured. These deaths are on me."

"I spoke with every man who survived that mission." Thompson rubbed the stubble on his chin and blinked bright blue eyes from inside the dark circles that made him look years older than the mid-twenties he had to be. "Never thought I'd hear so many Hunters defending Lycans and the man who protected his Lycan daughter, but they all said you and your actions saved lives. I'm keen to believe them. There's also something you need to see."

"What's that?"

"Proof your daughter may not be the monster we fear." He called out to one of the men at a table to put up a video from outside Dallas. "Be warned, it's disturbing."

A video clip taken on a cell phone appeared in the middle of the display. It showed a woman walk naked into a spotlight. Alien armor appeared to crawl out of her skin, burning red and cooling to shining onyx, like molten metal being forged in time-lapse. Grant had seen similar armor up close, but this was a darker, more twisted version.

"Athena," he almost whispered.

Thompson breathed heavy next to him. "That's the name we've heard too. It appears the Alpha Prime has a Summer Omega of his own. The prophesies never mentioned more than one."

As he spoke, Athena grabbed a woman, dragging her into the circle of light. A double-bladed scythe glowing a faint hue of purple appeared in her hand. It went to the woman's neck but did not cut. Instead, Athena half shifted, bit the woman's neck, then dumped the poor creature on the ground. Bullets bounced off her as she advanced, but she stopped short of entering the building. Instead, she threw the scythe at least fifty yards at whoever held the cell phone. The image lurched to the side. Blood splattered the ceiling, the walls, and the lens of the camera. A snarling wolf, as large as Mareus, raced past the still recording phone, wearing the dark armor.

"Show the other one," Thompson directed. He glanced at Grant. "This is what ultimately convinced me to let you in."

An image of Shelby appeared, standing between two men in some sort of confrontation. One had a weapon. The other was reaching for one.

Oh, Shelby, what are you doing? Her armor flashed into view and she held up her hands. There was no sound, but it looked like she was pleading with the men. All anger leaked from their faces. The gun fell to the ground, the conflict over.

Grant let out a pent-up breath. "That's my girl."

"Your daughter compared to that Athena woman? I'll take the traitor's spawn any day." He paused. "Um, that is, that's what Jack . . . called . . ."

The room fell silent except for the low hum of monitors all around them. Grant hardened, slowly turning and locking his gaze on Thompson. "I'm going to forget how you just referred to my daughter, but next time, I won't."

Thompson paled. "Apologies, Iron Ice. What do you think we should do now, sir?"

Grant had expected a question like that. "We get our intel buttoned up and our men and women out of harm's way. We fall back on every front until we have the concentrated numbers to attack." Grant stepped toward the table, putting his palms down as he leaned forward. "I'll do all I can until someone higher up makes it back to relieve me."

Thompson made a choking sound behind him. "Sorry. I didn't tell you, did I?"

"What?" Grant turned slowly.

Thompson's eyes had sunken in further. "We have been gutted from the inside out. Every sector head has been targeted. You are the highest-ranking Hunter in the United States that isn't dead, missing, or captured. Honestly, I'm not even sure if you still have any rank in our system but . . . well, you have more experience than anyone else here. So . . . I think that makes you in charge, sir."

"Well . . . feculence." Grant thought Sadie would be proud, and overly flirtatious.

"Not the word I'd have used, but accurate." Thompson walked around the table, pulled an ancient book off the worn wood, and handed it to Grant.

Grant took it, feeling the cracked leather in his massive hands. He turned it over, taking in the Hunter's shield and sword on the cover, parallel lines streaking away from the sword on either side. He'd seen the symbol hundreds of times, but never with these lines. "What's this?"

"Jack said it was the final solution, reserved for when everything went to feculence, as you say. It is for your eyes only." Thompson took a step back with a hint of reverence on his face. "I hope it helps."

Bryanne leaned against the side of the bus and stared at the sat-phone in Shelby's outstretched hand. "Shouldn't he want to talk to you?"

"We've been talking for a few minutes, but I gave him a full status update this morning." Shelby ran her other hand over her face, but failed to hide the smile creeping up her lips. "I suspect his insistence on a second report in one day is a thinly veiled excuse to talk to you."

"You do know I can hear you?" Grant's voice came from the phone as Bryanne took it. "This isn't a walkie-talkie. And these calls are expensive."

"Oh, I know," Shelby acknowledged. "That's why I cut my time short." Shelby walked toward the abandoned store they were using as a rest stop for the evening with only one sly glance back.

"Hi there, Iron Ice, sir. Your friendly neighborhood Druid lady reporting for duty." Bryanne gritted her teeth after she'd said it. She'd been trying to go for funny and charming, but wasn't sure if she'd pulled it off. There was also a slight delay with the sat-phone that always made conversations more awkward.

He sighed. "Grant is fine." But then he chuckled. "Sounds more helpful and less creepy than some teenager bitten by a radioactive spider any day."

"Glad you caught that." Bryanne relaxed, but still aware of time ticking by. Sat- phones could lose service at anytime. "What do you need, Grant?"

There came a long pause as the phone warmed against her cheek. Bryanne began to think she'd lost him, but his voice came through just as she was about to hang up and try dialing him back.

"How much do you know about the Hunters?"

Bryanne frowned. She'd been hoping to be more helpful. "Not much I'm afraid. We worked with them on occasion, against them other times." Bryanne bit her lip. "Humans, even humans doing bad things to the paranormal, wasn't part of my jurisdiction. We mainly mopped up the messes."

"I was afraid you'd say that." His voice grew distant, thin, but it wasn't a loss of service.

"Why? What could I tell you that your new…slash old coworkers couldn't?"

Grant grunted and something thudded in the background.

"You okay?" Bryanne felt the magic pouring into her along with the fear that the Hunter headquarters had just been attacked. *What can I do from here?* The delay killed her.

Grant apologized. "Sorry, just a heavy book I inherited meeting my desk. It seems the people who might have had answers are in short supply. I guess I'll have to read the whole thing. Was hoping you might be my Cliff Notes."

"Cheating only hurts yourself, Grant." Bryanne let the magic flow out of her and back into the ley lines. "Besides, I have my own book headache to deal with."

"How is that going?"

Bryanne took a deep breath. "Slowly. Those Mystics knew how to obfuscate."

Grant laughed. "Seems the Hunters liked their style. This book's written in English at least, but it also isn't, if you get me."

Bryanne nodded and realized that was foolish. "I do. I can reach out to some contacts in the government who might know more, but my connections are pretty thin at the moment."

Grant grunted again, and Bryanne thought she could hear pages turning. "No, I don't want you risking anyone else's life. I'll do the reading."

Bryanne bit her lip again. "It was nice to hear from you though. Stay safe, Grant."

"You too, Bryanne. And try to keep my daughter out of trouble."

"Oh, don't make me promise the impossible." Bryanne shook her head. "We both know she runs into it whenever it shows up."

Theo made it back to his downtown apartment unscathed, dodging several groups patrolling the streets with guns and silver knives. They were calling themselves militias or some nonsense. He'd picked up more of what was happening from the conversational snippets he heard as he passed other spatterings of humans. *The Lycans have gone mad.*

He'd almost sprinted the last two blocks. He stood out, walking the streets alone, and he received many distrustful glares for it. Best not to be mistaken for a werewolf, he'd have to pull his glamoured bow on relative innocents, or risk spilling any of his orange blood so soon after banishment. He didn't want exposing the Fae added to his list of crimes.

He leaned against the inside of the old door, paint chips falling to the stained hardwood floors. It was a modest studio that rested over a bakery on one side and a bar on the other, just off Main. The previous tenants hadn't appreciated the noise and scents early in the morning, followed by very different noise and scents in the evening, but Theo loved them all. It made him feel mostly human to be surrounded by the hum and odors of life.

Theo pressed his body against the door and balled his hands into fists as he thought, screwing his resolve. He had the means to begin looking for the resolution of his banishment or his brother's murderer, but not both at the same time. *I have a month to find the weird-eyed girl. The demon can cause more death and havoc if I let it live.*

"What would Alec say?" He knew the answer.

Theo unballed his fists and wiped away the orange crescents his fingernails had cut into his palms. "Duty." It felt like a swear word, bitter and full of anger, but it was also his only real choice. The demon would come first.

He pushed off the door and went to a wooden chest he had resting beneath the window that overlooked the graffitied brick walls of the alley. The lock was a complex mathematical puzzle no human could solve without hours and a supercomputer on hand. Theo knelt down, lifted the lock, and altered the entropy around it, pushing the unlikeliest patterns into the forefront, past the realms of possibility into necessity. The lock craved these patterns, the tiles on the front cycling through them rapidly. It clicked as the cipher fell into place.

The lid blew open, pushed from within. The Will-o'the-Wisp shot around the room, bumping into pictures, plants, walls. It tumbled into Theo, licking at him with happy flames.

Theo couldn't contain his laughter as a piece of the sentient fires of his homeland frolicked over his face like a happy puppy. "I know, I know, I've been away too long, little Fizz. Calm down."

The wisp nuzzled into his chest, humming with magic and

potential energy. Like him, his wisp had been a reject, lacking the usual reserve and finesse the Fae expected from their sentient servants. *It happens sometimes.* The fires of Mount Estorathi could be unpredictable, especially after the death of the Goddess, but Fizz had been a rare case of pure ecstatic joy. It loved to be alive, to dance, to hum its wordless songs, to chase fireflies through the caverns of Underhill.

Theo hugged the wisp and rubbed the blue flames with his hands, unconcerned about the fire. Wisps only hurt when commanded to. It wasn't in their nature to harm. Theo glanced down and noticed the fingernail marks in his palms had been healed. "Awww, thank you for that, Fizz. You're such a good wisp." Theo was glad again he'd managed to rescue Fizz from being cast back into the living fires to be reforged into a more appropriate companion for the queen.

She was in a generous mood that day . . . for once.

"I have a task for you, Fizzlet. You ready to play?"

Fizz zipped out of his grasp and around the room in dizzy loops, humming and spitting blue sparks of excitement. It knocked a mug off a table. The mug shattered. Fizz flitted to it and the shards lifted back together, cracks vanishing.

"My fault for leaving it out. Thank you again."

Fizz slowed to a more controlled loop around the apartment, still excited, but more careful with the décor, what little there was.

"Okay. I need you to find something for me. It's important."

The wisp stopped in front of him, expectant. Theo could feel the intelligence and curiosity in the hovering flame.

Theo pulled an arrow out of his quiver, the illusion that kept the quiver and arrows invisible falling away as he willed the arrow in his hand to be seen. He held the stained titanium tip out to Fizz. "I need you to find the demon this touched."

Fizz flashed red and sparked.

"I know. Demons suck. You have no idea how much."

Fizz seemed to sense the sadness in his words. It flitted forward and rubbed against his cheek for a second before flying to the extended arrow to sniff the blood on the titanium. Fizz sneezed a yellow flame that singed hairs on Theo's knuckles. "Watch it."

Fizz hummed an apologetic note.

"It's okay. Not your fault. Demon blood is nasty stuff. Messes with magic. Took a lot out of me to glamour it. You got it?"

The wisp bobbed and shot out the window, shattering the glass and reforming it at the same time, like a boomerang from Instagram played out in real life.

"Good luck, Fizzlet! You've so got this!"

A faint hum came back. Theo turned from the window to his studio. *Guess this is me for a while. Do I get a real job? Keep DJing on the weekends out at Salt Air? Any chance this mystery girl will just wander into a rave?"*

He pulled out a phone. "Okay, Google, red, green, and gold eyes."

The results weren't helpful, bringing up eyeshadow suggestions and rare eye colors. *Hurry, Fizz. I'd rather not be one of the screaming Fae. Drool and insanity won't look good on me.*

10

Taking the more scenic routes turned out to be one of the better decisions Kale made. They were able to get gas once more before the station owners got wise and stopped selling. *If the world tips into the apocalypse, gas will be gold. At least as much value as food in our end of days economy.*

Almost as much as toilet paper, mused Skotha.

Really? Kale chuckled. *You'd put that before alcohol and honey?*

You humans seem to really like the stuff. And you do not want to know what Daeglan used way back then as toilet paper.

Kale almost asked, but he felt a wave of uneasiness flow through him. It was only a second, but he recognized it as Shelby projecting an accident. A wave of calm reassurance came quick on its heels. *She noticed what she did and corrected it.* He was about to ask her through the pack link when her voice sounded in his head.

Sorry. We have another flat. Pretty sure we used the last spare.

Buses can run on a couple flats. We just have to move the tires around.

Silence came back.

What aren't you telling me? Kale asked.

Shelby's voice practically squeaked when she replied. *Remember that spike strip we dodged a while back?*

Yeah?

We didn't dodge it as well as I led you to believe. Sorry. I was trying to keep you from worrying.

Shelby! Kale didn't even know what he should be mad at her for. Telling him wouldn't have changed the current outcome. He calmed himself. *Okay. We'll pull over now.*

He stepped from the stuffy bus into a desert breeze that tossed his hair into his eyes, still crisp from the morning mountain air. It smelled like pine with hints of caramel. Iorna had told him all the trees of the Rockies had a distinct scent, some of butterscotch, vanilla, raspberry, even chocolate. He hadn't believed her, but he was beginning to.

He met Shelby between the still idling buses. She bit her lip, showing her anxiety. *Can't have her worrying. That's my job.* So, he hugged her and held her close. "It isn't your fault. I know you're our Omega. That doesn't mean you need to take on all our problems and cares as if they were your own."

"Doesn't it?" She pulled away slowly, painfully, but interlocked her fingers in his as she looked off to where the sun was rising above the tree-covered hills.

"A staff lends strength to the weary, but lean too hard and it snaps." Chenoa had come up behind them.

"Always helpful with the analogies, Chenoa," Shelby replied without looking back.

Chenoa put a hand on Shelby's arm, making the girl jump. "You do too much. The pack is growing. No one wants to see you snap."

Kale blinked at the hand still on Shelby. Chenoa wasn't one to touch people. She wasn't one to comfort. She'd also not loved exactly Shelby from the start. *This war is doing weird things to us,* Kale thought just to Skotha.

Skotha growled in agreement. *It will get worse before it's over.*

Some of the tension bled out of Shelby's shoulders. Kale could feel her grip relax.

"I'll try to be a smarter staff," she said. "What do we do about the flat tire in the meantime?"

Kale looked to the bus Shelby had been riding in, the one just behind his. "We siphon the gas, take the tires, scavenge any parts we think we might need, and cram ourselves onto one bus."

The tension returned to Shelby's grip. "The Feral won't handle that. We have over fifty of them on the bus now, not counting the ones loping along behind us, and there's way too many people. Everyone's barely keeping it together as it is."

Kale had already considered that. "We're only about a hundred miles from Salt Lake now. The Feral can make it on foot. They'll be happier running alongside the bus with the others anyway."

Chenoa grunted before she spoke. "And the pup becomes the hound, guiding the flock without nipping heels or getting kicked in the face."

Shelby chuckled. "I followed that one. I think your analogies are getting less opaque, Chen."

The elder woman shrugged. "Sometimes I enjoy your looks of puzzlement and sometimes I want you to understand my counsel." She paused and stared hard at Shelby, pulling her hand back, and crossing her arms. "But no nicknames." It came out as a cold warning.

"That's rich from someone who calls me destroyer, bringer of death, and a million other unpleasant nicknames." Shelby laughed. "Sad when 'staff' is actually one of the better ones, Chen."

Kale worried Shelby might offend the old Lycan, but the corners of Chenoa's mouth tugged up.

Kale grinned. *Shelby's getting good at reading and playing off emotions, when she can get Chenoa to almost smile.* But his grin vanished as a shadow raced through the tree line. He pointed. "More Feral?"

Shelby shook her head. "Not what they feel like."

"They?" Kale eyed the broken-down bus, wondering if he should risk running on a rim for a while. They'd managed to dodge the Advent, but luck always ran out.

"There's at least fifteen." Shelby closed her eyes. "They are a little anxious and excited, but I'm not feeling the usual pre-attack stuff."

"Pre-attack stuff?"

She huffed and squeezed his hand. "It's a thing. I'm not getting hungry excitement, anger, fear, or anything like those. I think they're friendly . . . ish."

"Ish? Love the confidence, love."

She leaned into him. "Well, they are still Lycans. We're touchy and territorial on a good day."

A howl came from the hills, moving closer.

Kale tensed. "We'll find out soon enough."

Chelsea ran through the incantation while the buses were stopped, Amanda watching from the side. The vibrations during travel made some spells more difficult.

"See, this finger runs across this finger and then you twist them like this. Got it?"

Amanda made a noncommittal noise and looked off to where Bubba checked and rechecked his many pockets, the wiener dog crawling over him and sniffing each one.

"Do you think Trish really liked him?"

Chelsea dropped her hands. She had been cruel to Trish for wanting to date DeShawn, calling him plenty of names she regretted, and not just because her words no longer fit his physique. "She went against my orders, so she must have." Chelsea eyed her friend. "Do *you* now?"

"I don't think so." But Amanda nodded at the same time.

Chelsea laughed. "You don't know is what you really mean."

Amanda bit her lip and looked at her hands. "Yeah. I guess." She wriggled her fingers in her lap. "Okay, show me one more time."

"No, I'm done teaching you this spell. You can't focus."

Amanda sat up straighter. "I'm good."

"Prove it. Try the spell on your own, for real this time."

Amanda's face went pale. "Inside the bus?"

"It's a strengthening spell. As long as you don't punch anything or anyone, we'll be fine." Chelsea smiled. "You feeling punchy?"

"No more than usual." Amanda grinned back. "My best friend *is* a bossy witch who has been manipulating my feelings for years so she could rule our high school."

Chelsea felt the blood drain from her own face. She'd stopped using such spells the last few weeks, and the feistiness of her friends returned with a vengeance. *Watching a friend die and living into the end of days changes your priorities.* She felt a twinge for Kale as she thought about all she'd done to win him and ultimate popularity over, but her feelings for him had waned as they'd moved away from the school. *I was obsessed.*

She swallowed the bitterness in the back of her throat. "I can't apologize enough."

Amanda put a hand on her arm. "Part of me wanted it too. It was fun and powerful being a piece of the whorey trinity."

Chelsea growled and glanced back at where Sean slept against a window. "I hate that nickname."

Amanda shrugged. "It fit."

Chelsea bristled. "We weren't whores!"

Amanda laughed. "Not in that way, maybe, but we still deserved the name."

"Maybe." Chelsea looked at her own hands. "But you're avoiding the assignment. Try it."

"Okay, fine." Amanda lifted her hands, ran through the movements, and spoke the words in a near whisper. A vibration came off her hands in the last moment. "Did it work?"

Chelsea blinked. "That was . . . perfect." She tamped down the envy that wanted to build and chose pride instead. "I'm such a good teacher!" She rummaged through the backpack beneath her seat and pulled out a metal stylus from a tablet that had lost power days ago. "Try to bend this with just one hand."

Amanda took it between thumb and forefinger. She pushed against it, her hand shaking with the effort. Nothing happened. "I didn't do it right."

Chelsea took the stylus back. "No, it was perfect. The words. The movements." She set the stylus down, ran through the spell herself. As the vibration came off her hands, she felt it drain away, pulled from her like a string unraveling. It was an unpleasant feeling. "That was weird." She tried to bend the stylus with both hands. It resisted.

Amanda bit her lip again as Chelsea looked up at her. "What is it? You have your freaked-out face on."

"May be nothing. Let me try another, one I know I get right every time." Chelsea ran through a spell meant to bolster her confidence. It was a spell she'd used every day for the past five years. The same unraveling, pulling sensation happened at the end. Her ego remained at its flagging level. She tried it again. Nothing. A third time, for luck. The magic fell apart.

Amanda squeezed her arm. "You've gone silent. That's never good."

The stylus rolled off her lap. She ignored it as it clattered against the rubberized floor of the bus. "I think we need to talk to the Druid."

Deep beneath Underhill, a pair of warrior Fae stood at attention, both staring at a portal. They knew this one had been the most active of the four demon gates in the past thousand years. And with Theophinus's banishment for failing at another, they were alert and well stocked with arrows.

The moment the portal flared, spitting off sparks, NaKyla loosed an arrow at the bell near the ceiling. The magical chime sent for help as a wispy claw reached through. They could hear reinforcements running through the tunnels to their aid as their arrows flew, biting into the shadowy flesh of the creatures pushing through.

But these demons were hard to hit. They leaked through the portal, flowing like smoke, hazy tendrils wavering from their indistinct bodies. Arrows flew through the smoke with little effect.

NaKyla recentered her aim. Her arrow thudded into the more solid flesh near the middle. The demon screamed, biting at itself with multiple mouths and rolling into a writhing ball. "They are smaller than they seem. The exterior is just smoke and ash, illusion."

She was partly right, but more wrong than she knew. Another of the creatures oozed through and raced her way. She focused and aimed slowly, locking on the center. A tendril of smoke touched her leg as she waited for the perfect shot.

Flesh tore open and burned. Sharp ash burrowed deep beneath skin and then burst out the far side. Smoke wrapped around the leg and pulled, sending her spinning. NaKyla's arrow flew ineffectively into the dark cavern and her skull cracked into stone. She did not see help flood into the room, even though her eyes were open and fixed on the entrance.

But she heard her brothers and sisters die.

The queen of Seely Court, Silphinaera, could hear the screams half a mile away. Alarms sounded higher in Underhill as demons escaped into other sections, working their way to the surface. A shadow, black as night with streaks of red, stole into the throne room. With a steady hand, she pulled a knife from her corset and sent it flying.

Smoke and ash pooled on the floor, dissipating in the shifting air. A twisted thing of mouths and limbs sat at the center, dripping black blood from the knife wound in its chest that caught fire as it sizzled to the floor. It tried to crawl her direction. A second knife sunk into an eye socket, barely a new stream of acrid smoke escaping the wound as the demon died.

The queen stood as more screams came from the halls above her. At least one of the demons was about to escape, moving toward the gates they held close to the surface. She pulled more titanium knives from hidden places and willed her wisps to follow her as she ran toward the screams.

She launched over smoldering corpses and moaning injured. Reaching one of their magical gateways, she found a shimmering sheet of light. The Fae who had stepped through it into Underhill stood staring at the charred hole in his chest, mouth open in a silent scream. He fell to his knees as the light behind him flickered and died. At least one demon had made it out.

"Hurry, Theo. We're running out of time."

Tarloch, Demon King of Bassindahr, felt the loss of each demon, but two survived the initial battle. He felt an immediate influx of energy from Earth as those two absorbed the life force of fallen kin, along with hints of Fae magic from Underhill. *Non-diffusers have made it through. It is time to hit harder.*

A thought sent a second wave of his creations surging toward the gates while he channeled some of the stolen magic toward the creation of a new portal, targeting a weakened section of the universe where a goddess had died.

S adie slid behind a dumpster across from the small Cajun restaurant owned by her target. His group met there often, and she could make out wolfish shadows inside, even with the blinds drawn. *They aren't the most subtle bunch.* She clawed her way into the pack link, not having the time to hack their communications gently. She normally liked to shadow someone, get to know them, ease into it without setting off any alarms.

I'm setting all the alarms off today. Listen up, pups of feminine persuasion, you need to get out. Get out now!

What the? Who are you? How are you doing this? The Alpha of this small-town Louisiana pack growled.

Sadie growled back. *No time to explain the amazingness that is me or admire your accent. The Advent is coming. You need to run. Head out the front and go south, that's where their numbers are thinnest. I'll meet you at the Slidell*

Bridge with more info and some dynamite I may have borrowed from some crazy fishermen.

Why should I trust you? the Alpha snapped back. *You might be Advent.*

Feculence! Why would I warn you, if I were?

You could be leadin' us into a trap. Blow us up on the bridge. Sounds like the Advent.

Sadie could hear the padding of wolf paws on gravel to the north. *Not gonna argue with that. It's so their style, but I'm seriously trying to save your lives right now. Please, get out. They're only a block away. Ya'll pissed em off good.*

We sure did. Had ourselves a gator feedin' party with them that tried to trick us before you.

I'm not copulating Advent! She howled into the night, hoping it would serve as an additional warning and spur the man to action. *I approve of your methods, if not the sanity behind them. I'm a friend.*

Her howl did get them moving, but not as she hoped. The pack barreled out the back door and into the larger group the Advent had sent there to prevent retreat. *No, you idiot, I said the front door!*

But she was too late. Sadie listened to the barked orders and then disconnected a moment later as the pack link filled with screams and death. *I failed them. I'm so sorry.* Releasing her hack didn't completely relieve her of the sounds that came from the far side of the restaurant. She curled up behind the dumpster and mimicked the scents of rotting garbage until the night fell silent again.

Bryanne sat with Gennesaret near the front of the bus, pouring over the ancient Lycan text. She gently touched a grouping of colorful letters, etched in ink from another world.

"Two sides of a coin, one to unlock the key, the other to grant consent. Both must be won together as living fires rebuild what was lost." Bryanne tapped the paragraph impatiently. "I hate this book."

Genn put her hand between Bryanne's and the pages. "Soft. The book is older than both of us combined."

"Sorry." Bryanne pulled her hand away. "I just wish the Mystics had written a little more straight forward. These puzzles are killing me."

"You must have some idea? You know the Fae better than I."

Bryanne pursed her lips. "I can guess. The Fae are split into two courts. That may be what it means. We have to get one thing from each court."

"Shelby has to."

"That's what I meant." Bryanne examined the words again. "Doesn't say which one will give us which part. Means we'll have to go to each." She let out a long breath.

"And that troubles you?" Genn asked.

"The Seely Court isn't too hard to deal with. They're slightly nuts, but manageable."

Genn caught on. "The other court is not as friendly?"

"They can be friendly, but they'll flip from friendly to homicidal in a second. The Unseely Court is completely insane. It's like Wonderland without the happy endings."

"Ah, something to look forward to. Any idea where we go after the Fae?"

Bryanne chuckled. "Ever the optimist. Just assuming we'll succeed?"

Genn lifted a delicate hand. "I have faith in the children."

Bryanne glanced to where Kale had just stepped from the bus to examine the other one and talk to Shelby. "They have managed some extraordinary things, but it's going to get harder. The Fae don't give gifts lightly."

"Hmmm." Genn mused as she closed the book to review the symbols once more, rubbing the indented lines of the last two.

Bryanne tapped the last. "I have no idea what to do about this. Grandmother said only four of the five races made it out of Alsvoira. She never named them. And the text here is even more garbled and mysterious than the rest, which I didn't think possible. It's going to take us weeks to unravel."

Genn smiled. "We will worry about that after we get the next key."

Bryanne felt the approach of two people from farther back, their slow movement shifting air. She turned to find Chelsea and Amanda picking their way past feet and backpacks in the aisle. The buses were well over capacity. *And they smell like wet dog.* "What brings two young Wiccans to us this morning?"

Chelsea froze, looked up, turned ashen, and opened her mouth several times.

Bryanne rolled her eyes. Wiccans were taught to respect the Bandrui from birth, which was nice, but it sometimes caused awkwardness. "Go ahead. The great Druid will hear you now."

Chelsea found her voice and stammered, "Magic is being weird. Like really weird. Pulling away from me and unraveling. I wondered if you noticed?"

Bryanne frowned. "I hadn't noticed, but I haven't tried any in a while. That's pretty common with new spells."

Chelsea gulped. "It did it with old spells I know by heart too. It felt . . . unpleasant."

Amanda nodded emphatically behind her.

Bryanne resisted the urge to send the children away. She and Genn had more to worry about than novices playing at magic they didn't know how to control yet. But she bit back the reply. "Fine. Let me check into it."

She closed her eyes and sought out the nearest ley lines. The closest were miles away, but she could still access those. Her magic would be slower and weaker, but no less real. She pulled from them, balling the energy together inside her.

She opened her eyes, seeing the world in tones of crimson with strings of energy flowing between the living souls on the bus. Bryanne smiled as Amanda and Chelsea both took three small steps back. Her red eyes disconcerted most people. Her scythe flashed into being in a hand she raised to keep it away from Genn and the *Isluxua*.

Her will flowed down her arm and through the scythe to create a simple light, something she might use in a dark cavern. The magic coalesced into being and then was ripped away, a streak of light flying downward. It hurt, scraping through nerves like sandpaper on fire. Tendrils of her magic ripped out of her body and mind with great friction and resistance. *Unpleasant indeed.*

Ice crept into Bryanne's heart. She knew of only one thing that could strip magic from creation. She staggered to her feet, but the magic was still being ripped from her. Her eyes cleared and her scythe vanished, but still the magic poured from her. Wounds tore open inside her. "We have to warn Kale and Shelby. We have to run."

Bryanne tried to walk toward the exit. Her vision narrowed, and she tripped over a sack of rations, falling against a seat before slumping to the ground. As darkness folded over her, she heard a howl that did not sound entirely friendly. *We don't have time for that. We don't have time for me to pass out either. Get up, Bry! Get up!* But the power of ley lines being pulled violently through her proved too much for her body to handle. The pain ended as the world went dark.

Anxiety flowed into Shelby from all sides as the small pack approached. *Small pack? We were barely that size a couple weeks ago.* Shelby calmed everyone as best she could, which was no easy task. The Feral felt cornered inside their bus. The other Lycans weren't much happier being stuffed onto a bus with strange humans. The Hunters still wondered if they'd made the right decision. The Wiccans were worried about their magic. Kale took on all responsibility for the growing pack and was having trouble letting others carry any of it. Shelby herself was a ball of concern for Kale and all the emotional beings who flooded her with their passions, fears, and insecurities.

Even the always stalwart Bryanne had a sudden spike of anxiety just as the wolves stepped from the trees. Shelby couldn't help the Druid much. She focused most of her energy on Kale and the approaching Lycans.

I'm spread too thin.

This is true, Thyra. You put too much pressure on yourself, Eira said.

Kale's emotional state changed. Confusion rolled off him in waves. He gave Shelby a puzzled look.

"What?" Shelby hissed.

He tapped his ear. "Sadie."

"Wait, what?" Shelby didn't know what else to say.

"Of course she waited until now to let me know."

"Don't make me say it again." Shelby growled at her boyfriend.

"Sorry. Sadie can talk to us when she feels like it, apparently. She sent our friends days ago and forgot to let me know. Nice timing."

Shelby reached inside and explored the connections she had with every pack member, including those who weren't Lycan. "I didn't feel her rejoin the pack."

He held up his hands. "She's getting good at that venatrix thing?"

"Seems like. What did she say about them?" Shelby pointed to the wolves who had reached the roadway.

Kale smiled. "Enough." He raised his voice. "Francis?"

One large brown wolf stepped forward and shifted into a young, handsome, and very fit man. Shelby averted her eyes from below his waist. She was sort of used to nudity within Elias's pack, but she had come to know them. It was a little weird still with new pack members . . . at least for her. Two black wolves stepped between Francis and the buses, a protective move that had the added benefit of covering much of his nakedness.

"That's me," Francis said. "So, the feisty one got you the message we were coming?"

Kale nodded. "Just a minute ago. She cut it close."

Francis laughed, loud and long. Shelby had a hard time not grinning with him. It was contagious.

"Sounds like the Sadie I met. Saved our wolfy bacon though."

"She mentioned that too. Seemed pretty proud of herself," Kale said.

"That's fair. She earned some pride." Francis then stared at Kale in silence for a while before broaching the subject. "She promised I'd get to meet the Summer Omega and the true Alpha Prime. So, that's you two?"

Kale gestured to Shelby. "She's the Summer Omega." Then quieter, "You want to show him?"

Shelby blinked at him for a second before she realized what he meant. Her armor flashed on over her clothes and she brought the scythe and wheat stalks into reality. She reached out to the ley lines to increase the effect, knowing her eyes would glow a brighter red and the lines of her armor would pulse with the power.

She held the magic within her, relishing the taste of it, the sense of something more inside her. It leaked away faster than it should have, but she'd done what she wanted, so she let it go. Francis whistled as she let the crimson drop from her eyes.

Chenoa put on her armor behind them.

Kale let his armor appear too. "I'm not the Alpha Prime though. I'm just an Alpha, doing the best I can for my pack."

"There's nobility in that." Francis glanced around at his little pack. "I'm convinced. How do we go about signing up? Do we have to fight? Or can I just swear to you and let you take over as Alpha from there?"

Shelby bolstered Kale's confidence as she noticed a spike of uncertainty rise.

Kale took a step forward as her strength filled him. The black wolves snarled. "No need for that. I don't want to strip you of your pack or your leadership."

Francis cocked his head to the side. "Isn't that kind of how this works?"

"I've had a few weeks to consider what I would do when faced with this decision. I want you to retain control of your group. Only you swear loyalty to me, not the rest. You stay their leader and I will become yours." Kale glanced at the bus that housed most of the remaining Hunters. "I've had the opportunity to watch military leadership in action. It has its benefits."

Francis looked from Shelby to Kale. "You think that'll work? I'm not as experienced as I seem."

Shelby again filled up Kale's flagging ego as uncertainty crept in once more.

Kale shrugged, but it was a confident shrug. "Me either, and I've never heard of a pack doing anything like this, but I believe it's worth a try. If it doesn't, I can always kill you later."

Francis flinched and Shelby sent forth reassurance. Kale slowly let a wicked smile creep on to his lips. "Kidding."

But he wasn't, Shelby could tell.

"Do we have a deal?" Kale asked.

"Don't have to ask me twice." Francis knelt, leaning on the two black wolves as he did so.

Shelby felt him join the pack, her heart expanding to accept him. Natural born. Young. Scared. Trying so hard to be half the leader his father was. He reminded her of Kale. His pack came with him as a package deal. She knew each by name and how to help them, as though they had joined the pack individually. She could sense Kale's influence over them as their ultimate Alpha. *I think Kale's plan worked.*

Of course it did, Eira replied. *He has revived the old ways. The pack structure before humans came to Alsvoira, before Lycans. Did you truly think Immortal Wolves fought over every scrap of authority?*

I guess I just assumed it has always been the same.

Change is a part of life, Thyra.

I know. One of the new additions snagged in her heart. "You have an Omega?"

Francis smiled. "My little sister was always good with people, from when she was three on. She helps us stay together and grounded." He waved a small wolf forward. "This is Wanda." He smirked at the look Shelby gave him. "My parents liked the old names no one used anymore."

Wanda shifted into a girl of maybe fourteen, cowering behind a black wolf. "Hi."

Shelby smiled. "Hi, and welcome. It will be nice to have another Omega around here." Shelby sent the girl a dose of support, encouragement, and comfort. That same mix of emotions poured out of the girl and into her pack. *Oh, that's going to be super helpful. We need to find more like her.*

Kale rubbed his chest and motioned for Francis to stand. "That's weird. I can feel you as part of the pack link. All your wolves are there too, to a lesser degree. I think we just made something new."

"Or something very old," Shelby corrected. She caught Chenoa's nod of approval.

"Welcome to our pack. We're an odd mix. Remind me to fill you in." Kale began walking back toward the bus they were about to abandon, staring at the shredded tire. "You showed up at a great time, just when we're soon to be busless."

Francis laughed his contagious laugh again. "We just ran across two states. We can handle a jog through the woods."

Kale's armor fell away. He glanced down and spoke in a hushed tone to Shelby. "Um . . . I didn't mean to do that."

Shelby's armor felt less solid now that he brought her attention to it. *That can't be good.* "Can you get it back?"

Sections of his armor appeared and disappeared. "Not completely."

Shelby lifted a hand and let her gauntlet vanish. She brought it back, the magical metal feeling thinner than before. "We'll have to talk to Bryanne, see what she thinks might be happening."

Shelby realized the sharp rise in anxiety from the Druid had gone, but it had been replaced with anxiety from the Wiccans and Genn. She was getting zero emotion from Bryanne. *Something's wrong.*

Shelby grabbed Kale's hand. "Let's ask her now."

Shelby found the Druid laying in the middle of the aisle, surrounded by Chelsea, Amanda, and Gennesaret. Several other people had stood to see what the commotion was about. Genn glanced up as the door hissed closed behind Kale.

"We wanted to get your attention, but we didn't want to interrupt."

Shelby waved Genn's apologetic tone away. "Probably for the best. Things were tense for a second. Is she okay?"

Genn leaned over Bryanne. "I think so. Her heartbeat and breathing are steady. She was saying something about magic and warning you before she passed out."

"Magic's been acting weird," Chelsea said.

Kale managed to hold a gauntlet on his hand, but that made his breastplate vanish in a spray of sparks. "We noticed."

Shelby knelt next to Genn. "When do you think—"

Bryanne gasped awake, coughing. She found Shelby's eyes and locked in on them. "Demon."

Shelby smiled, happy to have her friend back amongst the conscious. "I've been called worse."

Bryanne shook her head, absolutely no humor in her facial expressions. "No, demon close by, absorbing magic. It's the only explanation."

A demon? Why not? Shelby's world had only been blown up a few thousand times in the past months and year.

Kale leaned over Shelby, his breath warm on her neck, creating goosebumps up and down her arms. "What do we do about it?"

"We run." Bryanne tried to sit up, but that brought on more coughing. When she recovered, she continued. "The Fae can defeat demons. Our scythes might work on them too, but the rest are just targets and food to these things."

"You've met a demon?" Chelsea asked.

Bryanne wobbled as she finally succeeded in sitting up. "Only once. It sucked all the magic out of a town."

"That doesn't sound so horrible," Shelby said.

Chelsea gasped next to her. "You don't understand. A little magic goes into everything." She counted off on her fingers as she spoke. "Electronics, cars, computers, medicine, food prep and storage. It would be like an EMP went off."

Bryanne pulled on one of the seats to stand, but Genn put a hand on her shoulder to keep her down. "Worse. It was a town full of Bandrui."

"What difference does that make?" Kale didn't sound like he was being rude, just curious.

Bryanne pushed Genn's hand away and managed to get her feet underneath her, but she leaned heavily on the seat, out of breath. "It eats magic. We're magic. It killed everyone. Men, women, children, everyone."

Shelby caught on. "So, two buses overfull with magical creatures?"

"A freaking buffet." Kale replied.

"Exactly." Bryanne slumped into an empty seat. "It took five Fae warriors and ten Druids to bring the thing down after all the magic it consumed. They get bigger and stronger the more they do." She glanced south, the direction they'd been traveling from. "We need to move and hope it loses the trail or its interest in us." Her tone implied she wasn't sure that would happen. "Or we find some magic, demon-killing arrows, stat."

Athena followed her father through Houston. "Are you going to tell me what this surprise might be? It's not my birthday, and 'm not a little girl anymore."

Mareus chuckled. "Not a little girl, and yet she sulks at not being given more information. Convincing."

Athena fought an urge to pout. *You are the most powerful being on the planet. You can let him indulge in a minor fathering moment.*

Ptyas nodded inside her. *That is the kinder choice, though it could be debated that there remain a few beings more powerful. You haven't even met a Drake.*

She still wasn't used to feeling another being's movements and facial expressions, let alone another voice besides her own. *Screw kinder. Sometimes it's just easier to let my father play his games. He throws violent tantrums when I don't.*

Mareus stopped in front of a brick building with a neon martini glass with the simple phrase "The Spot" glowing beneath it.

The pulsing thump of base pounded through the thick walls and into Athena's chest. "You're taking me dancing? Is this some weird daddy-daughter bonding thing? Have you been reading relationship improvement books again?"

A dangerous, angry look appeared in Mareus's eyes.

That was less kind, Ptyas said.

No kidding.

Mareus pointed at the building. "Where are we, my lippy daughter?"

Athena sighed. "A club."

"Wrong. This is the swankiest, coolest club in the city." Mareus led her down steps that brought them to a door, guarded by a velvet rope and one large man who looked like he could throw Athena across a room, even as a wolf.

"You do have an eye for the best, Father."

He spun. "You have no idea what's about to happen. Your sarcasm will taste sour soon enough." Mareus stepped up to the man, whispered something and stepped back to Athena's side as the door swung open.

It was then that Athena noticed the odd scent to the man. He wasn't quite human. She didn't recognize the mix of nuts, flowers, and musk. But the door took her focus away from the smells. Where the portal should have opened to a loud club full of fog, lights, and music, there stood a sheet of shimmering light.

"What's that?"

"What? My rebellious daughter doesn't know all?"

She blinked. "Apparently not."

Mareus grinned at her and stepped through.

She followed.

Athena stepped from the humid street of Texas into a cool walkway lined with trees that sparkled with dangling pieces of metal and ghostly lights of every color. The air tasted like cotton candy and there was a musicality to the breeze. "Where are we?" She almost bumped into Mareus as she soaked in the wonder of the place.

He turned and put a hand on her arm, squeezing hard enough to sting. "Listen, this is important. Do not accept anything from anyone unless I say it's okay. Do not eat or drink anything unless I say it's okay. Do not thank anyone for anything. Try not to spill or be rude. And please refrain from killing anyone."

She could smell the guards who had taken up defensive positions on the other side of the trees. They did not smell like any human she had ever encountered. There was no sweat, no rot between teeth, no overuse of perfumes or cologne. If anything, they smelled mildly of spices and flowers. "Where are we?" She repeated the question.

He spread his hands wide. "Welcome to Underhill, the home of the Fae." He turned. "We're off to Unseely Court."

Kale supervised the siphoning of gas and transfer of supplies from one bus to the other. He gave commands to hurry things along and helped carry boxes of rations and bottles of water. Bubba helped too. Bottles, bags, and boxes flying from one luggage compartment to another like a scene from Mary Poppins.

Shelby released the Feral from the bus, the wolves frolicking amongst the trees while the work was done. More Feral arrived in the time they spent getting the bus ready. Kale felt them join the pack one by one. Kale guessed his pack was over two hundred strong now. *Still no match for the Advent.*

Skotha growled in his head. *You do not have to face the Advent today. Save that worry for another day.*

Kale growled back. *You're right. Today I just have to worry about a demon. Didn't even know those were real this morning.*

You did. You just don't remember. Daeglan fought many. You and Mareus drove them from Alsvoira.

Kale froze, holding a gallon of water in each hand. "We did what now?" The shock drove the words out of his mouth.

Skotha didn't reply.

You and Eira get all quiet sometimes when we'd rather you told us everything.

I've said more than I should have already. Knowing too much of the past locks you into one pattern of thinking, acting, reacting. You and Thyra are nimbler and more creative without it.

Kale set the jugs down in the compartment. *That actually makes sense. Such a better explanation than the you-aren't-ready argument.*

You're welcome.

Thanks, I think. Kale reached out through the pack link and gave a series of commands to his new sub-Alpha, to Shelby, and to the many Feral who would be loping along after his only remaining bus. *Let's hope we can ditch our demonic tagalong.*

The trees that lined the path became smaller and smaller, exposing the stone walls beyond and the elven guards who kept pace with them on their parallel paths. They wore armor, but it did not hide the slim, angular grace of the two men or women. Athena couldn't tell their gender, and it bothered her.

Soon they walked along a path that had become thick orange crystals with lights below, the trees on the edge of it only a couple inches tall, yet they resembled fully grown pine. Athena wondered if the air had narcotic effects or if the environment of the Fae was just that bizarre.

She probed her father for more information. "So, how did you know the portal would be there?"

He hummed as he walked, making her belief in the narcotic theory stronger. "The Fae love excess. You can usually find one of their kind guarding a door in the most lavish restaurants, hotels, and clubs in the world."

"Can you tell me more about them," she jerked a finger at one of the guards, "before we get where we're going? Maybe dig into some of that Viersin knowledge?"

"You could always ask Ptyas. Did you forget about your own Immortal Wolf already?"

She shook her head. "No, I just thought it would be nice to hear from you."

He eyed her appraisingly, perhaps gauging the sarcasm level. Finding it low enough he gave in to her request. "The Fae, before humans arrived on Alsvoira, were far different people. They were all logic and no emotion. More like Spock and his Vulcan kind."

Athena's jaw fell open. "You know who Spock is?"

Mareus's eyes twinkled as he continued. "They had a hard time understanding human nature when it was dropped in their lap by the Goddess. Addiction, lust, anger, deceit, fun, games, joy, madness— these were all alien to the Fae." He hopped over a river that literally giggled at them. "They decided to absorb the vices and virtues, the extremes of humanity, in an attempt to understand, to relate."

Athena thought of all the insane and illogical things she'd seen humans do, including herself and her father in that list. "Sounds dangerous."

"Very much so." Mareus stepped around a ring of toadstools. "They tied these extremes to their rules. In a way, all the Fae are OCD."

Athena smiled as she resisted the urge to kick over the same ring of toadstools. "So, they like to count things and touch lampposts?"

Mareus stopped walking, turned, and fixed her with a serious face that froze her in her tracks. "Do not mistake this for the quirky detectives on your streaming videos. The Fae are dangerous and unpredictable. When they feel their rules have been violated, they lash out. When rules are followed in a certain way, they are required to lash out. Sometimes that violence is directed at themselves, and sometimes it is heaped on another. Do you understand?"

Athena stared at her father, looking for any indications of jest. She could sense a slight tremor of trepidation in him. *He's afraid of the Fae. What scares the Alpha Prime? Fairies?*

You'll find your father has many fears, Ptyas answered. *Most run deep and are tied to legitimate threats to himself, his loved ones, and his race. He did terrible things on Alsvoira, but he did them for good reasons, at least in his mind. Do the ends justify the means? We have yet to see.*

Should I be afraid of the Fae too, then? Athena asked her Immortal Wolf.

Most definitely. Try not to be offensive, condescending, cruel, angry, or disrespectful.

We are in so much trouble, Athena half-joked with Ptyas.

Yes, yes we are. He didn't sound like he was joking back.

K ale stepped from the bus and shifted into his wolf, letting the armor shift with him.

Are you sure this is a good idea? Shelby padded up to his left. *It's not exactly the best time.*

I promised him I would give him an hour a day to start. Kale let his emotions flow easily into her, not resisting her at all, like he had to on occasion as Alpha. He wanted her to know he was as conflicted as her about this. *Do I go back on my promise, just because we have a little demon problem?*

She sent comfort with her sarcasm. *Yeah, just a tiny inconvenience . . .*

He always loved how her comfort projections felt like a hug. He could almost smell her in it too. That lilac soap mingling with the essence of Shelby. Intoxicating. *I know it's kind of huge, but if I let the big things get in the way of a promise, then it becomes easier to let any excuse become a justification. I won't be that guy.*

Shelby nuzzled into him. *I know. It's why I love you, even when I want to bite you.*

Oh? My girlfriend is so violent.

Just a nibble. He felt her link to the pack change. She'd given over to Eira.

Kale shook his head. *Ever the example, even as she argues with me.*

She felt it would make the decision you've already made easier, Eira spoke through the same link.

It does. He gave over autonomy to Skotha, sinking into the background to watch, listen, and comment if he chose.

Skotha and Eira loped into the woods around their makeshift camp, skirting the Feral, nipping at one another, laughing, and talking directly to one another. Kale felt a warmth grow inside him, hints of the bond he and Shelby had shared, but then it was gone, and he was in control once more.

What? No way was that an hour.

Skotha nodded. *No, but it was more than I should have taken with all you must manage. I am thankful you kept your promise. That is enough for today.*

Shelby came to his side, near silent. *Eira wanted me to say thank you. She is proud of both of us. I can't believe how selfless they both are. I'd have taken the whole hour with you, if roles had been reversed.*

Kale met her eyes. He'd been wondering if he'd be able to show such restraint as well. *Did you feel it? Our connection for a second?*

She nodded, eyes sad. *Yes.*

Don't worry. We'll get it back.

She rubbed her furry face against his neck. *I hope so. Giving up autonomy for an hour may be worth it, just to feel a fraction of the bond again. I'd give more.*

Me too. He glanced to where the bus waited, blankets and tents dotting the pristine landscape around it. *Back to work?*

Yeah. We can't stay long. Shelby looked off to the southwest. *The demon is getting closer.*

His eyes met hers. *You can feel him? How far?*

It's hard to explain and hard to guess distance. He's moving fast. She blinked her golden eyes.

Try.

She barked a laugh. *Eira just said the same thing. He's so hungry, so full of jealous rage. It feels like a vacuum, a void in my senses. Still a day or so away, I think.*

Wow. He turned and began a slow walk back toward the bus. *You're getting stronger.*

She grinned as she bumped his shoulder with her own. *Have to keep up with my ever-evolving Alpha boyfriend who's breaking all the rules.*

She's even stronger than she was on Alsvoira, Skotha added. *I'm not sure what she and Eira will become.*

I'm not sure if that's as comforting as you meant it to be, Kale replied to his Immortal Wolf.

It was not meant as a comfort, just a fact.

Race ya! Shelby jumped, bounded off of Kale's chest, and then sprinted down the mountainside.

Well, at least some things don't change.

For now, Skotha replied.

Shut up, my friend. Kale grinned and broke into his own sprint, silently dropping the ultra-light armor so he could run a tiny amount faster and laughing at Shelby's wolf face of surprise as he overtook her.

T heo woke to the usual hum of humanity below him. Salt Lake wasn't the busiest of cities, but it had its ebbs and flows. He had a moment of happiness before he remembered his brother was dead, and he was banished from Underhill. The hum grew louder. *Are they trying out a new mixer?*

Fizz blew through the wall above his bed, throwing plaster and splinters across the room. The wisp bounced off the far wall and collapsed to the floor with a puff of blue flames and a fizzling sound that meant exhaustion and had been the source of its name.

Theo pushed a chunk of plaster off his chest, stood, and dusted off his clothing. He looked out the hole in his wall into the stairwell and then out into the street beyond. "The landlord won't like that."

Fizz fizzled a reply that sounded like, "Not my problem," to Theo.

"Fine. I'll take care of it this time." He altered the entropy in the room until the broken pieces wanted to be in the same location they had been before Fizz's sudden entry. Dust, splinters, brick, mortar, plaster, and old paint that likely had lead in it, all crawled over each other to climb up the wall. The holes filled and repaired themselves. "But, if the pipes explode downstairs, know it was your fault for making me use my magic to fix your mess."

Fizz chirped a high-pitched note of agreement that made Theo smile.

"What did you find?"

Fizz danced over the wooden floorboards, laying down layers of soot to form a picture. It drew an image of a bus with mountains in the background. The accuracy of Fizz's soot images always astounded Theo. He could make out the license plate number and individual trees on the mountains.

"A bus? Really? The demon crossed dimensions, vibrated through stone, climbed to the surface, and hopped on a bus?"

Again, a high note of agreement.

"That makes about as much sense as a pixie with a ponytail." Fae aversion to imperfect knots made it unlikely. "Demons are drawn to powerful magic. They feed on it. They're parasites, not Greyhound customers."

Fizz bounced on top of the bus in its drawing, insistent.

"Okay, let's say there's magic on that bus, hypothetically. How is there enough to entice a demon away from the buffet of magic that is Underhill?"

Fizz let out a mid-tone questioning note.

"You don't know?" Theo sighed. "Fine. Any better landmarks than those mountains? That could be anywhere."

Fizz let out a low, negative, almost offended tone.

"I know, I know, your images are always perfect renditions of what you've seen. Sometimes I wish you had words though." Theo pulled out his phone, snapped a pic, and did an image search. It took longer than he liked, but the results came back with a close match near Fruitland, Utah. "Wait? Are they close?"

Fizz sang and bounced happily.

"Are they headed this direction?"

Again, Fizz bounced and sang.

"Well, that's convenient." Theo's alarm sounded. He glanced down. "Why did I set my alarm for seven in the morning?"

Fizz hummed an annoyed tone.

Time reoriented around Theo as he realized his mistake. "It's night, huh? Wow, I'm an idiot. Crap! I have a DJ gig in half an hour. Help me get ready, Fizz, if you have the energy."

His Will-o'-the-Wisp rose and began making his vacated bed.

Theo sighed then chuckled. "Not what I had in mind, but I'll take what I can get." He ran to the tiny bathroom to take the quickest shower. "Set out my clothes, will ya?"

A positive note.

"Thanks, Fizzlet. You're the best." He knew the wisp would most likely set out some bizarre combination, like a wetsuit, a dinner jacket, and a Halloween mask, but keeping Fizz busy made for fewer broken mugs. The wisp didn't always repair them perfectly. Half of Theo's cups, mugs, and glasses leaked.

Athena took deep breaths as the Will-o'-the-Wisps sniffed her face. It took everything in her not to slice one of the balls of blue fire in two with her scythe as they invaded her personal space and bumped against skin. Mostly she was curious what would happen if she did. "What are they doing?"

"Making sure you are who you say you are," Mareus growled behind a face full of his own wisps. "Let them finish. Then we can enter."

The wisps had swarmed out of an open doorway after their two guards had set up on both sides of it and tapped their spears to the ground. Athena had barely glimpsed the strange carvings in the wooden doors before being attacked. *At least dear daddy warned me a few seconds before, or I would have sliced one open.*

That would not be advisable, Ptyas said.

Why?

They are made of contained sentient fire. It would be like slicing open a live bomb.

Athena frowned as the last wisp finally pulled away from her. *Okay, that does sound unpleasant. Is it terrible that I want to try more now?*

Ptyas laughed. *Yes, but it is very you.*

"You may enter now." One of the guards pointed her staff at the doorway, her voice giving away her gender at last.

Athena let Mareus lead the way through, her eyes on the carvings that showed mischief, murder, and a mix of many other acts Athena wasn't completely comfortable with. Some she couldn't even place. *What is this?*

Ptyas sighed. *The Fae of Unseely Court lean toward the more dangerous, less benevolent, and areobscene elements of humanity. They integrated the worst of your kind into themselves.*

Athena bristled. *I'm not human. I'm Lycan.*

You are the unexpected result of a human and Immortal Wolf becoming one. We were unsure the mix would be capable of offspring. You are still more human than you pretend to be. Your thoughts and actions give you away.

Athena took another deep breath and calmed herself. She was beginning to understand how pointless arguing with the wolf could be. *It's like arguing with myself.*

Only I'm more enlightened. There was laughter in his voice.

Athena chuckled. *Shhh, something's happening.*

The wisps spun around the large, dark cavern ahead, their lights illuminating statues making grotesque faces and gestures. They then shot upward, punching into the crystalline ceiling. She let her eyes shift, so she could see into the darkness, but all she saw was a gray haze where the shadows had been.

Magic.

The wisps blazed brighter. Athena covered her eyes as the burst of light blinded her. She blinked as her eyes recovered, shifting them back to human. She glared at the wisps above her, but her anger subsided as she realized the ceiling was not crystal, but water, rippling where the wisps had entered and refracting their light into a blue-white glow that filled the entire cavern, revealing there were no statues.

She was surrounded by Fae, their faces no longer grotesque when illuminated, but each one staring at her and her father with disdain, like perfect, hateful CGI visages.

One sat on a throne made of red glass, maybe ruby, glaring at them. "How dare you come here uninvited!"

Athena could smell blood as his words reached her, as if carried with the sound. She gasped when the realization came. The throne wasn't glass or a precious stone. It flowed under the Fae, trapped in the shape of a regal seat, but made entirely of fresh blood.

Athena swallowed the retort that wanted to bubble out of her.

Someone's learning.

Shut it, Ptyas.

Shelby looked out the windshield as they drove down the winding road into Salt Lake. "Huh, it's grayer than I imagined."

Genn leaned against the back of the seat beside her. "Inversion. The valley traps the air, and all the fires haven't been helping. It's prettier after a storm blows the trapped air out."

"Guess I'll have to take your word for it." She glanced at where Bryanne was resting across the aisle. "You two figure out where we're going? The demon is closing in fast."

"Bryanne thinks she's narrowed it down, but I'm not so sure."

"Where the palace meets brine?" Shelby repeated the words she'd heard them discussing for days. "Is there a palace in the city?"

Genn nodded. "Two, of a sort. There is a convention center that has Bryanne's vote."

"Why?" Shelby could feel the Feral growing distant. They had to wait in the forested areas near the foothills where they wouldn't cause a panic and where food was still plentiful. She could also feel the void moving toward them from the opposite direction.

"It's actually called the Salt Palace."

"That's convenient." Shelby brought a gauntlet into existence on one hand, watching the magic flicker. "We could use convenient."

Genn gave a half smile. "Not convenient enough for my liking. It just doesn't fit the *Isluxua's* description. It's nowhere near any brine, despite the name. And it's not really a palace."

The gauntlet vanished at a thought from Shelby. "What's the other one?"

"The Mormons built a temple. It's practically a palace." Genn pulled out her phone and showed Shelby a few pictures of the building.

"Wow! And that has your vote?"

Genn put her phone away. "No. It's just a few blocks from the Salt Palace, still not anywhere close to the lake."

Shelby felt Kale come up behind her. She held out a hand, and he took it, leaning into the seat to stare outside. "You hear all that?"

He nodded. "So, where are you thinking this palace is, Mom?"

Genn folded her arms. "I don't really want to disagree with Bryanne, especially after what she's been through today."

"Bryanne isn't a child. She can speak for herself, in third person even." The Bandruí lifted her head, humming to herself. She waved away Genn's hand. "I'm fine, as long as I don't touch any magic." She hummed a bit more as a smile tugged at the corners of her mouth. "And I woke up with an old Pixies' song in my head. I change my vote."

"To what?" Kale asked, a hint of impatience in his tone.

Genn answered, as patient as ever. "There's an old event center right on the lake, called Salt Air. It was built to look like a palace. What made you change your mind?"

Bryanne sang a snatch of lyrics. "The song, of course. I can't believe I didn't make the connection earlier."

Genn laughed. "What? How?"

"It isn't their most popular song, but it was written shortly after the Pixies visited Salt Lake. It's a reference to Salt Air and how sad its clones have been when compared to the original. I saw the second one in person. It wasn't as beautiful as the first, and it's gone downhill since."

Shelby bit her lip, curious. "What's the song?"

"Palace on the Brine."

Shelby felt her mouth drop open.

Bryanne grinned. "Yeah, that's why I'm changing my vote. That's just the type of weird coincidence those Mystics seem to like."

Kale chuckled. "I'm so telling Iorna you said that." He made a disgusted face as they descended into the gray air, the scents of smoke sneaking in with it. "Salt Air it is. Let's hope you're both right and there's a Fae waiting for us, key at the ready."

Shelby squeezed his hand. "When has it been that simple?"

Bubba pulled the tab. The Vienna sausage container opened with a pleasant crack and hiss. "It ain't momma's fried chicken, but it will do. One for you." He held a sausage in front of his dog who snatched it up and wolfed it down. "Ya gotta chew, Oscar. You're not a Playa Killa, like me, so take it easy." Bubba pulled out another sausage. "Like this, and one for me." He chewed it with vigor.

"You're sweet with him," Amanda spoke from behind him where she leaned over the seat.

"Like I got a choice? Look at that face. Like honey." Oscar put a paw on Bubba's wrist and eyed the container. "Knows what he likes too, don't he?"

"Always a good thing to know. I think I like—" Chelsea tugged on her sleeve, and Amanda pushed the hand away, but didn't finish her thought. "Your first pet?"

"Momma's allergic, or least faking allergic so I don't get no idea bout bringing home strays." Bubba grinned up at her while Oscar snatched another sausage from his hand. "Cept her allergies always acted up after Kale came by, so maybe not faking. Been bringing home strays for years without her knowing."

Amanda giggled. "True." She reached into a pocket and slid something toward him over the top of the seat.

He finished the last sausage and took it. "Red Vines?"

She nodded. "I got them at a gas station a few days back. Road trip food. Thought you could use the calories in a more productive way than I ever could."

Bubba tried to hand it back. "You must've used the last of your cash, and there ain't no chance for more."

She ignored his attempts to give it back to her. "Don't worry, I'll loot a movie theater later." She smiled wider. "Or maybe a Costco, where I can get the big tub."

"Until then, hold on to it."

She folded her arms and glared at him. "DeShawn, quit being stubborn and chivalrous, and take the gift! If someone shoots at me, I want you to have the energy to stop that bullet. I'm being selfish, really."

He slipped the package into one of his many pockets. "I like this form of selfish. Everyone should be selfish and give me food." He winked at her.

She smiled. "That's a good idea. What do you think, Chelsea?"

The cheerleader hopped out of her seat and squeezed past Amanda. "I'll spread the word."

"I was joking, girl." But Chelsea was gone.

Amanda patted his arm and stared off to where Chelsea held a pillow case open as she berated two Lycans about snack salvation. "Too late. The Wiccan network has gone to work. Give that girl a cause, and she'll go after it, like a dog with a Vienna sausage."

"Speaking of." Bubba held up the container and tipped it over. The meaty liquid formed a rippling ball that sunk slowly toward Oscar. Jaws snapped, and the sausage residual vanished behind teeth. Bubba dropped the lid into the empty tin and ripped off the label.

"What are you doing?" Amanda asked.

"Saying thank you." Bubba dropped the tin in the air where it hovered. He then squeezed it into a ball. He pinched his fingers in the air and pulled his hands apart to focus his mind on the task as he blinked. "Details ain't easy."

Thin wavering tendrils pulled away from the ball of metal. He tugged at it with his mind, molding it bit by bit.

Amanda watched him work with interest. Her gasp of realization made Bubba happy.

"It's a giraffe! How did you know they're my favorite?"

Bubba grabbed the metal animal from the air and handed it over. "Oh, I've always been lucky, girl."

She took it, sniffed it, and laughed. "Sausage-raffe."

"Is there any other kind?"

Chelsea shoved a half full sack of goodies onto his lap. "Selfishness for the win."

"Thank you, Miss Chelsea, and thank ya'll too," Bubba said to the bus as he glanced inside. "Oooooh, that will recharge the sausage-raffe sculpting nicely." He ripped open a caramel filled candy bar.

Oscar whined and put his paw on his wrist again.

"Don't be silly. You can't have chocolate." Bubba rummaged through the sack. "But we got jerky. Oscar approved!"

Sadie slipped into the back of the high school gymnasium, wrinkling her nose at the scent of unwashed socks. *Someone needs to talk to these coaches about how often teenage boys should wash their gym clothes.*

She walked silently and took a seat near the back of the town hall style meeting where this pack's Alpha discussed the disturbing news he'd heard coming out of the south. *Here's hoping this one goes better than the last.* Sadie took a deep breath and let her scent shift to something similar to Shelby's wolfly smells. *She's always getting attention everywhere she goes.*

Every head whipped around. Several of the attendees began shifting, snarling.

Sadie raised her hands. "I know, I know. You aren't too trusting of outsider Lycans at the moment. Just give me a minute to talk." She nodded to a boy she'd spent days befriending. "Tyson will vouch for me."

The Alpha glared at the boy. "Is this true? You invited a stranger here when we're at war?" Tyson shrunk away and said nothing.

"Hades, I was counting on you to make this easier, Tyson. Do I know how to pick em?" Sadie let her Shelby scent dissipate, hoping the distrust might ease if the scent of a stranger went away. "I'll start with I'm not Advent."

The Alpha eyed her. "Yeah, I've heard they cull the weak."

Sadie bristled. "I'm small, but not weak. I'll have you know that Mareus himself tried to recruit me."

More snarls greeted her. *Easy, Sadie. This could go sideways really quick.*

"Look, I get it. I've got no love for the guy. I've seen up close and personal what the Advent is capable of. It's scary stuff. You did the right thing, but the right thing has consequences."

The Alpha gave her a suspicious look.

"Yeah, I've been spying on them . . . and you, but mostly them. I know they tried to sway you. I know you sent them packing. I also, unfortunately, know firsthand what they do when a pack turns them away. It ain't pretty, and it ain't far behind."

The Alpha sneered. "And you came here to warn us out of the kindness of your heart?"

Sadie nodded. "Pretty much. That and to let you know you aren't alone. There are others fighting. There's a growing group of us who don't want to see civilization burn under this so-called Alpha Prime."

"And you want us to join you? Be David to this Goliath?" The Alpha shook his head. "We're good on our own."

Sadie shrugged. "It's up to you, but you're the one who said you're at war. They will come in force next time, in two days, after a few more recruits arrive from the south. Allies are nice."

"How do you know this if you aren't with them?" The Alpha didn't sound as suspicious as his words.

"I know because I'm a spy for the true Alpha Prime and his Summer Omega." She let her hair change colors in waves while releasing the scent of summer rain. "Perhaps you've seen the gas station knight that's all over the internet . . . at least when the internet's working?"

The room nodded almost as one, wolves shifting back to their human forms.

"That's my friend and packmate. She and our Alpha are gathering their own group to stand against the Advent. Are you interested in hearing more, or do I walk away and let you fend for yourselves?"

The Alpha motioned toward a spot on the floor next to him. "You have five minutes."

A half-dozen heavily armed and armored Fae raced forward, bows drawn, arrows nocked. *That went well, Dad*, Athena thought. *Way to negotiate.*

Athena hissed, took a defensive stance, and let her armor appear, her dual-bladed scythe flashing into existence. She spun to take stock of the room and gauge the threats that could come from the other Fae in the room.

Mareus also wore his armor, but he held up his hands. "Wait, we're here to talk about the Keys of Ascension."

The king of the Fae raised one perfectly sculpted, bored eyebrow. The guards froze. "What is this glamour? How did you create such a perfect illusion of our ancient armor?"

Mareus kept his hands up and growled at Athena. "Put the scythe away. We cannot shed blood here." To the king he bowed slightly. "It is no illusion. These were forged by your hands before Alsvoira fell, Abdonius. Do you not remember me?"

The king squinted at her father while Athena contemplated letting the blades vanish. She chose to keep them in hand.

"I do recognize you, Alpha Prime pretender. I made that armor eons ago so you could save us all. You failed." The eyebrow dropped, and the guards advanced once more.

Mareus did not flinch. "I failed nothing. My mission was simply delayed and the location of the battle moved. We will still defeat Tarloch and his minions."

The Fae king laughed bitterly. "Without the Goddess? I think not."

Mareus growled deep and low, his anger making his body shake. "The Goddess let the demons in. I saw the alternate timelines where she defeated them easily. She chose to let us try to defend ourselves, knowing we would lose."

"You lie!" Abdonius leaned forward, spittle flying from his mouth.

"I do not and I can prove it."

Abdonius raised a finger. The guards retreated a few steps. "Show me."

A wisp shot forward and hovered before Mareus, who shook his head. "It isn't my memory to share." He pointed at Athena.

Athena stood straighter. "What? I don't know what you're talking about."

He means me, Ptyas spoke.

"Oh, my Immortal Wolf." She eyed the wisp that drew near with suspicion. "What do I do?"

Give it permission to see a memory. I will do the rest.

Athena looked the wisp in the upper middle, where she imagined eyes should be. "You have my permission to share a memory."

The wisp pulsed with light and then a picture formed in the air of the most perfect being Athena had ever seen. She made the Fae look ugly. *The Goddess?*

Yes, Ptyas answered, his tone sad and angry, but Athena couldn't tell who the anger was directed at.

Himself? My father? The Goddess?

Yes.

Oh, I was trying to keep those thoughts to myself.

There is no such refuge now.

Athena absorbed that bit without reacting. She was too entranced with the memory playing out.

The Goddess leaned down and reached out a delicate golden hand to stroke the side of her face, Ptyas's face. "Thank you for taking on this burden, my child. It is too much to ask of one. You will let Iorna rest."

The Goddess turned and walked away, but the vision followed her to where a sheet of glass hung in the middle of the room. Athena could see Ptyas reflected in it, the wolf standing tall and proud. *I've never seen you like that.*

I was young and so sure of everything, Ptyas said. *And a fool.*

The Goddess tapped the glass and it became a gateway, showing a desert landscape on the far side. "You will remember what you see here and work with a human you trust to record it. I will share a timeline that did not come to be."

The vision bobbed as Ptyas nodded.

She tapped the portal again.

Athena and the rest of the room stared at a field full of flowers. Water poured from a huge pillar of stone in the background in five directions. Blue mountains stood beyond that, topped in snow. *Alsvoira?*

Yes, watch.

A slash of black and red appeared at the center of the field, a portal to somewhere dark. Demons poured through the rift. The flowers fell as ash and flames spread out in all directions. A monster pushed through the gateway, huge, distorted, scorched skin blacker than the moonless night and a maw full of flame. A crown of molten metal topped his horned head. Where he stepped the world warped toward him as though he had a gravity all his own.

The Goddess appeared, stepping over ash, fresh flowers sprouting in her footsteps. An assembly of the five races stood behind her, dressed in bright gold Fae armor. A battle ensued, the Goddess forcing the demons back into the shadows of their own world, light flowing from her hands in streams that the demon king tried to absorb, but it was more than even he could devour.

He staggered backward through his rift, abandoning many of his demons as the portal closed behind him. The vision flickered and fell apart.

Athena stared at the wisp again. It swam lazily through the air back to the king's side. The king sat, mouth open, staring at where it had been. "That's not what happened."

"No," Mareus replied. "She let them destroy our world. She stood by and let them devour your sacred pools. She watched our cities burn. She failed us, not me. But I won't let that happen again. Earth will not fall like Alsvoira did. We're here for the key."

Abdonius shook his head and closed his mouth. "You have come to the wrong court. You will find no keys here." The guards advanced once more.

I knew it. Athena tapped into the ley lines she'd found deep beneath them. It wasn't as easy to draw from these as the ones she'd leached into at the manor, but she found holes punched in these as well. *Demons?* She pulled the magic in, the world taking on a tinge of purple.

Illusions vanished as the magic filled her. The room remained beautiful, but the population halved. Ghosts of Fae looked on, held together by orange light. Even a few of the guards weren't real. *Tricks and lies. I don't think I like the Fae.*

"If they won't give us the key, Father, we'll take it by force." She lashed out, sending a burst of Druid magic at the throne. Not all of the ill-made spell made it to her target as some of it siphoned away with a painful tug at her soul, but enough landed home. The Fae spells holding the throne together shattered. The king fell in the pool of unbound blood. It splattered the silver, gold, and bejeweled shoes of the crowd. Athena swung her scythe at the neck of the closest real guard.

Her father caught her blades in his gauntleted hand, the one that hadn't fully healed, fingers curled at odd angles around her blades. "No, Daughter. This is not the way. Force never works with Fae." He bowed toward where the king glared at them, soaked in blood, his perfect face blotchy with orange and splattered with red. "Blood has been spilt, but no Fae blood. And payment has already been offered."

Mareus lifted his hand, letting the gauntlet vanish. His gnarled fingers barely covered a gash to the bone from her scythe, blood dripping down his palm to splatter against the floor.

Athena went to take his hand. "Oh, Father, I'm so sorry. I did not intend to hurt you."

He ripped his hand away from her. "I allowed you to hurt me to undo the damage you had already done. Silence, child! You've said and done enough." He turned back to the king. "Accept my apology for a daughter who is overly eager and lacks patience."

Athena took a step back, stung by his tone and words. She bit back another angry retort and was grateful Ptyas said nothing.

The king sat staring at his bloodied pants and then began to laugh. It kept going for several minutes, high-pitched and manic as he kicked his feet and gasped for air. He finally managed to stop and stand, but giggles kept bubbling up. "That was a surprise, dear Athena." He smiled at her surprise. "Yes, I know who you are. I'm king. Surprises are rare for someone my age. Thank you." He gestured to the room. "Leave us. And someone bring me a few chairs."

Half the Fae vanished in a flash of fire and smoke. The others shuffled out. Someone dragged three chairs into the center of the pool of blood.

Athena released her hold on the ley lines as she took the seat next to the king. The scythe disappeared. "Sorry and you're welcome."

Abdonius chuckled. "You made a feisty one, Mar-Bar."

Mareus growled. "Really? Still with that nickname?"

The king shrugged. "It is law to give nicknames to those we care for. A human affectation we're still attempting to understand. You were one of my dearest friends. Seems you remain so. I can't believe the Goddess let Alsvoira fall. It is madness."

"And that's coming from you." Athena realized what she'd said too late to stop herself.

The king eyed her and laughed again, slapping her shoulder with a heavy hand covered in blood. "I like her. Madness is another law here. You humans fall into it so easily. We have to work so hard to hold onto it."

Athena wiped at her shoulder with a gauntlet, trying not to let her disgust show. "Doesn't seem like it."

"That is the kindest thing anyone has ever said to me." The king looked at her with pure sincerity, a tear in one eye. "Refreshments!" He shouted the word in her face so forcefully Athena's hair moved, and she wondered if she was supposed to get up and find some for him.

But a thin Fae woman carried a tray in before Athena could stand. The king took an assortment of fruit, meat, and cheeses, stuffing them into his mouth quickly before letting the tray pass on to the others.

Mareus waved the tray away but nodded at Athena's unspoken question.

She took a skewer with strange fruit on it and a fluted glass with a pink liquid inside that smelled faintly like strawberries. "Thank . . ." Athena trailed off as she caught her father's widened eyes.

The Fae with the tray was leaning forward, a look of rising anger on her face, with an undercurrent of eager excitement.

". . . goodness the weather's been so nice. Am I right?"

"That was close. Did your father explain what happens when you thank a Fae?" Abdonius waved the servant away after Mareus showed no interest in the refreshments.

Athena shook her head as she sipped the beverage, aware within seconds that it was laced with something that felt more magical than narcotic. She fought an urge to giggle and shook her head harder to clear it.

The king frowned at Mareus. "You didn't prepare her well." He turned back to Athena and threw a grape in his mouth. "Humans arrived on Alsvoira, so thankful for everything. It didn't take us long to realize you use those words to dismiss what was done for you. You speak the words and then promptly forget all the work, the anguish, the heart that went into the acts. Nothing angers a Fae like being thanked. Not a single one here is your servant and not a single one wants you to dismiss any kindness they do."

"I can handle one angry Fae." Athena sipped again and couldn't suppress the giggle that bubbled out.

"You misunderstand. You also would have owed her something to show your gratitude was not a simple spell to forget. It is law. You would not be able to refuse, not here, not with Fae air in your lungs and Fae drink in your mouth." He watched the woman with the tray slip out a side entrance to the throne room, giving a disappointed glance back at the Lycan. "That one is partial to eyes."

Like I'd let her take one of my eyes.

No, you would have plucked it out yourself and handed it to her. Ptyas snapped, obviously angry at her flippant attitude.

Athena shrugged. *Eyes heal.*

Ptyas growled inside her. *Not in this case. She would have kept it alive and whole. Your body would have never recognized the wound. You would have seen glimpses of whatever maddening glamour she cast upon it for the rest of your life. And she would have been in possession of a piece of you, given freely. That's a magic that can be used against you, even decades later. You need to take this seriously.*

Athena swallowed what was in her mouth but set the glass down on the bloodied floor next to her chair. *Fine.*

Athena looked up to find the king contemplating her.

"Talking to yourself? Who's mad here?"

"To Ptyas, not myself," she corrected him.

Abdonius laughed, only slightly manic this time. "Is he not a part of you? Just because the voice in your head has a name does not make you less of a shattered creature than the rest of humanity."

Athena swallowed her argument. She'd already lost that one with Ptyas. "What about the key? Are you willing to give it to us now?"

The king smiled, his lips curving farther than human lips could. It was disconcerting. "I told you. There are no keys here."

"Riddles." Mareus said. "Fae love them. So, no keys here, but they are somewhere? Seely Court?"

The king winked at Athena before turning to his old friend. "Always so clever. The Goddess, taking into account the unique nature of the Fae, divided the key between us. Only royal Seely blood can unlock the key, in the place where keys were forged."

Mareus leaned forward. "That means there is a second part that you can offer."

Abdonius grinned, revealing perfect white teeth with tiny silver designs carved into them. "I am the singular individual that can give consent."

Athena scooted to the edge of her seat. "Do you? Give it?"

"Of course. I give consent. You have it."

Athena felt an electrical sensation in her bones, a tingling that rolled from toes to crown. "Yes, I do. How do we get the key?"

"I've told you."

Mareus leaned back. "Silphinaera will never give me or my daughter the key. That's why I came to you."

"And I'll never give consent to Thyra-mit-Eira, not after all she did to me and mine. So many Fae deaths at her hand." The king's countenance had gone pale, his eyes dark and far away, but then he cackled, slapping his thigh. Blood droplets flew everywhere. "The Goddess set up the perfect ironic logical trap. Two want the key and neither can get the whole of it. Perhaps you are right, Mar-Bar. Maybe she really did want the demons to win. Maybe our sweet Goddess embraced madness at the end too."

Athena wiped drops of blood from her face. "What now, Father?"

The king answered before Mareus could say anything. "I can get you to the right place. Maybe that will be enough."

T heo's powder-blue Vespa skidded on the gravel as he parked too fast near the side entrance to Salt Air, kicking up a cloud of dust that blew out over the water. Brine flies dodged his dust as Theo set the kickstand, pulled off his helmet, and grabbed his meager gear from the compartment.

He relied on the current owner of Salt Air to provide most of the equipment. Theo could have had the best gear, a swanky apartment, and a better vehicle, but he didn't like leaning on Fae contacts if he didn't have to.

The stuffy interior of the helmet was replaced by the scent of salt and decay. *Ah, the beauty of Stank Air.* That was a common nickname for the location, but it was one of the largest venues in Salt Lake area and well away from the city, so the concerts and events could get loud and go late.

Theo pulled the door open and stepped into one of the employee's areas, which was as run down as they come. The building had been moved, rebuilt, and changed hands too many times to count. The original had been a sight to see, with copper-topped towers, polished wood, fancy pavilions, and plenty of boardwalk space to take in the view. The latest version was a squat warehouse made of concrete. The dome-roofed towers were reminiscent of the original Moscow-esque architecture, but they were fiberglass and sun-rotten. People didn't show up for the fancy décor. Salt Air was all about the wild parties and the music.

Theo ran up the concrete stairs to the landing where all the equipment waited. The venue owner paid a company to set it all up for him beforehand, get the lights running, kick on the fog machines, and play a pulsing track on repeat in the background so the early comers didn't file in to silence.

Theo checked the soundboards, adjusted a few levels, plugged in a mic, booted up his laptop, and put on the most expensive thing he owned: his headphones. When he felt good about starting, he flipped a switch that swung multi-colored lights his way as he dropped his glamour to reveal lavender eyes that were larger than most humans, pointed ears, and long hair that shifted colors in the light. He stared out at the mob of humanity that huddled in the dark between cinder block walls painted black.

"Are you ready to dance?" he shouted into the microphone.

The crowd screamed. Theo loved that moment, the pure excitement and anticipatory joy. "DJ Elf is in the house! Let's get it on!"

He kicked on the first track and then blended it with another, pumping the bass into overdrive. It was always good to start with something fast-paced and thumping. The crowd came alive, pulsing in rhythmic movements that created rippling patterns through the room.

Theo hit a program that would run the lights through a series of movements with his music. He also cracked opened a spell-lined shoebox and whispered inside. "You know the drill. Stay high, don't bump into people." He widened the crack and Fizz shot up to dance among the lights and artificial smoke near the ceiling.

Theo tapped into his magic, altering entropy enough that unusual and unlikely patterns formed in that smoke. Checkers, swirling designs, and fractals filled the air above the crowd, highlighted by lights and lasers. The crowd went crazy, pointing upward as they danced, picking out images, like kids do with clouds. Theo grinned, let one track end and slid another into the background, and he turned on the projector that sent psychedelic video splashing along one large wall. Yeah, he definitely liked his job.

Athena followed the elf-like woman who had almost taken her eye through the winding and weird paths of Underhill. Her father had remained behind. He couldn't join her in the quest for this key. There was too much going on in the world for him to take the time, especially as the king hadn't been specific on how long she might be waiting in Alsvoira. *Why can't he leave a lieutenant in charge for a couple more hours at least?*

Ptyas answered the question she'd posed to herself. *Because you are his most trusted, and he can't leave you behind. I suspect he also wants to avoid Alsvoira.*

Athena managed not to flinch, despite his sudden voice surprising her. She smiled inwardly at her control, but then realized he was grinning at her. *Weird to feel someone grinning inside me. You noticed you startled me, didn't you?*

Of course. We are one.

When will I get used to that?

Probably never. It is unusual for me too. I tried to be a comfort for my previous host, but we didn't really converse. Thank you, again, for what you're doing for her.

Athena shrugged. *I made a promise. I usually keep those.*

Ptyas chuckled but said nothing more.

They walked in silence again for a few more minutes, staring at the perfect backside of the Fae woman, rustling silk, before Athena spoke again to her Immortal Wolf. *Why?*

Pardon?

Why wouldn't my father wish to see Alsvoira? It was his home. He talks about it all the time. He's kind of obsessed really.

Ptyas sighed. *It isn't what it once was. He is partly responsible for that. I'm sure it would pain him more than it will me to see the corpse of our world.*

Athena mused over his answer. *That makes sense. Are you sure you can handle it?*

I have to. You need the key, and I am not in charge of this body.

Sorry. Athena didn't know why she said it.

It's okay. I was barely in charge of the last body, so it is kind of nice to sit back and stop fighting for every tortuous movement. You have no idea how hard hunting is when every nerve resists you.

Did it hurt?

It was agony.

They fell silent again.

"We are entering Seely Court territory," the Fae woman said.

Athena grinned as she felt Ptyas jump at the Fae's voice.

She hadn't needed to say so. There was a sharp distinction when their journey crossed from the Unseely madness into the more orderly Seely weirdness. The paths were less winding, the landscape less bizarre, but there was still an otherness about the place that reminded Athena she was not in the world she knew.

"How far now?"

The Fae woman glanced back, her perfect blue eyes too large in her skull as she blinked languidly at Athena. "Not far to the demon gate and then a short hike to your destination. Do you still have the token?"

Athena rubbed the silver coin in her pocket, given to her by the Unseely king. "Of course. I would not lose a Fae gift so easily."

The woman nodded as if Athena had just passed a test. "This way." She stepped off the main path into a wall that swirled around her like smoke before it solidified back into the wall.

Athena stared at the solid stone for only a second before stepping through. *Here's hoping this isn't some Fae trick to make me break my nose and spill more blood.*

It wasn't a trick. Athena passed through without harm, though it felt like walking through spider webs. She rubbed the tickles on her nose away as she stepped through the smoky illusion, almost running into two Fae draped in silver and green armor. Two more stood near the center of the chamber, staring at each other. She froze, but neither of the guards closest to her acknowledged her presence, so she stepped forward, admiring the strange metal. *So much like my own.*

Ptyas answered her thought. *They made it, remember, though my . . . now your armor was crafted by Unseely hands, so it has some more flare.*

Thank you, Ptyas. I know. She elongated the last word, sounding snippier than she intended, but didn't apologize. *I would love to see how it's made.*

You will get to. That coin in your pocket isn't really a coin. It's a complex weaving of spells with instructions for the sentient fire. The king intends to forge something for you.

She rubbed at the silver token in her pocket again, feeling the ridges of the design that resembled a circuit board, if the ancient Celts had created circuit boards. *Huh, cool.*

You modern women are so hard to impress.

She smiled. *That's true. So, where's this portal thing?*

Demon gate. I assume there. Athena felt him gesture forward with his nose.

You know I can't really see where you're pointing, right?

He chuckled. *You know where I'm pointing though, even if you can't see it.*

And she did. She looked to where the two guards at the center of the cavern stared. It was where her guide also gazed.

The Fae woman spoke. "She's here at the king's request. Reveal it. We're going through." She held out her hand to one of the guards where the king had stamped a silver tree.

The guard nodded. A gash of fire appeared at the center of the room, gold electricity sparking off the edges. The center rippled, like a pond in the breeze. It had a mirror-like quality, reflecting Athena's astonished face, while also revealing the red sky and black earth on the far side.

The Fae nodded at her. "Be prepared. There may be demons waiting on the far side, though we believe they moved on to another part of Alsvoira." She stepped through.

Demons may be waiting?

Ptyas chuckled, but there was no humor in it. *Why do you think they call it a demon gate? They made these after we abandoned Alsvoira, trying to follow.*

Athena hesitated, knowing this was no smoke or spiderwebbed illusion. She would be on another world once she stepped through.

Look who's finally impressed, Ptyas chided.

She smiled. *I feel like an astronaut, or part of SG1.* Her scythe appeared in her hand.

Athena stuck it into the portal. Her hand tingled, turned cold, and then went entirely numb. She yelped and pulled it back. Her hand returned fine, warm and whole. *This is safe, right?*

Ptyas shrugged his wolf shoulders inside her. *Depends on if the demons really moved on.*

Athena held her breath and stepped through.

She lost all feeling in her body for a few seconds and then staggered out onto sharp black sand, choking on the cold, sulfurous air. *An astronaut sent to explore icy hell. In many ways that's exactly what Alsvoira has become,* Ptyas replied. *Though the residents do seem to be elsewhere.*

The smell was terrible. "Sometimes I wish I could turn this off." Kale held one of his cleanest t-shirts over his face. "Tell me we're close."

The driver looked over his shoulder. "Maybe two miles." He sniffed. "It's not great, but it's not that bad."

"You're human. You can't smell it, not really. When we got close to the lake, I could smell the salt and water. Now it's all rot, decay, death." Kale pulled his shirt away. "Want a lesson on how the Lycan nose works?"

The man shook his head.

"Too bad. The lake doesn't really smell, but they're pumping wastewater into it near here. Know how I know this?" Kale walked up right behind the driver.

The man remained silent.

"Because I can smell the waste in it. Wrap your head around that for a second and imagine what that means."

Kale could see the look of disgust reflected in the windshield. "Exactly. Gross. On top of that I can pick out the scents coming off the bacteria that bloom and then die off in the salty water. I can tell this is choking off the nutrients and killing the brine shrimp too, which brings in flies. I can almost hear the flies!"

The driver grunted. "I smell rotten eggs. Is that part of it?"

Kale built up a new rant in his head about how that was sulfur from the bacteria, not anything to do with eggs, but as a car passed them on the left, the bus shuddered and the engine in the back made a screeching sound as metal tore. The bus came to a stop as the lights went out. "Maybe threw a belt?"

"Sounded worse than a belt. Something else."

Lights came on inside the bus as people pulled out flashlights or lit up their phones, the few who still had battery life remaining.

Shelby took his hand and squeezed, her own hand clammy. She leaned into him in a pleasant way, but hissed in his ear. "The demon is here. Can't you feel it?"

Kale couldn't, but he didn't want to tell her that. He went rigid. "Where?"

In the flickering light of moving flashlights, she closed her eyes and pointed down. "Storage."

"Bubba, Francis, Sean, with me. Let's take a look at the engine." Kale didn't want to alarm too many of his pack just yet.

"Chelsea, Amanda, Genn, Bryanne, with me. Let's take a quick inventory, in case we need to walk from here." Shelby gave him a scared smile. "The girls here kick gluteus too."

Kale nodded. "Didn't mean anything by excluding you. I

welcome the help. I'm sure you all kick mechanical and inventorial gluteus." *Demon gluteus too*, he thought.

"And don't forget it."

They filled in their volunteers quietly after stepping down the stairs and off the bus, making a loose plan to open the storage door, see what they were dealing with, and either hit it with all they had, or call the rest of the pack out to fight with them. Kale felt a group of Feral several miles out. He sent a call for them to move closer.

Bubba pulled out a candy bar and began devouring it. "Know what I really wish I had right now?"

Kale put a hand on his friend's shoulder, still surprised at the iron cable like muscles he found there. "Your momma's fried chicken?"

"Dang straight! Nothing like a plate of crispy chicken when you're about to tangle with a demon for the first time. Oscar's worried." He pointed to the window where the outline of a wiener dog could be seen backlit by flashlights. A whine reached them through the glass.

"We'll be fine," Kale said it with more confidence than he felt. "Ready?" That question was for all of them.

He looked from face to face, getting a silent nod from each. "Okay. Let's do this. Which one, Shelby?"

She pointed. "It's there."

Kale stepped toward the bus. "I'll open it."

"No, I'll not let my Alpha put himself in needless danger." Francis stepped forward faster and pulled the handle. He jumped back as the hydraulics lifted the hatch.

Bryanne shined a flashlight inside.

Bits of luggage sat with blankets, a cardboard box with lentils and a few cans inside, and a tent that hadn't been packed well, canvas bulging out of a zipper. A silver pellet zipped into the box, sending lentils flying, but nothing else moved.

"Just making sure." Bubba recalled the pellet. "I don't see nothing. Can demons go invisible? Are we dealing with them ninja demons?"

Bryanne traced her hand through the air, leaving a streak of crimson light. It shot away from her and into the storage area, breaking into a million dots of light that hung in the air or spotted the supplies inside. She staggered, but pushed Genn's hand away. "I only held enough magic to do that one spell. I'm okay. It's definitely in there, but it seems to be in pieces."

Kale allowed himself a breath of relief. "It's dead then?"

Shelby held up her scythe, glowing bright red. "No, it's very much alive. It's hiding." She slashed at one of the bright dots. It shattered and went dark. "Not enough?" She slashed another and another. Ten went dark in quick succession as her blade flew through the space with Lycan enhanced speed and grace.

The lights shot together.

Amanda screamed and tripped backward over a loose rock. She didn't hit the ground. She stopped inches from the ground and then tipped forward to her feet. "Thanks, Bubba."

"I won't let nothing happen to that sweet backside."

"Gross and kinda tender."

"Focus, you two." Chelsea hissed as her hands ran through complicated gestures. Amanda did the same. Sean joined them.

Kale hoped the spell to protect their magic worked. The Wiccans had been practicing it all day, but Chelsea said it only partially worked. *I'll take any advantage we can get.*

The demon materialized amid flames as boxes of supplies caught fire next to its smoldering body. The bulk of the beast more than filled the storage area. Black eyes stared, wings curled, claws tore into the flooring, and talons braced against the sidewall.

It bellowed, sharp black teeth dripping green saliva that sizzled in the flames sparked by molten skin. And it crawled out, fast as lightning.

Kale shifted and pounced, knocking the creature against the side of the bus. It rocked violently. Faces appeared in the windows. *So much for keeping this quiet.* He slashed and bit and whined as his teeth slammed into what felt like concrete.

Another wolf attacked it from the other side. Francis fared no better. His claws and teeth doing no damage. Kale dodged a swipe at his belly from one of the talons. The sharp claws still scraped against armor with enough force to vibrate his bones. The armor wasn't flickering in and out of existence, which meant Chelsea's spell was helping.

Another slash sent Francis flying backward. The sub-Alpha lay silent, but sent Kale a message that he was hurt, but healing. Genn took his place, snarling as she bit at what would be the softer, vulnerable parts of most animals. They proved hard and impenetrable. Genn's teeth didn't even break the thin skin of its wings.

It slashed at her neck. Kale jumped, knocking his mother to the side, his face shifting into something closer to human that formed raspy, growled words. "Now, Bubba!"

Silver pellets flew like bullets, whizzing through the air. A few bounced off. One chipped a spine at the beast's elbow. Several others melted and spattered against scaly red skin to drip down molten muscles to fall ineffectual to the ground.

Genn licked the wound on her ribs that would have destroyed her neck. It was healing slower than it should.

That was close, Kale said.

I'll be fine, his mother said. *Get back to the battle.*

Shelby spun forward, half shifted. Her scythe sliced through the air.

Kale turned away from his mother to watch his girlfriend fight. *Please work.*

The blade cut into a pectoral muscle, exposing red blood that flowed like lava down its chest. It bellowed again and pushed Shelby hard with a claw in her chest. Shelby slid across gravel, but kept her feet. It unfurled its wings and began flapping hard. The wind pushed everyone else back. It opened its mouth wide.

Kale felt his armor thin around him.

"No you don't." Bryanne lifted her hands, her eyes red. A whip of sizzling light appeared in her hand, dotted with golden leaves. With a flick of her wrist it wrapped around the beast's maw, closing it. Another whip appeared in her other hand. "We can't let it get into the air." She sent the second to wrap around a wing. She pulled.

"I'm on it." Shelby's voice was deep and raspy as she ran forward. Her scythe tore through the thin material of the lashed wing. The other wing flapped wildly, slapping against Shelby and knocking her to the ground. She rolled to her feet and prepared to dash in again.

The demon glared at Bryanne as it calmed itself, squatting low.

Bryanne swore as it jumped, pulling the whips and the Druid into the air with it. Bryanne fell and slammed into the ground, scattering gravel. She let go of the vine-like restraints.

The demon tore the whip from its mouth with razored black claws and shoved it inside. The wound on its chest healed.

It forced open the damaged wing, the second restraint ripping to illuminated pieces. It opened its maw toward the broken magic. Glowing fragments flew toward the gaping mouth. Behind it, people were coming off the bus to watch or try to help.

Kale lifted a clawed hand, shifting more. "Stay back."

Shelby slashed into the exposed side of the beast's neck, cutting deep. A claw flew sideways, catching Shelby in the waist. She spun through the air and landed hard. Kale ran to her side, wolf once more. *You okay?*

She shifted too, to heal faster. *Armor took most of it. Just knocked the wind out. Couldn't let it fly away.*

The demon bellowed. Stolen magic healed the more dire neck wound, leaving the wing damaged. It screeched at the group of attackers and said something in a guttural language, spitting acidic saliva.

Bryanne stood on shaky legs and created another whip. "You've got that right. It won't be as easy as you hoped to steal what she has."

Shelby stood too, shifting back to human now that her ribs healed. "You understand that thing?"

Bryanne cracked her whip. "Unfortunately. It called you some names there aren't even translations for."

"Let's teach it some manners." Shelby snarled as she strafed around the creature, scythe glowing red and held at eye level between them. Her eyes changed from amber to a matching red as Druid magic filled her.

The demon sniffed the air, growled something, kicked gravel at Shelby, forcing her to duck, and ran off into the dark.

Everyone gaped at where it had been. Retreat didn't seem to be a demonic attribute.

Shelby coughed and sucked in more air, her teeth stained with blood from her fall. "We have it on the run?"

Bryanne curled her whip in on itself. "No. It said something about there being other magic nearby it could use against us."

Kale cocked his head to the side, listening to the crunch of gravel as the demon ran into the night. There was another sound in the background, thumping and pulsing. "Music. There's a concert or a dance or something happening not far from here." There was a hint of sweat and artificial smoke in the air, along with a chemical tang Kale recognized from cutting a glow stick open as a kid. "Maybe a rave."

Shelby stared off into the dark, the red draining from her amber eyes. "There are hundreds of people there, happy, excited, enjoying the music. We have to protect them. It will cut through humans like paper."

Kale shifted and sent out directions. *We go after the monster together. Let the smaller group lead, but be ready to jump in. We'll also need anyone with medical training to stay human and help any wounded we find. Spread the word to the non-Lycan members of our pack.*

He ran, feeling Shelby sending out her own version of instructions as she shifted and followed. His courage got a boost, despite the worry inside him, as his paws padded along the chilled pavement of the freeway exit toward the lake. He hit a hot patch where the demon must have stepped, tar sticking to fur. *That thing almost killed Francis and my mother, and all we've really managed to do is clip one wing. The wounds it leaves heal like they were made with silver.*

But we can hurt it, Shelby said. *We know it. It knows it.*

We? Pretty sure you're the only one of us who can.

Maybe, but I still need your help.

The sound of music grew louder. Then the screams began.

Kale ran faster, pushing his body to the limits.

Shelby matched his speed.

It wasn't Theo's best show, but it was on track to be in the top five, despite all his concerns and the recent situation of the world going nuts. The distraction was good. *Maybe that's why all these people are here too, trying to escape the madness outside and just feel purely human for a second. To forget. To feel safe and alive.*

He transitioned to another track, dancing along to the beat with the crowd, and a demon fell from the ceiling to land in the middle of the crowd, tossing several dancers to the side with its bulk. Theo stopped dancing and sneered. The little creature that came through the portal had grown.

It clawed at a group nearby, slashing someone across the ribs. Another girl fell, holding her cheek.

The crowd parted, panicked teens running for the exits, trampling one another, the screams louder than the music for a moment. But a large chunk of the crowd stood and stared, perhaps thinking it was planned. Theo pulled the cord between his laptop and the soundboards. The music died. He spoke through the mic. "This is not part of my show. Make your way calmly to the exits." People froze. *Of course, that made sense. Idiot humans.* "Go!"

They began to move again, faster, but more organized. Theo aided their departure with his magic, creating patterns in the crowd that reduced the likelihood of trampling and injury. A few teens huddled near the demon's feet.

"Get the injured out of here!"

A man turned back, braving the demon to help lift the bleeding and broken. The demon lumbered toward him. Theo concentrated his magic directly above the beast, the patterns in the smoke becoming firm, distinct, and complex. The demon stopped chasing the man and focused on the magic-infused fog, mouth full of obsidian teeth gaping wide.

Tendrils of light left the fog and flowed into the beastly mouth that dribbled green saliva. The patterns fell apart above it. It lumbered after another group of helpers who were lifting a girl dressed all in black whom Theo hoped wasn't dead. *That didn't last as long as I'd hoped.* He poured more magic into the fog, feeling it leave him. *Can't keep this up all night.* There wasn't a finite supply of magic inside him, but it took energy to shift entropy. He'd pass out at some point if he didn't stop the beast.

His quiver was in the Vespa. He needed the crowd safe before he made a break for it. The demon devoured his magic in seconds again. It stalked toward the stragglers. "I wish Alec was here." Fizz came to his aid, zipping around the monster and bumping into it. Massive clawed hands swatted at the wisp, but Fizz was too agile, dodging around the hands and slapping them.

The demon, snarling with what Theo swore was frustration, opened its mouth wide. Fizz slowed as tendrils of light pulled away from its flaming body.

"Get out of there, Fizz. It'll break your containment spells." But Theo's friend was moving sluggishly, spurts of colored flames leaking out of the blue. "No!"

A light ripped away from the ceiling and slammed into the demon's open maw hard enough to send the beast staggering backward. Fizz darted away. Theo blinked down from his perch, confused.

An impossibly fit boy walked through the few trickling streams of survivors. This boy was wearing a tactical vest with bulging pockets. He pulled out a candy bar and began eating. "Oh, there's bout to be more where that came from, ugly."

Wolves darted into the room, several wearing Fae armor.

"What in the Unseely Court is happening?" Theo said.

One of the Lycans shifted, the armor hugging her transforming body. Theo watched as her amber eyes turned green and then flashed red as a scythe appeared in her hand. Theo's mouth went dry. *It's her!*

thena staggered, choking on the cold, poisonous air.

Ptyas came to her aid. *Put on the helm and breathe through your nose.*

She followed his counsel. Fresh, clean air flowed into her nostrils from the alien metal. "Clever." She choked again as she breathed in through her mouth after speaking. *Teach me not to be a mouth breather.*

The Fae woman waited for her, a smirk on her lips.

"You could have warned me!" Athena said.

"Where's the fun in that? It is part of my nature to be evasive and misleading. Would you have me break Fae tradition for your miserable comfort?"

Athena let the myriad replies fall from her lips, though they did play out in an internal rant about what she'd like to do with Fae tradition in respect to the woman's perfect backside.

Wow, that last one was . . . colorful. Ptyas sounded breathless.

Not used to hearing a modern woman speak her mind, eh, old man?

I'm just glad it was reserved for only my ears, and not our host. We need her.

Athena sucked a long breath in through her nose. *Fine.* "I wouldn't dream of encouraging you to break your law. Will you kindly lead on?"

The woman cocked her head to the side in an alien way. Her bones did not align exactly the same way as human bones. "Cordiality? With fire in her eyes? You might have made a decent member of Unseely Court . . . with a few decades of training."

Athena felt her eyes sting and lip begin to curl.

Athena, Ptyas warned.

She swallowed her anger. "Tha . . . that's nice of you to say."

"Your human proclivity toward those words is a hard habit to break."

Athena smiled as she mused over how true the Fae view of human gratitude might be. "It really is. But I want to keep my eyes, so . . ."

The Fae shrugged as she spun. "Tongues are fun too." She wandered out into the desolate landscape, toward a black peak that jutted out of the ash and sand. "Come, before any demons note our arrival."

Athena rubbed the grit in her mouth with her tongue. *Yeah, I want to keep that too.*

Then maybe keep it inside your mouth? Ptyas suggested.

Nice.

She followed the Fae into the icy whipping winds. It was colder than she expected from the image she'd seen before stepping through the portal. Her armored feet crunched through rime on the sandy soil. Hell had frozen over.

It took half an hour to reach the mountain. Athena's tongue was held in check, though mainly from her desperate breathing through her nose. The air was thin and lacking in oxygen, even after magically filtered and enhanced by her helm. Despite the nuclear winter on Alsvoira, the hike had Athena dripping with sweat inside her armor. She was grateful for the warmth though. She thought she'd be shivering without it. *I'd have to go wolf to stay warm.*

That might not have been enough either, Ptyas replied. *It's colder than it seems. Fae control entropy. Our guide is holding warmer air around us.*

That's convenient and kind of nice.

I assume it's mainly for her benefit.

Athena noticed steam rising from her arms. *What's that?*

Your armor releasing the moisture. Otherwise, you'd be swimming by now.

How does it know to do these things? Programming?

Ptyas laughed. *It has a heart of living fire. It is alive.*

Athena eyed the glowing red lines of her armor again, watching them pulse, much like a heartbeat. *Can it hear me?*

Of course. How do you think it appears and disappears at will?

Great, another listener. At least it doesn't chime in every few seconds.

Ptyas said nothing, making Athena laugh out loud and then choke again.

The Fae glanced back, arched one perfect eyebrow, and then went back to climbing the trail. Drifts of ash covered the path for long stretches, but the woman didn't seem to need the visual to know where they were heading.

"Where are we going, if you don't mind me asking?" Athena decided to break the silence, despite her voice coming out thinner and weaker than she liked.

The Fae woman said nothing, but pointed one pale, slender finger upward.

Athena followed the gesture to a dark hole in the side of the mountain. A cave.

The cave was not warmer than the outside, but it did offer an escape from the winds that whipped ash into their faces. The Fae pulled a glass globe from somewhere and tapped it to release light. She held it on her palm as they walked deeper into the cavern.

Athena held her tongue. There was a sacred feeling to the place that even she dared not disturb. Ageless carvings illuminated by magic lined the halls. This was the original Underhill, the home of the Fae before they had to abandon it for Earth.

Athena tripped over something as she tried to make out a set of carvings that depicted what looked vaguely like a dragon swallowing a sun while serpents swam around it in the starry sky.

She caught herself and glanced down to see a piece of obsidian. She picked it up, the glass scraping against stone with a distinct ring.

"You should leave the dead be." The Fae woman spoke without looking back.

"What?"

"The demon bone in your hand. It is unwise to disturb them. Who knows what might draw the attention of their kind and bring them back to this place?"

Athena examined the obsidian closer, there were bits of red clinging to one end. "Bone?"

Those red bits are tendons, Ptyas added.

Athena dropped it, half expecting it to shatter, but the demon glass was stronger than it looked. Instead, it bounced against stone with a clang that echoed through the abandoned halls. "Sorry."

"No apologies necessary, of course." Oh, how Athena hated the woman's prissy smirk. "Just know the bones will become more frequent as we near our destination," the Fae woman said.

Athena noticed shadowed mounds everywhere, now that she knew what to look for, glass bones gleaming under the leathery remnants of skin. She kept an eye on them, wondering if one might just be a slumbering demon waiting for just such an intrusion into their tomb. "Why are there no other bones? Didn't Fae die here too? Was it too long ago for any to remain?"

The woman stopped, and Athena almost ran into her. "We placed a few small spells on the entry after the demons departed to keep the ash outside from entering what remained of our home, to keep the winds from burying this place forever."

Athena kicked at a pile of ash. "Must be broken. There's a ton of ash in here."

"The spells were unbroken when we arrived. It is why I am certain no demons lay in wait."

"Then all the ash came from before you placed the spells?" Athena asked.

The Fae woman shook her head. "We do not leave bones behind when we die."

Athena started to speak, but bit her tongue. She looked down at the pile of ash she had kicked. "Oh."

She avoided stepping on obsidian and ash from then on, at least until they reached a chamber that was too full of demon bones and ash to avoid. Even the Fae woman waded through it, tipping piles of glass to roll over one another with macabre music. Athena debated bringing a few bones back to make wind chimes.

She almost ran into the back of her guide as she debated the logistics of such a creation. "What?"

"We have arrived, as far as I can take you anyway."

"So, we just wait?" Athena resisted the urge to kick another pile of ash.

"Correct." The Fae gestured. "Unless you want to try what the demons failed to do?"

Athena looked at the wall ahead. There were hundreds of demon bones fused with the stone, gaping black skulls half buried, rib cages jutting beneath those, obsidian vertebra dangling. "What happened to them?"

"They tried to phase through the wall, but it was thickened from within by a hundred Fae weaving spells to protect the last pool of sentient flame." The woman held a finger against her forehead and bowed. "Their sacrifice saved something irreplaceable."

Athena touched the wall with a gauntlet. "They sealed themselves in?"

"It was the only way."

"And you haven't opened it since? What if the fire has gone out?"

The Fae rolled her large eyes. "Of course we've opened it since. We've made arrows and armor and wisps, but we are careful and selective so as not to draw attention to a part of Alsvoira the demons have left behind. And only one of the royals can open the doorway."

"Why the hells, including Alsvoira in that list, didn't the king come then?"

The Fae woman whirled on Athena. "You forget yourself. It is not your place to question his logic."

"Logic? I haven't seen much of that from your kind so far, Miss Elf."

"Miss Elf?" Her large eyes narrowed. "What is my name?"

Athena's mouth fell open. "Your name?"

"I gave it to you at the beginning of our journey. Have you forgotten it already?"

"What does it matter?"

The woman ran a finger over the glass globe. "It matters to me."

Athena thought. *Kiera? Keena? It was a K name, right? You remember, Ptyas?*

I remember everything.

Then what is it?

He said nothing more.

You stubborn son of a—

A silver dagger pegged into the wall next to Athena's face, the sharp metal sinking inches into the stone. She spun, her scythe warm in her hand. "That was a mistake, whatever your name is."

"The pretentiousness of you humans."

"I'm Lycan!" Athena darted forward, partially shifting her legs to propel her at breakneck speed. Her scythe slashed through the air, the twin blades whistling. And they hit nothing.

The Fae had taken one step to the side a fraction of a second before the blade could find its home in her neck. She smiled as the razor edges slid an inch from her nose and punched Athena in the ribs.

Athena felt as if she'd been hit by a truck, the force sending her flying against a pillar hard enough to crack stone. Her ribs and spine didn't fare better, even with the protection of magical armor.

She slid down the pillar and crumpled to the floor, her vision darkening with pain and lack of oxygen. She'd need at least a minute or two to heal that kind of damage in this environment.

The Fae woman stood over her, kicked her once, breaking an ankle. "I was told to stay with you as long as I felt comfortable doing so. That time has passed. Here." She tossed a handful of silver packets at Athena's prone body, spun on a heel, and walked away, taking the light with her.

Her name was Keanierah. She is part of the Cereus family.

Athena winced as she slid herself into a more comfortable position. *Why didn't you tell me earlier?!*

You are accustomed to winning. It is good for you to learn a touch of humility. You constantly assume you are the smartest, strongest, most capable. You underestimate everyone else. You won't always be the most powerful being in the room.

Okay, thanks Yoda. I could have taken her.

He laughed long and hard inside her head. *No, she could have defeated you without touching you. I told you the Fae control entropy. She could have encouraged every oxygen molecule in this room to choose the unlikely position next to her and watched you suffocate.*

Athena sat in silence, letting her eyes adjust to the new levels of light, most coming from her armor. Her bones knitted together and a punctured lung healed. *Okay, lesson learned.*

I hope so, young Padawan.

Wait, you actually knew that Star Wars' reference?

Chewbacca was always my favorite. Felt like a distant cousin.

How did a Feral barely in control of his wolf body sneak into a movie theater?

Drive-ins, naturally.

Shelby shifted and brought her scythe into existence. Her armor and blade held together well now that the demon was focused on other magic. Bubba sent a trash can at the beast's face while a blue ball of fire, leaking spurts of orange, distracted it.

Where did that come from? Shelby asked Eira. *Bryanne? The Wiccans?*

It's Fae, Eira replied. *There must be one here, and not just any Fae can have a wisp.*

The Lycan pack formed a circle around the demon, but no one was venturing close. Kale had instructed them to only engage if necessary. The fighting was reserved for those he thought could do the most damage.

He means me, Shelby thought. *My blade is the only thing we've seen do anything.*

She jumped over the nearest Lycan, her legs half shifting without a thought. It had become natural, instinctive. She landed and sprinted toward the monster, slashing at hamstrings while it focused on Bubba and the wisp.

I don't even know if it has hamstrings.

Regardless, her scythe didn't cut deep enough to cut tendons. It still bellowed, turning faster than Shelby expected. It swung a massive claw, spikes sprouting from its wrist and elbow.

Shelby dodged, knowing she wasn't fast enough, but jaws clamped down on the demon forearm. Kale had come to her aid.

The demon shook him off, sending his massive form tumbling into several Lycans like they were bowling pins. A hunk of metal flew past Shelby's face and slammed into the red, scaly skin of the demonic chest. It barely reacted to something that would have killed any human and many a Lycan, brushing metallic shards from its skin while eyeing Shelby.

She staggered back as her Omega gift gave her insight into the monster. So much hate, pain, resentment, and anger inside the creature, it overwhelmed her. With this came glimpses of brutal battles to the death while demons cheered the carnage, worlds on fire, and an inhuman face that, despite the horrific monstrosity of it, reminded her of the Goddess.

The images blinded Shelby but she felt the floor shudder as the demon stepped toward her.

Gold whips wrapped around its neck, but it still advanced, hissing out something in its vile language before opening its maw wide, revealing rows of sharp black teeth and a green tongue.

"It said something about a rare magic in you, something broken." Bryanne tugged hard on the whip, but she slid on the sweat slicked concrete floor. "Don't let it near you."

Shelby screamed. The shreds of her bond with Kale burned within her, like someone had set her nerve endings on fire. She heard him scream as well. He'd extricated himself from the pile of Lycans and was nearly at her side. They both fell, her to her knees and Kale to his side as a wolf.

The hollow feeling she'd come to associate with the broken bond became an endless void of pain and despair. The pieces of it ripped away from her soul one by one, leaving her empty, alone, shattered. There was nothing she could do.

Part of her could still see the demon advancing. The wisp was falling apart, spurting flames from several holes in its shell of blue fire. Bubba had stopped to eat a bar, his skin loose on thinning muscles. Lycans were being thrown from arms and legs as the demon stepped closer, swatting them away like pesky flies.

Another part of her welcomed the coming death. She would be forever alone, a broken thing, after it had finished taking what was left of Kale from her. She held her arms out in an embrace.

The wisp spun a jet of flame into the open mouth, melting teeth and sizzling saliva away into steam. A net of golden light was forming on its jaw at the same time. The net knit together and pulled the maw shut.

"It's about time someone muzzled that nasty hole."

Shelby came back to herself, her soul scarred, but intact. She glanced back, expecting to find Bryanne, but it was *Chelsea*, the banshee herself, hands held in an intricate pattern, her mouth moving in chants. She was saving Shelby.

Bryanne had one vine-like whip around the demon's neck still and another wrapped around the wing. She staked one into the ground with a mallet and a spike that looked like they were hewn from gnarled wood. Rivulets of golden light flared from the seams of the magical wood. A stalk of wheat appeared in a hand and transformed into another stake to tie the second whip to the ground.

Chelsea looked down pointedly at Shelby and then nodded toward the demon. "Want to do something about that? I can feel it absorbing my magic, slower than it has been, but still." One of the strings of golden light snapped as though to punctuate her point.

"Oh, yeah." Shelby staggered to her feet, jumped, and slashed at the demon's throat. She felt the vibration of her scythe cut deep against the beast's hardened flesh, but the wound began healing as soon as she landed. The muzzle was dissolving, the magic from it fueling its healing. Then, an arrowhead sprouted out of its neck just below its gash. Then another and another.

She looked up to see a man with long white hair and large lavender eyes standing on the railing around the DJ's booth holding a large bow. He pulled another arrow and nocked it, but held his fire as the demon growled something before toppling backward.

Is that the DJ?

"Bryanne, move!" Kale shouted.

The Bandruí dropped her magical aids and jumped to the side. From the ceiling, the demon free fell right onto one of Bryanne's magical stakes, impaling itself through the chest. Concrete shattered as it hit the ground, sending chunks the size of basketballs high into the air and cracks shooting out from the epicenter of its meteoric crash. The scene appeared as though a bomb had just exploded.

Bryanne cried out. Shelby whirled, seeing her leg pinned—crushed—under the demon. Time seemed to slow as the chunks of concrete shrapnel reversed its upward flight and began to rain down. Bryanne covered her head in reflex. She had a small gash across her cheek, obviously from concrete debris.

Shelby jumped over her fallen friend, landing with her knees on the demon's chest and shielding Bryanne with her own body. Concrete chunks bounced off her armor, hitting her square in the middle of her back. It sounded like a storm of lethal hail and almost felt like getting shot. Yes, she remembered that excruciating pain well from the warehouse with Sherman and Lucas. A final crunching thud ended the storm. Shelby started, stunned by the vibrations she felt reverberating in her bones. The final piece of concrete was the size of Elias's old desk in his study. It missed Shelby and Bryanne by no more than two inches.

Bubba fell to a knee.

"Yeah, I need more fuel, son," Bubba said. "Quick like, ya feel? That was too close."

"You okay?" Shelby said to Bryanne.

Bryanne nodded. "Had worse." Her eyes flashed red and Shelby felt herself and the demon lift slow as the golden spike of wood grew branches and climbed upward, sprouting leaves. The Druid slid her leg out from under the beast, wincing. "That's a lie. This leg is shattered and the demon blood is bad. I'm no Lycan, but I can speed the healing process. I'll need your help."

The DJ with the bow jumped from his balcony, landed easily, and ran to his wisp. The flame looked dimmer, still spouting jets of orange flame.

"Fizz!" He wrapped his hands around the wisp, ignoring the fire. His hands covered the tiny creature of flame for a moment. When he opened them again, the wisp looked healthier, though his hands were a mess of third-degree burns, some all the way through from palm to back of hand, showing bone between.

"We'll need to help him too." Shelby began reaching out to the ley lines, but Bryanne grabbed her hand.

"You need to know what it said just before it died."

Shelby blinked at the white knuckles on her own. "What?"

"The Summer Omega will not complete Ascension. He is coming. Tarloch rises."

Grant swore as another of their strongholds fell. Someone was definitely feeding the Advent pack intel. "We need to be unpredictable. Have the remaining survivors fall back to places we would never consider. Non-Christian churches, YMCAs, homeless shelters, rehab centers, nunneries, orphanages, Wiccan gathering halls."

"What?" a woman in camo asked from the next table over.

"You heard me. Find such a place in every city where we have troops and get them safe." The group at a row of computers began searching maps online and shouting out coordinates. "And someone put me in contact with Wiccan Supreme. We should probably warn her that Hunters will be showing up on her doorsteps around the world."

A sat-phone slapped into his palm.

Hours later, Collins placed a steaming bowl of something in front of him. Grant blinked tired eyes. "What's this?"

"Chili, sir. It's my grandpappy's recipe. Has some kick, both due to spice and the secret ingredient: caffeine."

"Sounds perfect." Most of the remaining Hunters in the world were somewhere relatively safe for the night. There wasn't much more he could do, but he knew he wouldn't sleep. Grant picked up the spoon and cracked open the book he'd inherited from Jack.

The first few lines froze a spoonful of chili a few inches from his mouth, the steam crossing in front of the words. *It is time you knew the truth. There is no hope of winning this war. Earth is doomed to repeat the fall of Alsvoira. It is simply a matter of time.*

Grant put the spoon back into the bowl and kept reading.

You have been lied to, and you will now be required to continue the lies. Once you complete the higher vows, you will know all the unseen horrors, but you will dole out hope, bedtime stories of Hunters prevailing. But there is no stopping the death of this world. It was set in motion long ago by a being more powerful than any we know.

It has always been a Hunter's solemn duty to slow the process, to give humanity one brief, shining moment in the sun, before destruction and ruin. We keep magic in the shadows where it cannot grow in the light of day and entice those who wait for such a feast. Magic will still grow.

The Summer Omega, Alpha Prime, and Advent will bring to pass Ascension, a time when magic reigns, flaunting it before the beasts of ash and flame. A flood of darkness will soon follow.

It is true, we have stopped this in the past, but time repeats itself. We may stop Ascension a thousand times, but the one time we fail will be the end of everything.

Grant pushed the book away. "What is this garbage?" His

stomach growled. He finished off the chili in seconds. The book waiting patiently beyond the bowl.

Grant growled as he licked the spoon. It almost felt like the parchment called to him. There were whispers in the air. He grabbed it, debated chucking it across the room, but decided to skim ahead first, see if it gave him anything of worth further in.

He flipped several pages, but felt compelled to turn one more. He recognized the feeling as coming from outside himself.

Ice ran through his bones and a bead of sweat crawled down his temple, but he flipped the page. *The vows Hunters make during initiation are a pale imitation of the higher vows, which must be earned through patience and dedication.*

Grant thought back to his initiation, which had been an intense ritual involving blood, pain, and fire while making sacred vows to give his life in service to eradicating magic and the abominations that use it. "A pale imitation. I'm not sure I want the real thing."

"What was that, sir?" Collins placed a second bowl of chili in front of him and retrieved the empty bowl.

"Just arguing with the sacred book of our fearless leaders you put in my hands."

"Jack carried it for months, talking to it constantly. Honestly, sir, it always gave me the willies. Feels like it's watching you, if you know what I mean."

Grant stared at the book. It stared back. "I do." He grabbed the boy's wrist before he could leave. "Get me Bryanne. If anyone knows anything about this book, it'll be her."

Collins looked like he might protest. Grant glared at him, daring him to say something. The boy swallowed and set off at a sprint to find a sat-phone. Grant turned the page and read. "It will be nice to talk to the Bandruí again anyway."

Bryanne filled herself with magic as her bones knit back together. It was nice wielding it again without the painful drain caused by their recently deceased stowaway. Some of the magic still flowed away, but slower and in smaller amounts, spiraling off in more than one direction, which wasn't the best of omens.

There are more demons in this world today than yesterday. Not great, not great. Oooh, that wisp is pretty.

The Fae's companion hovered over her legs, helping along the healing. Chelsea and Shelby also leaned over her. Someone put something in her hand.

Bryanne stared at the sat-phone for several moments before realizing what it was and what it meant. She put the small brick of plastic to her ear. "Hiya, Grant. Did you hear we killed a demon? It was mean."

"Yes, what did I say about keeping my daughter out of trouble?"

"Hey, it rode the bus with us. What's a Druid to do? Ask for its ticket?"

"Are you okay?" Grant hesitated before continuing. "You sound drunk."

Bryanne giggled. "A lot of magic in these veins. Fae magic, Bandrui magic, Wiccan magic, even a little Lycan thrown in. It's an unusual, and heady mix. I broke some stuff. I'll be right as rain in a minute though. You should ask me out when the world isn't ending."

"What?"

Bryanne smiled, even as part of her felt a rising horror at her words. "You heard me."

Grant chuckled. "Deal. If we survive the coming apocalypse, and you remember this conversation, I will ask you out. In the meantime, can you tell me about magic books?"

"Grimoires?" Bryanne closed her eyes and tried to focus. "You can't use one."

"No," Grant seemed to be searching for the words too, "more of a possessed book that guides me to the spots it thinks I should read."

"Ghosts were never my thing." She opened her eyes and swished a hand at the wisp. "They could hide in books I suppose."

"I'm not sure if it's a ghost. Just something odd about it. Keeps trying to get me to do some ritual."

"Then do the ritual." Bryanne scrunched up her face. "Depends on if it's a good ghost or a bad ghost though. Could be a spell too. I'd have to see it in person to know for sure."

"I may have to fly it out to you or you to it then."

"That's a weird first date, Grant." She picked at a newly formed scab. "I like it!"

"Ummmm . . . I should probably try back when you have less magic in you."

Bryanne nodded several times. "Okay, buh bye." She clicked the button to end the call.

The Fae called his wisp back with a short whistle and spoke to Shelby. "That's as good as it's going to get with magic, at least for now. Demon blood is nasty stuff. Your friend is going to need time."

Chelsea stopped her chanting. Shelby leaned back. Bryanne let her magic go too and rolled an ankle to check on the healing. Fire tore through her leg. "Yep, that's going to sting, but it's not broken any longer." She glanced at Shelby, groaned, and put her head in her hands. "Did I really just command your father to ask me out? Tell me that was a hallucination."

Shelby grimaced. "Nope, that happened alright. It was painful to watch."

Bryanne looked up from her hands. "Wait, did he say yes?"

Niff set down the crate of fruit he'd been carrying as a section of stone wall to his left fell away. A rush of warm, humid air poured out of the opening. *Someone just added to Underhill? We aren't in a building phase.* He glanced inside the newly added cavern and swore at his idiocy. There was an exception to building phases. Underhill would extend itself to absorb any newly created demon gate, to protect the world from easy incursion.

Bells warning of the addition tolled down the hall. More bells began ringing in the distance as other gates became active. *Goddess give me strength.*

Niff reached for the bow on his back as sparks flew from the edge of the gateway. He killed a dozen demons before anyone arrived to aid him, but the Fae woman fell to teeth and claw seconds after she arrived.

Niff went through every arrow in his quiver, leaving a body on the floor for each one. When the quiver was empty, he pulled a short staff from his back and twisted it to release the concealed blades at either end.

Twenty more demons fell, their black blood coating his skin in streaks of onyx. Arrows flew past him as more of his people came to his aid, but the demons continued to pour from the portal, crawling over their fallen kin with no sign of remorse or mourning. *They more slither than crawl*, Niff thought, *like serpents, without love or affection.*

He staggered back as four fought him at once, claws and spines flashing in the electrical light of the demon gate. He sensed a fifth demon fall from above, one he hadn't seen. He had a moment of surprise before a talon pierced his heart.

Niff fell, eyes glued to his chest as the obsidian spine retracted. His orange blood mingled with the black on the floor. *Like my favorite human holiday, Halloween. I would have preferred a treat instead of a trick.* It was his last thought.

Bells tolled throughout Underhill. Silphinaera sat up in her bed as she recognized the three distinct tones that let her know which portals were active. She'd posted hundreds of guards outside each chamber after the last incident, but feared even those might not be enough. Another bell tolled, and her fear grew. *A new gate. It's been centuries. We are not ready.*

She pulled several rings from concealed slits in her nightgown. The rings sprouted titanium blades as her will flowed into the living metal.

Shadows clattered through the entrance to her bedchamber, spindly spidery things that crawled up the walls and across the roof with awkward staggering movements. Their faces were a purplish-red full of jet-black eyes. Each of their nine legs had a mouth.

"Well, aren't you lovely?" One of her knives dropped the nearest. It twitched on the floor as it died, spitting green venom and hissing loudly.

A second knife removed two legs of the second. The third flew at her, kicking off the wall with all its legs. She spun, her gown twirling with ironic grace, and skewered the abomination mid-flight. She dodged to the side as it hit her dresser with enough force to splinter the thick wood.

"That was an antique." She sighed and danced away as the now seven-legged one shot spines from its mouths. One caught her in the thigh, and she sneered. "That's a neat trick."

She ripped it from her leg, knowing it surely held some nasty poison. It burned, and her vision fogged. She took a second to alter the entropy in her leg, encouraging the poison to want to be outside her body. Green liquid oozed out, followed by orange. Her blood. Clicking came from behind her just as a mouth bit into her neck.

She swung a blade up, severing the thing's leg at one of the segments. The venom leaked out of her again, but it took more effort, and more shadows were crawling through the entrance. *I'll not fall so easily, miscreants.*

A larger shadow came through, but Silphinaera was having trouble focusing her vision. She threw a knife, but silver metal flashed in the air and knocked her blade aside.

"You'd think you'd welcome the help."

Silphinaera squinted. "The King of Unseely Court in my bedchamber? What will the Fae think?"

He stabbed a spider demon off a wall with his spear and threw the carcass at another. "That this is hardly the first time."

She chuckled and fell against a wall. "Might be the last."

"Well, then let's make it a night to remember, shall we? Let's take half this demon army with us."

She pushed off the wall and pulled another knife. "Yes. Let's."

Thick scents of decay and death wafted out of the demon's mouth after the magic holding it shut dissolved. Theo stood over the body, not happy about the task in front of him. He held out an arm to motion the odd group of Lycans, Wiccans, Hunters, a Druid, and one PK back. "This is going to be gross. I need to bring the head back with me to Underhill as proof I took care of my mistake."

The Lycan with Druid eyes lifted her hand, the scythe appearing there. "This felt like a butter knife against that skin. How will you do that?"

"You'll see." Fizz landed on his shoulder. Theo opened the front pocket of his ruined jacket. "Here ya go, buddy. You did so great. Rest up now."

Everyone stared at him. It was the PK, now back to his fit self after half a dozen candy bars, who finally said something. "Ain't nobody gonna say nothing bout the fireball that just crawled up in his jacket?" A girl at his side shushed him. "Oh, yeah, I'm the crazy one for asking?"

"It's my wisp. I'll explain later." Theo grimaced at the demon. "First things first."

He poured his will into the demon's body, but not the head, increasing entropy more than he ever had before, more than he thought he could, inviting decay, increasing friction, and encouraging molecular bonds to break. The crimson skin went dark purple, hints of gray appearing in splotches. The stomach bloated, distending itself to huge proportions before collapsing in on itself with a wheeze of foul-smelling gasses. The group stepped back farther.

Theo continued. Skin pulled away from skin, flesh rotting beneath it and falling away with wet smacks inside exposed onyx ribs. Finally, the entire body deflated and fell as dust to the concrete floor, leaving the still fresh head behind.

The Alpha Lycan held out a trash bag he'd had someone retrieve from one of the bins at the fringe of the room. "Well, that was the freakiest thing I've ever seen."

Theo dropped the head in the bag, took it from the Lycan, and tied a knot in it to seal the stench inside. He glanced at the fading flower on his wrist and then locked eyes with the Alpha, expecting some resistance to his next request. "I need the green, gold, and red eyed girl to come with me too. It's kind of important in undoing my banishment."

The Alpha nodded. "Of course. She won't go alone though."

Theo frowned. "I was only told to bring the girl."

The Druid took a step forward. "Were you expressly told not to bring anyone else?"

Theo rubbed his jaw, the new skin of his hands stinging at the familiar habit. "No. Looks like someone knows how to handle the Fae."

The Druid smiled back and then winced. Her leg hadn't fully healed.

Theo examined his palms. He suspected she'd put most of her magic and energy into healing him. He could return the favor. "We have magic that can finish healing you too. Will you be joining us?"

"Wouldn't dream of missing it. You'll need to bring about five or six of us, or none at all. We're a package deal." The Druid crossed her arms.

Theo sighed. "Holding a portal open to Underhill that long is going to hurt, after all the magic I've used tonight."

The Lycan-Druid girl partially shifted. "We can move fast." She was at his side a half second later to prove her point.

"Okay."

Kale sprinted through the portal to Underhill as soon as it opened, dodging to the side so Shelby wouldn't run into him. She still bumped into his back but gently and totally on purpose.

"Sorry, didn't see you there." She winked at him, but her eyes widened, and her scythe appeared in her hand. "Something's wrong."

Kale had enjoyed the physical contact for a second too. Their bond was beyond repair now, the shreds of it seemingly cauterized by the demon's hunger. Touch was the closest they had to it now, and Kale did not mind that one bit. Bonded or not, Shelby was still fully tempting to him. But something *was* wrong. There was a thick, sweet aroma in the air that he didn't recognize, but it mingled with smoke and a familiar stench he had recently become very acquainted with. Demon breath.

Kale wished he had a scythe of his own. Instead, he partially shifted, letting his claws extend the gauntlet into sharp points. *That'll do.*

The rest of their party arrived. Bryanne knew the Fae better than any of them, so she had to come. Genn insisted she get to see Underhill. And Chelsea had volunteered to help. She'd been too instrumental in defeating the demon to be refused, and she'd reminded them of that fact quite vehemently until they relented. Kale had to refuse Bubba's request though, at Bryanne's urging. He was too loose of a cannon to drop into the weird rules of Underhill.

Kale felt bad leaving his best friend behind, but he needed Bubba and Francis to take care of the pack while he was away. He could still feel the link though, and he informed Francis they had all arrived safely as Theo came through and the sheet of light in the shape of a door vanished.

Theo stopped, eyeing Kale and Shelby. "What is it?"

"Demons," Shelby answered. "Lots of demons. Can't you smell them?"

"Fae nostrils are not as sensitive as Lycan, thank the Goddess." But he looked concerned. "Follow me. Stay close, stay alert." He ran, almost as fast as a Lycan on his long legs.

He jumped over demonic bodies, barely glancing at them, though he slowed as he passed piles of ash.

He's looking for someone in particular, Kale said to his wolf.

The queen, Skotha said. *She is of the Morning Glory House. He's royalty. How do you know that?*

The mark on his wrist.

Kale noted the tattoo on his wrist of the flower. It had darkened since they'd arrived in Underhill. He had no time to ask about it.

They raced through a throne room. There were plenty of demon bodies there and a few injured Fae, but none Theo seemed to care about. *That's not fair. He does care, you can see it on his face. He's just hoping not to see one person in particular.*

Kale also discovered the source of the strange, sweet scent. Fae blood.

Theo staggered into a posh room full of silk, fine wood, and elegant lighting, or at least it had been before it had been spattered in red, black, green, and orange. Theo dropped the black trash bag and ran to a woman sprawled on the floor surrounded in spidery demon carcasses. She had fought well.

She gasped as Theo lifted her. "Careful, son. I'm dying fast enough. I don't need the push."

Theo put a hand against the large gash in her neck. Worry washed over his face. In a frantic voice, he said, "I did it, Mother. I brought the girl with eyes of green, orange, and red. See?"

He pointed to Shelby, and the woman, Theo's mother apparently, weakly rolled her head to take in Shelby. A small smile tugged at the corner of her mouth.

"Greetings, Eira-mit-Thyra." She lifted heavy eyes to Kale. "And Daeglan-mit-Skotha. I wish . . . I wish I could have stood beside you again. The magic is rent. Tarloch is coming. The Advent—" The woman broke off in a weak cough that sounded wet.

Kale felt Skotha's hollowness, that feeling of inevitable loss.

She was noble and great once, Skotha said. *She would have been a valuable ally.*

"We can heal you, Mother," Theo said. "Just hold on." He tried to influence the entropy around her but it did not change. Theo punched the ground, and Kale empathized with the tortured cry that escaped clenched teeth. Pleadingly, Theo looked to Shelby. "Please."

Shelby shook her head. "We're trying, but it's not working."

"Try harder!" Theo said.

"No time," the woman said. She pulled a decorative silver coin from the front of her gown and pressed it into Theo's hand. "You must take her to Mount Estorathi."

He took the coin and stared at it. "You're sending me alone to open the doors in the midst of a demonic invasion?"

"That gate was not used. It seems the demons have found a new point of ingress somewhere else on Alsvoira." She coughed.

"Even if the way is clear, I've never forged anything without you. I'm not even sure if I can, half human and all." Theo stared at his hands as though they revealed something ugly about himself.

She hissed darkly. "That was a lie I told you to protect you and your brother. You never were rejected from the Changeling Program. You never could have qualified."

Theo's knuckles went white around the coin. "What are you saying?"

"I dared not lose my darling boys to Unseely Court." She gestured toward where a Fae man slumped against a wall, unconscious or dead. "He would have claimed one of you. How could I break you up, especially after the Goddess promised me a son would be my most important possession." She coughed. Orange dribbling down her porcelain chin.

Theo sat back, hard on the tile floor. "You pushed me away. You made me guard the gate that killed my brother."

"All to protect you. That was the least active gate. I thought I . . . was keeping you safe. I . . . was wrong. I'm so sorry, Son." She pushed on his hand. "Go now. Who knows how many escaped to the surface. They will be sending magic back to fuel more arrivals. We must abandon Underhill."

Bryanne stepped forward. "Go, Genn and I can take care of her and the king, if he's alive. We'll search for other survivors too. We'll meet back here, or Salt Lake if we find someone well enough to open a portal."

"Chelsea might as well stay here too. She's pretty good at healing spells."

"Oh no, not gonna shake me that easily, Kale. I'm your third wheel through this whole thing." She took Shelby's hand. "Besides, you might need an extra spell-slinger wherever that one's taking you." She whispered to Shelby. "I don't trust him. His eyes are too big to be honest."

Theo stood, slow, concern all over his face for his mother. "Unlike our sense of smell, Fae hearing rivals Lycan. Fine, the witch can come." He glanced at the garbage bag. "I got the one that killed Alec. Doesn't seem to matter now. It wasn't why you banished me, was it?"

She smiled. "My clever boy." The smile turned sad. "When Alec died, I knew it was you who had to be the one to find the Summer Omega. You are the child of both courts. You alone can both give consent and unlock the key."

Theo shook his head. "I'm really not half human?"

"You really aren't. Now, go. She needs the key sooner than later. The end is coming." She coughed again, harder.

Bryanne began working a spell, pushing light into her chest, but her expression said she wasn't sure it would work.

Kale turned to Shelby. "You want to try?"

"Eira isn't sure it will work on a Fae."

"What?" Theo asked.

Shelby stepped toward the queen. "My Immortal Wolf is a healer."

"No, leave me to die. You are more important." The queen tried to sit up and move away from Shelby, but didn't get far before collapsing.

"All children of the Goddess are important."

Kale didn't recognize her voice. "Shelby?"

"It's okay, sweet Daeglan. She gave me permission to try." Eira, having been granted control by Shelby, shifted into her wolf body and held her head over the Fae queen, eyes closed.

Silphinaera squirmed and then went still with a soft sigh.

"No!" Theo ran forward and pushed Eira away.

Eira shifted into a human and stood, but then it was Shelby's voice when she spoke again. "We are so sorry. Eira was able to take her pain, but not undo the damage. The demon wounds resist our magic. She has minutes left."

Theo cradled his mother's neck, pulling her head into his lap.

The queen smiled up at him. "You will make a great king." She coughed, her body vibrating. Skin and flesh dissolved into flower petals that caught on fire and fell as ash around Theo.

He sat in silence. Shelby put a hand on his shoulder. Theo tried to shrug it off, but then leaned into it as tears streamed down his face, streaked with ash. When he stood, his jaw was clenched and his eyes clear. "Let's go see Alsvoira."

Kale glanced at Shelby. "Is that safe?"

Theo pointed around the room at the shattered furniture and blood, before staring hard at the dark pile at his feet. "Where's safe anymore?"

Kale took Shelby's hand, looking back at Theo. "Lead the way."

Athena threw another bone at the wall, enjoying the musical echoes it made through the halls. She picked up a new one, bouncing it from hand to hand like she might start juggling. She tossed it at the wall.

Must you? Ptyas asked.

Not much else to do. Besides, it's pretty. But Athena took a break from her new musical sport to tear open one of the silver packets left behind by her angry Fae guide. Keanie Meanie would become her nickname if it didn't sound so petulant. Or childish. But, it did help Athena remember the Fae woman's name.

She was happy to find that the silver color of the packets was not from real silver like she suspected. It had to be aluminum. Inside was a heavenly honey colored paste that tasted like fresh cinnamon rolls drizzled in caramel. It was also much more filling than she expected. The assortment left for her would probably keep her alive a couple days. Longer, if she could find water.

You don't happen to know if there's an elvish drinking fountain around here?

Ptyas showed her a memory, layering the dark cavern with warmer, brighter images of what it once was. *That way.* He gestured with his nose, and she knew where he meant.

Wait, I was joking. There's an actual elf drinking fountain?

Not exactly, but it may still be there, if it isn't frozen over.

Athena rubbed her arms, though she really rubbed her gauntlets over the metal covering her arms. It had grown distinctly colder since the Fae had abandoned them. The armor kept her from freezing, but she wasn't comfortable.

She followed the memory images that overlaid the actual cavern, tripping over bones and rubble absent from Ptyas's recollections. *Do you think you can make those more transparent?*

Hmmm, never tried. Let me see. The memories thinned, becoming ghostly.

Athena picked her way through reality and the memories with more ease. *It was beautiful once, wasn't it?*

His head dipped in agreement, but he said nothing. She let him relive the past in silence until they reached the fountain, happily bubbling in his memory, but cold and dark in the present.

She punched a chunk of ice free. *Don't suppose we can build a fire and melt this down? And I forgot a pan.*

Ancient warriors used their helm as a cooking vessel and to boil drinking water, Ptyas replied.

Really? Too bad mine's keeping me alive and all. It doesn't come off either, so much as just disappear.

Guess you're sucking on ice chips until the Seely Fae show up and unlock the key for you. Do you know how you're going to get it this time?

She rolled the coin across her knuckles. *Pretty sure this puppy will do most of the work, along with proximity. I have consent. That's all I needed the first time.* She gathered up several chunks of ice. *Will you show me what Alsvoira looked like before everything went to hell?*

Ptyas filled her mind with rolling fields of perfect grass and wildflowers. Wolves raced one another through the grass and into the forest beyond. The purple leaves of the trees flashed blue in the wind, like aspen trees alternate between green and silver.

Athena felt the ice fall from her hands. *Show me more.*

Ptyas led her past falls that tumbled down from an impossible spire of stone into dreamlands she had never thought possible. Each race had their own section of Alsvoira, filled with wondrous life. The Druids lived in hilly territory full of wheat fields interspersed with dense forests of gnarled old trees and glowing mushrooms the size of cars.

The Fae had their beautiful mountain, green, but topped with snow. The inside was a maze of corridors, silken dividers, and living barricades. There were hedges, trees, grass, and a million varieties of flowers all growing within the mountain. They were masters of herbs, medicine, fruits, and vegetables. The Fae traded with all the other races for anything else they might want or need.

What happened?

Ptyas showed her a crystal doorway, a small human girl stepping through it. She was young, but familiar in a way that made Athena's jaw clench. *Was that Shelby?*

Thyra was the first to arrive.

Of course she was.

More humans arrived, coming in small groups after that first glimpse of Athena's rival. They introduced joy, laughter, love, and mourning to the five races. But the population grew. With more humanity came crime, deceit, disagreements, greed, hoarding, dissention, and a hundred other problems. The five races fought and warred. Peace shattered.

Wait, you're showing me thousands of years. How did Shelby live so long?

Ptyas showed the Goddess once more, a stunning being of gold and light. *She didn't let any of the humans who came to Alsvoira die, not of old age anyway.*

The vision faded and then reappeared, showing the demons ripping open holes into the world, flowing like blood from a wound. The Goddess refused to fight back. She even forbade her creations from engaging their new enemy. Alsvoira burned while many escaped to Earth through the crystal portal.

The Goddess's gateway was never meant to be used more than once, Ptyas chimed in. *It isn't like the demon gates, holes in reality. It's more passive than that, so many Immortal Wolves sacrificed themselves so humans could cross the threshold once more. It came with costs.*

Athena nodded. *Loss of autonomy.*

More than that. The human sides were stripped of memory, even when linked to another soul. The gate was kinder to the other races, especially those who left early.

In the vision, a group led by Mareus ignored the Goddess's commands, bringing war to the demons. Thyra led a group against him, enforcing the Goddess's wishes with violence, bringing death to her own.

I left before the end, at your father's command, so I don't know exactly what happened after that, but I do know Mareus killed the Goddess. He, Thyra, and Daeglan were the last to leave Alsvoira.

Athena picked up the ice once more as the apparitions of the past faded to black, not caring about the sediment on it. The dim halls held even less life for her, knowing what they had once been. *Why did the Goddess give up on her world?*

That is the ultimate question, and your father took the answer from us. Perhaps she was tired and wanted it all over. Perhaps she was ashamed of her creations. Perhaps she, like the Fae, absorbed some of humanity's madness. Perhaps she did what she thought best for her children. I do not know. She is gone, so I suppose it no longer matters what her reasons were.

Athena picked her way back to the wall of embedded demon bones and sat across from it. She used a rib bone to chip off a small piece of ice. She popped this in her mouth, only worrying about alien ice viruses for a second. "I'm Lycan. I can heal almost anything." The water was also sweet on her tongue as the chip melted, hints of a floral taste. The Fae didn't do anything without flare.

Shhh!

Athena had tossed a larger piece of ice into her mouth now that she trusted it more, but it was so cold it froze her saliva and stuck to her tongue. "Whub?

I think I hear someone, Ptyas warned.

The clattering of bones echoed down the halls from near the entrance.

Demon, Fae, or Lycan? I can't smell anything through this filtered air.

Hide. We'll have to wait and see.

Athena dodged behind the largest mound of bones. The demon would have been the size of a dump truck.

"You can do this, right?" Sadie waited an extra second to see if her Immortal Wolf would appear and say something encouraging back. "Talking to myself would be a lot more fun if you were real, Sexy Lexi." She stood naked in the cool Louisiana rain. "That armor would be nice too."

She gulped and then ran into the warehouse, shifting as she did so, letting her fur change to a mottled gray and brown that mimicked mud stains. Her pelt reeked of mud, ivy, and pine, with just a touch of humanity. She wanted to appear wild, but not one of the Feral.

Sadie had infiltrated and convinced another dozen small packs and one larger one, sending them to Salt Lake to meet up with the rest of her strange packmates. A few more were on the fence, but she suspected they would tip soon enough. The Advent had spread like a plague across the country, and small, independent groups wouldn't be allowed to exist for long.

Today wasn't her usual mission. *Can I call them missions, when I give them to myself?* She had avoided the packs that had joined the Advent, other than to spy on its movements against those she hoped to turn toward Kale.

Here's hoping this goes better than my last attempt. I'd rather not get anyone killed this time . . . especially since it's just me here. But she needed to reestablish a link to the Advent if she wanted to keep spying. Her hack through Athena no longer seemed to work. Either Mareus's daughter was dead—*A girl can copulating hope!*—Or Athena had discovered the hack and severed the link. *Or something else. Athena felt strange, like a different person, and then my hack stopped working.*

Sadie didn't avoid the sentries this time, instead following the sounds of their breathing past empty metal barrels and rotting wooden crates. *Here we go.* She steeled her nerves and stepped around a cement pillar to almost run right into one.

He snarled while she shrank back and whimpered, letting out a tiny hint of fear and urine scents. She shifted, covering herself and cowering into the shadows. "Please don't hurt me. I'm so hungry." It came out with a pitiful rasping squeak to her voice.

"Who are you?" The man stood tall, ignoring his nudity while he growled in a husky voice.

Sadie shrank back more and tried not to giggle at the dad-bod this sentry sported. *Like I can talk.* She had starved herself for three days and smeared soot and dirt on her body for good measure. "I'm Kallie, sir."

"And why are you here?"

She whimpered again. "I miss having a pack. Been hiding in the woods since my parents died a few weeks ago."

The man's face softened. "You aren't the only one who lost people when the Advent first arrived. Order has a price, and I paid it in blood. Come." He turned and strode off into the darkened warehouse. "We got Chinese takeout for dinner. There should be some left."

Sadie's stomach growled, and the man chuckled at the sound. *Feculence, I couldn't have planned that better if I tried. Good job, rumbly tumbly!*

"I'm Phil, by the way. I'm in charge of this group."

"You're the Alpha!?" Sadie didn't manage to hide her shock as much as she might have wanted. "Sorry, no offense."

But he laughed. "Not Alpha, just a lieutenant." Phil paused and tapped his chin. "Was it my appearance that threw you off?"

Sadie shook her head and made her eyes wider than she normally would. "You're serving sentry duty."

Phil started walking again. "A good leader does his share of the work."

Sadie stared at the man, surprised at his response and his appearance. The distraction caused her to stub a toe on a piece of rebar. "Fecu . . ." but she caught herself. "Fetch! That hurt." *Athena might have circulated my literal swearing as a way to identify me. Have to be more careful.* She wasn't sure if stupid made up swear words would be a giveaway, either.

Phil kept walking with only a glance back. "Sorry, it's a mess in here. We just took it, so we haven't done any cleaning yet. I should make a chore wheel."

Sadie studied his every movement, facial expression, tone of voice. She'd decided he would be her perfect new hack. High enough to get some information not given to the masses, but low enough not to raise suspicion for her. She had to get to know the man quickly to do this well. He was probably not a bad person, just trying to survive the Advent's take over.

He stopped at a row of hooks by a metal door where hard hats or equipment might have once hung, but it now held robes and clothing.

Phil took a silk, paisley robe and gestured at a soft, cotton terry one for Sadie. She took it, marveling at the kindness in the act. *He gave me his robe. It smells like him.*

It also smelled of fresh laundry and fabric softener, warming against her skin and easing the chill from the rain.

Phil led her through the door into a warmly lit room with beds and couches crammed into it. A massive table sat in the center of the room where a few people joked, ate, drank, and played cards. They looked up and nodded toward Phil with respect.

Phil grabbed a plate and tossed an egg roll and a couple scoops of rice and stir-fry on it. "Sorry, it's only vaguely warm."

It smelled amazing. Sadie's stomach growled again. "It's perfect." She took the plate, sat, and began devouring it greedily, stuffing it into her mouth as fast as she could chew.

"Guess you won't need this." Phil held up a plastic fork.

Sadie looked down at her fistful of lo mein. "Sorry."

"No worries. Eat how you want." He pointed off to a twin bed against a cinder block wall. "Sleep when you're done. We'll talk about joining after you wake up."

A pang of guilt went through Sadie. *He's such a nice guy. How the Hades did the Advent get him on board?* But she nodded while she stuffed some beef and broccoli into her mouth with one hand and grabbed another egg roll with her other. She held it up questioningly.

Phil smiled and nodded. Sadie finished it off in two bites.

She crawled into the bed a few minutes later, not faking her fatigue. She'd kept herself awake for three nights along with her fast. The bed smelled like Phil too. *Of course he gave me his bed! That man is going to make taking advantage of him really easy and terribly difficult. Underworld, I may even join the Advent for real at this rate.*

But Mareus, he would never trust her again. He would likely just kill her at first glance. *Such nice thoughts to fall asleep to.*

Thick roots draped down along the walls, sparkling with dots of light and releasing fluffballs from yellow flowers. The cottony seeds danced in the wind currents as Theo led Kale and Shelby down a path he had only trod once before.

Kale spat. "One got in my mouth."

Theo rolled his eyes. "We Fae like our elegant ambiences. Breathe through your nose."

Shelby elbowed her mate. "Mouth breather."

"Please don't call me that in front of the pack."

"No promises."

Theo managed a smile. He enjoyed their banter, but then it fell apart as he remembered his mother. "We're almost there."

"Do you guard this one too?" Chelsea asked.

Theo shook his head. "We do, but it's just a formality. Alsvoira is dead. The demons abandoned it long ago. We go back only to use what's left of the fires on rare occasions."

"You . . . go back?" Shelby asked. "To Alsvoira?"

"Rarely."

"What's left? You lost some of the fire?" The concern in Shelby's voice touched Theo.

"The demons consumed all they could find, but a pool was hidden deep inside the mountain. The sentient fires reproduce very slowly, so we are careful with our forges. It will take thousands of years to refill the upper pools."

"That's so sad." Shelby looked to where Fizz bobbed along beside Theo.

"Don't worry. They didn't feel pain." Theo held a hand out and let Fizz kiss his fingertips as they walked, the cool flames making tiny sucking noises. "We call them sentient because they absorb personality and will from those forging. We can create living pieces, like Fizz. They also go into armor and weapons that respond to the will of the wielder. But they are not like you and I."

"So, they aren't alive before then?" Kale willed a gauntlet onto his hand and poked at the metal with an uncovered finger. "I can almost feel the intelligence in this."

"They are alive." Theo thought hard. He'd never had to explain this to anyone. All the Fae just knew how it worked. "The flames are more like bacteria. Each one microscopic, simple, but alive. We forge them into multicellular organisms that can do more, even think on their own."

Shelby held out her own hand, and Fizz darted over to lick her fingers. She laughed. "How many flames went into making your wisp then?"

"Millions. He's more complex than even your armor."

She wiggled her fingers, letting Fizz dance along them in a tiny game of tag. "I believe it. He's brilliant."

"And not a 'he.' Wisps have no gender. The fires reproduce in a process similar to mitosis." Theo held up a hand. "And we're here. Squint, it's bright."

He pushed another vine curtain aside. The cavern ahead opened up into a dazzling display of crystal that refracted and reflected the light from above into rainbow streaks. A pool of crystal-clear water sat in the middle of the room beneath a pulsing portal of white light. Two guards stood at attention on the lush carpet of grass along the pool's edge.

Theo heard Shelby's intake of breath.

"It's beautiful," Chelsea added.

He turned, making his tone grave. "We made this side of the gate reflect the way we feel about Alsvoira. I must warn you, the other side is not what you remember." Theo spoke mainly to Shelby, but looked deeper, meaning to speak to Eira.

"She knows. She saw where it was heading in the end."

Theo nodded and led them to the stepping stones. He hopped from one to the other and jumped through the gate without hesitation, barely noting the tickling sensation on his skin that preceded numbness and prickling as his body came to exist once more. He scoured the horizon, looking for signs of demonic activity. A pillar of smoke billowed into the sky, but it had to be hundreds of miles from where he stood. Mother was right. The demons found a new place to gather. He took a step back and waited for his companions to follow, knowing it might be harder for some of them, while he kept an eye on smoke.

Wind tore at his clothing, blowing ash and dirt into his eyes. He started shivering. Theo hugged his chest. *I forgot how cold it is here.*

Chelsea appeared a moment later. The girl immediately gasped and fell to her knees. Theo swore inwardly at his lack of preparation for the human while he formed a shell of heat and oxygen around her. She began recovering, but the others didn't show.

"Come on, you two, you can do this. Nothing to fear, except the ashes of a ruined world, and maybe an army of demons."

Shelby and Kale stood before the portal leading to Alsvoira, bathed in bright shimmering light. Theo and Chelsea had already stepped through.

"Eira isn't excited." Shelby could taste her Immortal Wolf's apprehension. That was still so cool to her, tasting emotions.

"Skotha either." Kale picked up a pebble and tossed it through. "They blame themselves."

"Which is stupid." Shelby growled before Eira could reply. "And don't argue. You did everything you could."

Maybe not everything.

"You couldn't have been expected to kill Viersin and my son."

Expected, maybe not, but I should have.

"Could you have?"

Probably, at the end, but by then it was too late.

"Exactly, which takes us back to the beginning. You did all you could. I win the argument."

You must have driven your father crazy with such dazzling logic. Eira's tone was joking, but there was sadness in it too.

Shelby winced. She hadn't heard much from her dad since he'd gone with the Hunters. *I hope he's okay.*

Sorry, I did not intend to hurt you. He's the strongest man I've met. I'm sure he is better than fine. I'd worry about the Hunters.

Shelby smiled at that. *Right?*

If it helps, Skotha agrees, Kale said, interrupting through the packlink. *You did all you could. All four of you did, and yes, I'm counting our former lives in the mix, which hurts my head. It just wasn't enough. That happens sometimes.*

That wasn't smart. Eira sighed. *All this internal talk about fathers and sons is hard on Skotha.*

Yeah, we're idiots sometimes, Shelby said. *You'd think an ancient wolf would grow out of that.*

Not yet, Eira said. *Give him a thousand more years.*

Shelby stepped up to the portal. *If we survive the next few weeks, I will.* She crossed the prickling and numbing threshold to stagger into icy wind that pelted her with ash and sand.

"About time!" Chelsea glared at her with hands on her hips. "You're lucky I know a spell to concentrate heat, or I'd be frozen to death by now. As is, it'll run out of gas in an hour, and my magic doesn't seem to work well here. It's like it has a bad fuel pump."

Kale stopped. "You know cars?"

She put a hand on her hip. "There's quite a bit about me you never bothered to learn."

"Excuse you?" Shelby said, stepping in front of Kale, head lowered.

"It's whatever," Chelsea said dismissively.

Theo waved a hand over Chelsea. "I'm also helping her with air. You two should don your helms. Magic will weaken as we move away from the gate. There isn't much left in Alsvoira. And any we use will be siphoned in that direction. Best we keep it minimal, lest we get noticed." He pointed to a dark line of smoke on the horizon.

Shelby summoned the helm and felt it materialize around her head and face. She smiled. "I never get tired of that."

They followed him through a blinding dust storm to the base of a mountain, up switchbacks, and into a cavern system.

Theo's sadness as they entered was almost visible in the air around him to Shelby. She could smell it and taste it, even with her helm filtering out most scents. *His people died here by the thousands. I can feel the ghosts all around us.*

Not just his people, Eira added. *All the five races came together to defend the sentient flames. They weren't quite a sixth race, but we all thought highly of them. It would be like the demons coming to Earth and eating all the puppies.*

Shelby winced at the analogy. *That's monstrous!*

Eira nodded. *Yes, that's demons. They consume without thought, without care, without love.*

Then that's how we'll beat them.

Eira's silence spoke volumes. When she spoke, it was distant. *That didn't work last time.*

A pile of demon bones toppled like a deranged game of Jenga as they passed, upset by the vibrations of their footfalls and the shifting air currents from their movements.

Chelsea blasted it with a small burst of fire in reflex, her fingers moving rapidly despite the cold. The flames rolled around the obsidian, harmless.

"Fire isn't the best against demons," Theo noted. Fizz puffed up defensively at his words, but deflated as though accepting the truth of them.

"Thanks for the obvious, elf-boy," Chelsea snapped back. "It's just my go-to kill-it-dead-before-it-kills-me spell. What would you suggest?"

"Reinforced titanium or diamond blades would be better. You got a spell for that?"

Chelsea's glare transformed into pure disappointment. "No, not really. I can make magic knives, but they aren't much better than steel, just cooler looking."

Shelby had her doubts. She'd seen the girl's magic up close and personal. Chelsea was stronger than she thought.

"You also have to throw them fast," Theo said, "or the demons strip the magic away before they hit. It's one reason we like our bows."

Chelsea took up stride next to the Fae. "Why not guns then?"

Theo made a face as if he'd just smelled something repugnant. "Human weapons."

"Racist!"

Theo started to protest, but then stopped himself. "You may be right. We've tried hard to understand your kind, but we never truly embraced you as equals, not like the Immortal Wolves did, even before they sacrificed themselves so you could go home."

"What?" Chelsea was running her fingers through movements. Golden knives appeared in her hands, but they flickered out. "I've always been home."

"Sorry." Theo gestured behind him at Shelby and Kale. "Mostly talking about them. Humans wouldn't have survived what the demons did to Alsvoira long enough to make it through the gate without them."

"Makes sense," Chelsea said as she created another set of knives. "Sort of."

It was more complex than that, of course, but we did what we felt was right for you and your people. The gate wouldn't have let you cross. Eira sounded far away. Seeing her world in ruin was a torture. *So few made it through, even with our sacrifice.*

Shelby wanted to hug her wolf. *I'm not sure if Thyra said so, but thank you for all you did then and now. I know Kale and I are glad to be here. I also know you gave up everything to make that possible.* Shelby used her Omega gifts to send comfort inward. She'd never tried before, but it seemed to work.

Thyra did thank me . . . and curse me for giving up my autonomy for her sake, but it's still nice to hear. You are a lot like her, but also warmer, kinder in many ways, like the best of the woman I knew.

Shelby felt her cheeks redden inside her helm. *I try. But, aren't I her? Her spirit or whatever?*

Yes, but genetics and your environment growing up as Shelby have changed some things.

Theo held up a hand. "We're here." He touched a wall where the demon bones piled up thick against it, and many had been imbedded into the stone. "The pool is on the other side."

The stone hummed in the Fae's presence, like he'd awakened something within it.

"That is you, right?" Shelby took a step back and grabbed Kale's hand. She couldn't feel his warmth through her gauntlet, but the weight of it was a small comfort. Whatever the demon they fought had done to them, it still hurt. There was a fresh wound where the bond had begun to go numb. The pain made it harder than the cold void it had been. *I miss the bond.*

"Yeah, that's me," Theo answered her. "It opens for royal blood, as long as there are no demons around." He glanced over his shoulder. "Almost certain we're good, but, if it doesn't open, be ready to fight."

Kale squeezed her hand. She felt that at least. Chelsea frowned at their hands, but said nothing.

Shelby felt Eira growl within her.

Has to be hard on her too, Shelby said to her wolf. *She had so many hopes and dreams wrapped up in Kale once. I know how that feels.*

When did you become the rational one?

They waited in silence as the wall hummed and buzzed. It took forever, and Shelby began to fear a demon hid in the darkness. *Maybe it wasn't our steps that tipped those bones. It's hoping we open the way.*

But a loud crack echoed down the empty halls, and the wall slid open. A swirl of color came from the crack. Shelby had expected blue, like the wisp that followed Theo, not a million shades all at once.

"It's beautiful." Chelsea could have spoken for Shelby. The witch took a step forward.

Theo held out a hand. "Go slow. The fires are skittish around new people."

Chelsea smiled, seemed to realize he wasn't joking, blinked at the light with her mouth open, and took a step forward, slowly.

"Now you two." Theo waved them forward. "Go to the edge of the pool, but no closer than two or three feet."

Kale tugged Shelby along as the light transfixed her. She could hear each flame's tiny soul in her mind, yearning to create beauty, to be a part of something bigger. Kale brought her to the edge of the small pool, maybe ten feet across, where Chelsea stopped and stared.

The pool pulled away, ever so slightly, notes of trepidation and concern in a million flaming hearts. "They are alive." Shelby poured out comfort. *We mean you no harm, little ones. We need your help.* The pool relaxed and lapped against the solid stone near their feet, tendrils of multicolored fire crawled up to reach toward Shelby.

Theo came up next to her. "I've never seen them accept someone so fast."

Kale grinned. "That's my Shelby. The best Omega you'll find anywhere."

"So it seems. Or they just recognize the armor." Theo pulled out the large coin his mother had given him. Fizz launched itself from his shoulder and flew over the pool, glowing brightly as the flames made ripples in their evermoving surface around the wisp. "Let's get to forging this key of yours before any demons smell our magic." He handed the metal disk to Shelby. "You have my consent."

She took it and flipped it over in her hands to see the carvings on each side. She could make out the shape of a lock in the center, surrounded by lines of circuitry. The other side showed two wolves facing off, a curved line above them with two arrows pointing downward. "What do I do?"

Fizz flew over and bumped against her hands, gentle, but curious.

Theo laughed. "You do very little. Give it to the flames. They will do the doing." He paused and looked up. "You can give them some additional instructions though. They listen. Mind you, they don't always follow through, but they listen."

"I wouldn't even know what to say." Shelby knelt next to the pool and set the coin on top of the shifting fire. "I wish you could fix so many things for us, but I'll take what the queen thought we needed. Forge well. I trust you."

The medallion floated on the surface for a moment and then

sank under the flames. Only a few heartbeats later, a silver key rose from the same spot.

Kale shifted his footing next to her. "Is that it? I expected something more spectacular."

Shelby smiled. "Don't listen to him. You did perfect." She reached down and took the key, but as soon as she touched it, fire shot up in a fountain and fell down on her like rain. She tried to back away, but flames had curled around her hand, holding her in place. "Theo?" The fiery rain also began swirling over her body, but it did not burn.

"I don't know! I've never seen them act like this . . . well, except for once." Theo grabbed her shoulders, but an explosion of light and fire sent him flying. He slammed against a stalactite and fell hard. Fizz buzzed to his aid. Chelsea did as well, weaving spells as she ran.

Kale came up beside Shelby, his hands extended.

"Wait, Kale," she said. "They aren't hurting me."

"I have to try something." Kale took her free hand, and Shelby feared the flames would send him flying. Instead, they wrapped around him too, pulling him closer to her and to his knees.

More flames shot from the pool, streams of light that slammed into their chests, burrowing deep into armor and flesh beneath. Shelby tried to scream, but flames poured into her open mouth. It still did not hurt. If anything, it was warm, the sentient flames urgent, but not malicious. *What is happening?*

Eira answered her. The Wolf didn't sound calm, but also not fearful. You *are what they are forging, not a simple bow, arrow, or sword. You.*

Shelby closed her eyes, calmed her body, and listened to the songs within each tiny spark of life as they followed the instructions carved onto the coin and from her. She also felt Kale trying to free himself.

"No, it's okay, Kale." She brought a fire enveloped hand to his face, running her fingers down his gruff. She loved the feel of it. "Let them do what they need to do."

Warmth flowed into her chest. The flames found the tatters of her bond and dissolved it with fire. She thought she had known pain and loss, but it was nothing to the last of her connection to Kale being devoured before her mind's eye. She did scream then, wailed and howled. She cried for them to stop, to undo what they had done. Then Kale screamed next to her as his own bond burned to ash. She grabbed him, embraced him, plowing her head into his hard chest with such desperation.

I'm so sorry, Kale. I didn't know. I didn't know. But, of course, he couldn't hear or feel her thoughts, not even through the pack link. All trace of that powerful magic was gone.

Molten will poured into the open wound within her heart and soul. It was too much. Too painful. Things turned blurry then dark as she let go of consciousness.

Athena crept quietly in behind Kale and Shelby. Another Fae and that Chelsea witch were with them. She held the coin in her hand from the king. *How am I supposed to get this into the pool without them noticing? I am so getting caught while outnumbered. Maybe I should just put a scythe in Shelby's back and toss mine in.*

Ptyas let out a long sigh inside her.

What do you want to say, old man?

She is the one unlocking it. If you kill her now, no one gets the key. Wait and watch for an opening.

What, you think distractions just happen? It's not like I can send the annoying voice in my head down the hall to make noise, can I?

Ptyas grunted. *That might work.*

She growled at him. *How would that work?*

He pointed forward with his nose. *Not that,* that!

Flames shot out of the pool and fell on Shelby. *Oh, yes, that,* Athena thought to Ptyas. The Fae was flung across the room, distracting the Wiccan. Then Kale got caught up in the flame. *Okay, I guess distractions do sometimes just happen.* Athena squinted. Strange how the fire seemed to consciously envelope Kale, as if protecting him rather than scorching him to ash. There was always hope, she guessed.

Now, quick, Ptyas urged.

She rolled her own coin across the stone and into the pool. It sunk. *Now what?*

Wait.

She did. A stream of fire pulled away from the pool and rolled across stone toward her and formed into a smaller pool. When it receded, a silver bow with a single arrow remained. She picked them up. A jolt of electricity shot through her, and she felt a connection to the bow like it was alive and a part of her, a limb that had long been asleep, reawakened.

The bow dissolved in her hand. The arrow dissolved in the other. She cursed. *Where did they go?* They reappeared at her summons. *Ah, they're one with the armor now.* It was more than that. She could feel something growing inside her, something powerful and orderly. *I have my key.* She snuck out the way she had come in, glancing back. *Good luck getting yours without the king's consent, Shelby darling.*

Shelby screamed and then slumped to the floor. Kale did the same.

Yep, getting a key without consent has to hurt. Serves you right. She froze as she saw their bodies go limp, the Fae down and the Wiccan distracted. *Is it killing them? Is that what happens without consent? This I have to see.* She turned, strafing behind a rock formation as the bow flowed into her hand from the armor and an arrow appeared in her other palm. *I can make sure of it.*

There is no honor in this, Ptyas scolded.

When has honor done me any good?

When have you given it a chance?

Athena thought back over her life. *A couple times. Disasters all. Over it.*

You are very much like your father, the ends justifying the means.

I guess I am. Enough. I'm doing this.

Ptyas sighed. *If you must do this, aim true. Do not make her suffer.*

Athena wanted to shake her Immortal Wolf. *I thought you were beginning to know me. It's the only way I aim.* She climbed up a stalagmite and drew the bow. The arrow was cold along her forearm, the bowstring feeling somewhat electric against her cheek as she sighted in her prey.

She's waking, Ptyas hissed.

Athena ducked back behind the stalagmite at his warning.

We should leave while they remain distracted, Ptyas added. *I do not imagine we would fare well once the door closes.*

I have the key. Father will be glad of that, but will he forgive me for not taking advantage of this opportunity dropped at my feet?

Ptyas didn't answer, leaving the possible answers in her own mind.

Minutes passed as she debated whether to engage or flee. The murmur of their voices echoed through the cavern, and her anger at her indecision grew with the sound of happy conversation. Her resolve hardened into steel inside her heart. *Distracted is almost as good as unconscious. We end this now.*

"I am the Summer Omega," she whispered as she leaned around

the stone formation once more, focusing her aim and hatred. *Goodbye, Shelby.*

The arrow flew.

ire softly caressed Shelby's face. Kale lay at the edge of the pool next to her. He had passed out it seemed. *That hurt.* But the pain had stopped and his face appeared tranquil and relaxed.

She saw his dream as if she were experiencing it, a dream of a hunt, chasing elk through the Colorado mountains. Not a dream, really, but a memory of an actual hunt the first couple weeks after Elias died, when they were on run, when—

She bolted upright. *Wait, how do I know that?*

That sense of belonging and wholeness flowed through her once again, the same that had budded within her upon first meeting Kale, even just unknowingly being around him. It felt like a release. It felt like warmth. It felt like *home.* She inhaled sharply and put a hand to her chest, not wanting to believe for her heart's sake.

Kale was waking up. She knew it without looking at him, sensed the veil of sleep leaving. The elk had eluded him. That hadn't happened in real life, but the dream changed . . .

The bond! She blinked rapidly, letting only a few drops of hope seep into her heart. *They . . . reforged the bond?* The fire had eaten away the remnants of the old bond, and she had felt a molten something pour into her heart. "The sentient fires," she said breathlessly, "they reforged the bond . . . using my heart as a mold." Or something like that. Shelby couldn't explain it, but the love that filled her being, that ancient connection to Kale . . . her eyes brimmed with tears of pure wonder and delight.

Chelsea and Theo rushed to her side. Chelsea wove a healing spell. Shelby had begun to recognize some of the more common patterns she wove in the air. "Are you okay?"

I was having the best dream. Kale's sleepy, resonant, sexy voice came to her through the bond, and Shelby's heart felt as though it might explode.

Shelby gently put her hand on one of Chelsea's, shaking her head. "I have never been better." Shelby smiled. "Well, not never, but it has been a while." She leaned down and deeply, slowly, kissed her boyfriend, her soul mate, her everything.

His eyes fluttered open as he became fully awake. *That's nice,* he said through the bond.

Shelby tingled all over. *Isn't it?* She let her love for him flow down the renewed connection.

He sat up, confusion in his eyes. "Wait, I thought I heard you inside my head."

Chelsea huffed. "I knew it. You're both insane. Explains so much."

Shelby nodded and licked her lips, tasting the remnants of their kiss. *You did,* she said through bond and kissed him again.

He pulled her close and she fell into his embrace, wrapping her legs around his hips. "I never want to lose you again," he whispered, and Shelby's chest fluttered at the sound of his gruff voice against her ear and inside her heart. Chills raced from her neck to the small of her back. She buried her face into his neck. Oh, that scent! She had lost so much of him when Athena severed their bond, so much more than she had realized.

"I think it's even stronger than before. I don't have to work to talk to you at all."

Chelsea's voice came next. "Um, like, what's happening?"

Shelby reached out, not lifting her head from Kale's neck, and grabbed the girl, pulling her into their hug. "It's back. The bond is back."

Chelsea took a deep breath. "Right. I'm, like, so happy for you."

Shelby knew she meant it, at least mostly.

The Wiccan pulled away. "The gifts don't stop there." She pointed to a set of bows and arrows and the hilts of two knives. "The fire left those behind. Theo thought we should let you sleep though, rough wedding night and all."

Kale sat back. "What?"

"Yeah, the elf guy said the fire acted like it does during Fae weddings."

Theo came to the edge of the pool, healed from any injury by Fae or Wiccan magic. "It's only a theory, though the fire usually won't do that without three witnesses. They like threes."

Kale blinked at Shelby, his mouth open.

"What? You don't want to marry me?" she snapped with a sarcastic glare.

He choked. "Of course I do, I just wanted my mom and your dad there when it happened." He grinned. "Oh, you're messing with me."

"You heard Theo. It isn't legal. We'll just have to do it again in front of more witnesses, preferably on Earth."

Kale looked to Chelsea and then Theo. "Did she just propose?"

"Sounded like it." Chelsea coughed and then pointed to the weapons. "Open the engagement gifts already."

Kale pulled away from Shelby and stood. He picked up the larger bow and an arrow. It flowed into his armor and a sly smile formed on those full lips. "Cool."

Shelby didn't mind him pulling away. She stood and took her own bow and arrow. *I freaking love this!*

Something sparked within her as she touched the bow. *I have the key.* She willed the bow into her armor and back out. *Those clever Fae.* She reached down for the knife hilts, but a tendril of fire smacked her hand and pointed at Chelsea.

"Looks like Kale and I aren't the only ones getting gifts. I think those are yours, Chelsea."

The girl's eyes widened. "Really? I was wishing for magical knives that could defeat a demon ever since Theo mentioned they were possible. How convenient."

Theo pushed her toward the hilts. "I told you, they listen."

Chelsea reached down, her fingers just brushing the metal. "But they have no blades."

Theo smiled wickedly. "Pick them up."

Chelsea did, then closed her eyes. Diamond blades extended from the tops of the hilts. She opened her eyes and almost dropped her new toys. "I want to hug a pool of fire right now."

Shelby watched the blades disappear. "Try a different shape or length."

"What?" Chelsea looked down at her hilts. "You think?"

"I do."

Curved blades extended out, farther than before. Chelsea swung them through the air, the diamond whistling. "The balance adjusted too." She let the blades retract again. "Now where will I keep them."

She was bringing the hilts toward her pockets when the metal shrank and curled around a finger on each hand.

Shelby laughed. "That answers that. Nice rings."

Chelsea held up her hands and admired the silver with diamond stones. "I wonder." Tiny sharp knives extended from the middle of each ring. "Yep, elf-boy's flames are the coolest."

Shelby enjoyed Kale's laughter as it flowed to her, making her tingle with delight and desire. She leaned forward and stole another kiss.

Pain seared through her shoulder. Something had hit her, pierced her, even through her armor. Kale went rigid with surprise, and she knew he felt her pain through the bond. Fire raced through her now, not the caressing fire of the sentient flames, but the agonizing, pulsing fire of an open wound. She screamed and toppled forward into the pool of living flames.

ryanne leaned against the table, coating the luxurious honeyed grain with sticky orange blood. She and Genn, with the help of survivors, had managed to move all the injured to the two throne rooms, which were mirrors of one another with this small meeting room between.

Bryanne sat and put her head in her hands.

The ley lines beneath Underhill were in tatters, shredded by hungry demons. Her magic couldn't heal anyone. She'd watched helplessly as too many of the Fae disintegrated into flowers and ash. Bryanne had to lean on more human means, applying pressure, makeshift bandages, stitches, and cauterizations.

Fae magic worked slightly better, so the more whole survivors were set to work staunching the flow of blood from serious injuries and preventing infection. The wisps bobbed around listless and unhelpful.

Genn burst through the door that lead from Seely Court. "The king is waking up."

Bryanne lifted her head. What little magic she could cobble together had gone into that man. *I'm not letting Theo lose both parents today.* "Good."

Bryanne stood and followed Genn to where the king sat up from the mattress they'd placed him on.

"Why am I in Seely Court?"

"Because that is where you were when the demons attacked, sire." Bryanne put a hand to the gash in his stomach. His movements had opened the wound. "You need to lay back down."

He pushed her hand away and glared at the bloody bandage, then up at a passing blue wisp. "Why is Silphinaera not healing my wounds? That vindictive woman!"

Genn knelt next to him, wiping tears from her eyes. "She is dead, sire. I am so sorry."

The king slumped at her words. Real loss flashed in his eyes. "And Theo?"

"Alive and in Alsvoira," Bryanne answered.

The king sighed. "Something of her lives on." He swallowed hard. "That is good."

"So, you do know." Bryanne gently pulled his hand away and placed a fresh strip of torn sheet on the gash, pushing to stop the bleeding.

He sat back up, brow knitted. "Do you dare presume to know something I do not? I know my champion will gain the key while yours does not!"

Something inside Bryanne hardened and she pushed harder against the king's wound. "Your champion?" She couldn't keep the sneer from her tone. "What have you done, sire?"

"Stop, you are hurting my royal flesh."

"I know, sire." Bryanne dug a thumb into the wound.

"Guards!"

"You will find no guards in this room who will respond to your calls. Is your champion Mareus's daughter?"

The king gasped as Bryanne dug a little deeper.

"Is it *Athena?*" Bryanne asked.

"Of course, I would never give consent to the woman who butchered my soldiers." The king pushed against her, but his hands were weak. Bryanne batted them down.

"My grandmother was there. She spoke of the Unseely Fae who turned on the Goddess. And your *son* gave us consent, so your attempt to hurt Shelby for your past wrongs has failed." She pulled her thumb from his wound and applied another strip against the wound. A last burst of magic poured from her fingertips and into the wound, sealing it. She almost regretted it. "And I save your life for Theo's sake, not your own."

Bryanne staggered back. Using magic here hurt. Genn caught her and dragged her a few paces away from the king who struggled to his feet, anger on his beautiful face.

"Your grandmother didn't see the Goddess turn a blind eye to her people's suffering," the king said. "The demons tore through us like we were made of the flowers we love." Orange tinged spittle sprayed from his mouth as he staggered toward them. "We wanted only to force her to action. We never wanted her blood on our hands." He stopped and stared at his shaking hands. "Did you say my son has given consent?"

Bryanne nodded. "Theo is your son, he is a royal of both courts."

"That treacherous, beautiful, wonderful woman." The king fell to his knees. "I will miss her." He wiped at his eye. "I have a son, an heir to reunite the courts." He lifted a hand to his lips and whistled loud and long.

Orange wisps flew through walls and to his side. He smiled up at them. "Heal as many Fae as you can in both courts. Get your lazy cousins to help, if you can convince them to act without Seely royalty." He glanced at his healers and tormentors, eyes tightening. "Prepare Underhill Five Point Oh. We can't stay here. And bind those two while you're at it."

The wisps buzzed about their duties, several blue ones joined them in healing wounds, while two orange spun around Genn and Bryanne, cocooning them in amber threads.

Bryanne slumped against Genn, her magic too exhausted to free her. They both fell to the floor. "At least I don't have to watch another die, thank the Goddess."

The king frowned down at her. "Thank the Goddess all you like, but I doubt we've seen the last of death."

Terror flowed down the bond and into Shelby's heart. Cold, so cold. Like the bitterness in her bones that night outside Odessa with Nicholas's pack. She saw Kale's strong arm flailing above her in the pool fire, reaching blindly for her, but she let herself sink deeper. The fire truly felt like liquid as she floated away from Kale's reach, even down to the fluid friction on the object sticking out of her right shoulder. Gingerly, she raised her left hand and traced the arrow's shaft. *Athena.* So, there had been a third witness after all. Eira growled and lent Shelby strength. With a swift rip, Shelby tore the arrow free. Its barbed tip tore flesh, and streams of blood trickled away, floating in the liquid fire.

Shelby!

Kale's voice, through the bond.

I'm fine. The fire seemed to lick her wound. *Already healing. Now fight!*

She felt his mind turn toward assessing the threat. Her own instinct kicked in, and half-shifted, pushing hard against the stone bottom of the sentient pool. She launched into the cavern, trailing streams of multicolored fire. A howl tore free from her mid-flight.

Shelby landed as a wolf, eyes trained in the direction of the arrow's flight. A shadow ducked behind a set of crystal studded stalagmites as an arrow pinged off the stone inches away. Kale stepped to her side, his bow drawn, a second arrow appearing from his gauntlet.

"It's Athena." He glanced toward the opening to the cave. "How did she get in here?"

And is she alone? Shelby added through the bond.

"Theo, Chelsea, get to cover. We don't know if she's got company." An arrow bounced off of Kale's helm with enough force to send him back a step. He focused all his attention back on Athena. "I'll keep her busy." He shot another arrow, forcing Athena to duck once more.

Shelby heard Chelsea and Theo scramble over a stone outcropping. She shifted and pulled her own bow, pinning Athena down with a few more arrows. Shelby also reached out with her Omega abilities to sense how many other enemies might be near. She felt nothing, but Athena had blocked her before.

"I don't feel anyone else, but I also don't feel Athena, so . . ." Shelby trailed off, not wanting to admit her uncertainties out loud.

Kale grimaced and knelt next to her, making himself a smaller target, even as he partially shifted to strengthen arms. "I trust your feelings." His next arrow punched through stone. A chunk of demolished stalagmite bounced off metal, Athena's armor.

Athena swore and rolled to the side behind thicker mineral deposits.

A flash of red light to Shelby's right made her stand, her scythe appearing in one hand and an arrow clenched in her other fist with the point extending between her fingers, but it was Chelsea. The Wiccan stood in the open, spreading a net of light over the opening.

"Get down!" Shelby hissed at the girl and Theo who stepped out to aid her.

"Not yet. It's, like, really close to done." But Chelsea sounded out of breath, and the last few threads of the net looked thinner and dimmer than the rest. "My magic's fading, but it'll still slow anyone down trying to come in." Her words slurred, and she wobbled to the side.

Theo caught Chelsea before she cracked her head open on the stone floor, but Shelby felt Kale tense. Theo's hand came up. An arrow curved around Chelsea's head. Another was caught midair by Fizz and incinerated.

"Get her out of the open." Shelby yelled as she spun back and down. An arrow punched into her thigh just as her knee touched stone. She bit back her scream for Kale's sake, realizing he'd know she was hurt through the bond a moment later.

He started to turn her direction, but she cut him off. *Still fine. Still healing. Focus, my Alpha, on the enemy. I might get shot less if you do.*

He grunted and nodded. "She has better aim than me."

"Me too," Shelby admitted through clenched teeth. Her shots all pulled hard to the left, and she didn't know how to correct it. When she tried, her aim became even more unpredictable.

"That's because some of us studied archery and other weapons," Athena taunted from behind a crystalline formation, "while others went to human schools where they learned how to use crayons and solve for x." She kicked off a stalagmite and ran along the side wall of the cavern, arrows forming and flying in a smooth coordinated motion that appeared effortless. She spun around a stalactite using the curved blades of her scythe as a counterpoint, bounded off a boulder, and sent three arrows at once before she landed again.

Shelby managed to cut an arrow out of the air with her scythe and lifted her left hand to deflect several others, a small shield forming from the armor as she used it in defense. She bit her tongue as titanium punched through metal and into her wrist. The shield dissolved, and two arrows clattered to the floor, but one remained behind to make it impossible for Shelby to draw the string on her own bow. She pulled it out, nearly missing the twinge of pain that came to her through the bond.

Kale had been hit. He fell backward, clutching his chest.

Fear and sweat prickled Shelby's neck and trickled down her forehead. She crawled to Kale's side and put a hand around the arrow over his wound, willing him to be okay.

I'm fine. Healing. Focus. He used her words. He shifted into his wolf. *And I'm a better weapon like this.*

She could taste his anger. He wasn't fine, but he'd be worse if her loss of concentration let more arrows through. *Okay.* She turned back to Athena, a growl in the back of her throat, but it transformed into a yelp as she found Athena running across open ground toward her, bow pulled back. The arrow flew.

Shelby rolled to the side, but Athena's arrow curved to follow, ricocheting off a vambrace. *How did she do that?* Shelby had no time to contemplate Athena's newfound skill as a glowing blade whistled through the air a fraction of an inch from Shelby's nose.

Shelby scrambled backward, her armor deflecting most of the next few blows, her own scythe used purely in defense.

Athena pushed her advance. A small crossbow formed on one arm, punching a bolt into Shelby's side. The scythe swung cutting into her arm. A second crossbow formed on the other arm as soon as the scythe passed, sending another arrow into Shelby's leg as Athena swung the dual blades at her middle.

Shelby's wooden shield blocked the blow, but Athena didn't miss a beat. The scythe appeared in Athena's other hand as it swung toward Shelby's neck. The magical armor kept Shelby from losing her head as blood sprayed from a shallow gash. Her hands shot to her throat as she staggered back.

Kale caught Athena's wrist in his jaws before it came for the second killing blow, armored claws ripping at her back.

Watch out! Shelby tried to shout it, but her vocal cords were still healing.

A bolt slammed into Kale's neck from point blank range, and Athena arched her back, her armor forming spikes along her spine. She spun as he fell, pulling her dual bladed scythe into two, both cutting through his armor in twin gashes over his stomach. He snarled as he landed and lunged, jaws clamping hard around Athena's thigh. Magical armor bent under the pressure.

Athena grunted and put two new bolts into Kale's hide, but the Alpha bit down harder. Armor tore, and Athena screamed. She punched Kale in the head over and over, her gauntlets spiked and spraying blood. He bit harder, and bone snapped.

Athena dragged her scythes across his ribs, but Kale would not let go.

Shelby felt every new injury lash through her own body. "Stop!" she managed to yell, her voice raw and new, inhuman to her ears. She pulled a hand away from her still bleeding neck to throw her scythe.

A gauntlet slick with blood didn't help her aim. The blade sliced through Athena's side and then along Kale's spine.

Forgive me. Shelby felt the bite of her own blade and Kale finally let go.

It did draw the woman's attention away from Kale, though she hobbled on her ruined leg. Already, Shelby saw her healing take effect.

Athena pulled back on the string of her bow while it was still forming from her armor. An arrow grew from the fingertips of her right hand in less than an eye blink. It slammed into Shelby's foot, pinning her to the ground.

Shelby fell backward as another arrow punched through the armor, flesh, and bone of her other foot. Another found her wrist as soon as it hit stone. The fourth punched through her forearm. Holy Hell, Athena was fast. Shelby's eyes blazed with Eira's fury. She started to shift, but something blocked her.

Eria?

I'm not alone, her Immortal Wolf answered.

Athena stood over Shelby, scythes forming before the bow completely dissolved back into the armor.

I don't know what you mean, but we need to shift! Shelby screamed inwardly. To her side, Kale languidly rose.

Too slow, too slow. Eira, why can't I shift?

Eira didn't answer, and Shelby's heart thudded frantically. Then, she noticed Athena's eyes, that they flared with amber pin pricks like stars in the night sky but did not turn fully to those of her wolf.

Ptyas, Eira gasped. *He's . . . here. With me.*

She felt it then, another presence within her. A streak of cold raced through her veins, somewhat paralyzing her. Athena was interfering with her and Eira's bond, and had somehow—on some level—projected her Immortal Wolf *into* Shelby.

Shelby dropped onto a lush carpet of green grass surrounded by tall trees. There was no moon, but the stars felt brighter than Shelby had ever experienced, a swirl of them cutting through the sky in a way the milky way never managed. Its pulsing light illuminated a path toward the jagged mountain on the horizon in streaks of silver. She recognized it. *Of course, Eira lives inside a recreation of Alsvoira in my head.*

A large wolf darted out from behind a tree, sniffing the air. *Ptyas. How is he here?* He slipped back into the trees, seeming not to notice Shelby, or not to care about her aspect in this fight. Shelby felt Eira more than saw her as her Immortal Wolf darted over an outcropping of stone covered in a blue moss and blanketed in shadow. *She's sneakier than you.*

Pain ripped into Shelby's side. She looked down to find her blood glowing in the starlight. *What?* She realized her peril. *Athena. I'm still fighting Athena.*

Shelby split, half of her inside her mind, following Eira and Ptyas, and half of her facing the blades of her enemy, who had knelt down to slide a scythe into her ribs. Shelby ran toward where Ptyas closed on her internal companion while she ripped a hand free to punch Athena in the face as hard as she could. Magical metal cracked and healed in seconds, but it was enough to force the woman back.

Kale slammed into her, toppling her over and allowing Shelby a few seconds to fall back into the hidden landscape of her mind. She was almost on top of Ptyas, but the wolf had also found Eira, backing her into a corner formed by a fallen log and cracked stone. Eira could still escape. Shelby knew how agile her wolf could be. *Why isn't she escaping?*

Eira snarled at the attacker who advanced slowly. *Get out of my head, Ptyas. I will kill you if I must.*

Ptyas shook his muzzle. *I do not want to hurt you, Eira. I simply want to sever your bond with the girl. You will live.*

Why would you do that? And how?

Ptyas bared more of his teeth, glinting in the starlight. *So there will be only one Summer Omega. The prophesies will make sense again. Athena has the power, and so do I as a part of her.*

Shelby saw past the imagery of the realm. Eira was not cornered. She guarded something. The log and stone melted away into a stream of energy. *Our bond. That's why she isn't running.* Shelby stepped between them. *Not gonna happen, dogbreath.*

Ptyas laughed. *You aren't really here, sweet girl.* He walked through Shelby to punctuate his point. *You are a ghost in this realm where we who sacrificed our autonomy are banished. You can do nothing to me.*

Shelby stared down at her translucent form. Past her flesh she could see shadows fighting. Kale had Athena on the ground, pinned while he bit into her. Her armor buckled and tore under the shear force of his attacks. *Goddess is he powerful!* But he did not see the crossbow forming on her vambrace, angled toward his chest. *No!*

A cold seeped into Shelby's bones, starting in her fingers and toes, curling inward, as though all the warmth of her body and the surrounding air crawled toward her middle where it was devoured. She had felt this once before, when Nicholas and his pack attacked her and her father.

Something burned inside her heart, eating up all the surrounding energy. *I give you autonomy, Eira.* Shelby's voice came out low, hints of thunder in it.

Her wolf stared at her, shock on her canine face just before she vanished. Shelby felt her body spring to life outside herself, shifting, but it felt even farther away than before. Eira rolled over Kale, the bolt lodging in Shelby's side, but she felt almost nothing.

Ptyas pounced on the bond, tearing into it with teeth and claws.

Shelby lifted her hands, which were no longer translucent. Every inch of her body felt like ice, except a flare of heat at her center and a pulsating link to her mind. *Enough!*

Ptyas turned to face her, his jaws dripping golden light, the blood of her bond with Eira. He growled. *You are too late.* He made to bite into the bond once more.

Stop, she felt the ice grow as she said it, heat channeled into the fire inside her.

He froze inches from the glimmering stream of it, shaking with tension and snapping empty jaws on air. *What is this?*

Shelby smiled. *I am here now, this is my mind, and I can hurt you.*

She slammed her hands together, releasing all the energy inside her at once. A wave of fire flew from her pressed palms. Ptyas blew into the starry sky, pushed by air and flame. He vanished, his face a mask of confusion.

Shelby collapsed. The last time she'd used this power, she'd fallen unconscious and forgotten everything. *I must hold on this time.*

But whatever magic she'd wrought had taken a toll on Eira as well. Shelby felt herself collapse in the real world. Athena kicked Kale in the chest while he was distracted with Shelby's sudden fall and raised her scythe. Shelby looked through Eira's eyes, unable to lift a paw as death swung toward her neck. *I don't think we can win this.*

Fizz streaked in front of her, buzzing through the air and into Athena's face. Mareus's daughter swung at the wisp, but the flame creature zigged and zagged at blinding speeds, bumping into Athena's legs and chest before darting away again. "Get away from me, you pest!"

Kale stood, recovering, but moved too slow to her aid.

It isn't over, Eira screamed at her. *Take back autonomy and kick!*

Shelby did as she was told. Her skin tore and melted, legs finding the powerful middle between wolf and human. Shelby fought back the spiraling darkness that wanted to overtake her. *I am not giving up after just getting Kale back!* But the darkness closed in on her fast. Through shadows, she could see Athena pushing the wisp aside, blades spinning past it toward Shelby's neck once more.

Shelby's vision went black, but she rolled into a ball on her back. Her legs came up as powerful muscles coiled. She kicked.

The force of it crumpled armor and shattered bone on both sides. A magical zapping sound came to Shelby's ears, followed by the music of metal colliding with demon bones and solid rock. A palm slapped against stone, and thick walls ground together with thunderous vibrations that set Shelby's teeth rattling.

Grant dropped into the bed and fell asleep immediately, but his dreams came feverish and chaotic. Dragons poured through a portal, spilling fire across the sky. Blood poured from a golden chalice into a fountain, a fountain he'd seen before.

His heart beat fast in his chest, rhythmic, thumping hard as the water of the fountain changed from clear to red. The thumping grew insistent, and a part of Grant realized it wasn't his heart.

He opened his eyes and found he still clutched the book to his chest. The cover pulsed softly against his sternum.

"Now what?" Grant sat up, leaning against a cinder block wall. "I haven't slept in days, book. I need rest if I'm to save what remains of the Hunters."

But he opened the book, flipping past pages and pages, guided by something, to land on a diagram of the fountain. It was the same fountain Grant had drunk from when he'd taken the vows to become a Hunter. He read the first paragraph.

Once the Fae key has been unlocked, if we hope to defeat the Advent and prevent annihilation once more, the true ceremony of blood and fire must be completed. The Hunters must be prepared.

"Haven't I already done that?" Jack had cut himself, dripping blood into the water before handing the recruits a golden cup. They had all dipped, drunk, and spoke an oath binding themselves to the order.

The ritual performed for initiates is a shadow of the true rite. Speak the words. Open the floodgates.

Grant remembered the change that had come upon him when he tasted the water of the fountain and spoke the words that made him one with the other Hunters. He had felt powerful, more awake, quicker. He was certain the reason the Hunters could stand against the Lycans and other magical creatures was because they were made more by the ceremony.

"What's in the fountain?"

The next paragraph simply detailed the dimensions of the fountain and talked about the type of stone used in its creation.

"Where is this fountain?"

More paragraphs about the carvings. He closed his eyes and flipped pages, waiting for the guidance he'd been feeling, but it did not come. He opened his eyes to a diagram of a Lycan, highlighting the weak points of their physiology. He slammed the cover.

That's what I get for thinking a book is having a conversation with me. This isn't Harry Potter. He swung his legs off the bed. But he knew the book was trying to get him to do something, even if it didn't exactly talk. *I have no idea where the fountain is.*

That wasn't quite true. He'd been blindfolded throughout the flight there and as they returned, but his senses were keener on the return. He'd smelled fresh snow, pine, and stone. He'd heard the fluttering of aspen leaves. He'd experienced the same thing years later on a ski trip to Colorado. "Guess we're heading to Colorado. I need to call Bryanne again and ask around if anyone knows where the fountain is exactly." He glanced around the sparse room. "And stop talking to myself so much."

Athena slid into a pillar, knocking what breath she had left out of her shattered chest. She tried to stand and collapsed, the healing taking longer than it should thanks to the Wiccan magic she'd passed through. That half of a second had felt like she'd been thrown into an electrical storm wearing a suit studded with silver lightning rods. *I'll kill that somersaulting banshee.*

She's more powerful than she looks, Ptyas said.

Please don't praise the witch who almost killed us.

Sorry. Something else is slowing down your healing too though. Can't you feel it?

Athena could. She reached around and pulled a sharp obsidian bone out of her back. The wound didn't close right away, leaking blood out onto the ashy stone until the armor repaired itself. *Demons suck, even when they're dead.*

You have no idea. Some explode when they die.

Athena punched the ground, cracking stone and breaking a knuckle. *I was winning!* She rolled onto her side and stared at the demon bones embedded in the wall, her armor providing enough illumination to see through partially shifted eyes. *We could wait them out and try again.*

Don't even think about it, Ptyas scolded. *You're not healing, and they're regrouping. You had the advantage for a minute when you caught them by surprise, but we'll be outnumbered and outmatched when that door opens again.*

She knew he was right and hated him for it. She couldn't help but pout. *I'm better than they are.*

No doubt, Ptyas agreed. *You did things I wasn't even aware you could do with your armor and your new toys. It was impressive, but staying would be stupid and suicidal. You aren't either . . . at least not simultaneously.*

She coughed a laugh as she pulled another piece of demon glass out of her thigh. Blood oozed out before the armor sealed the wound. *Still feel more.* She banished the armor and ran shaking hands along her skin until she found every shard and pried them from her flesh with frozen fingers.

Athena shivered uncontrollably as her armor reappeared. It warmed slowly as she sucked down filtered air in gulps. Each breath burned. At least one lung had been punctured by her own ribs, if not by a demon rib too. *Yeah, you win. I can't fight anyone like this, not even the voice in my head.*

Wasn't trying to win anything, so much as keep us both alive a little longer, but I'll take it. I expect a trophy.

Athena shifted into a wolf and limped her way out of the caverns and down the mountain. *How about a Scooby snack when we get back to Earth?*

Even better.

Do you ever get pissed off?

Were you trying to anger me?

Athena only grunted as she made her way toward the portal.

Shelby flopped onto her side as the door closed, fully shifting into her human form. "That was too close."

Chelsea came to her aid. "Yeah it was. You look like my gran's pin cushion on sewing Sundays." The Wiccan tapped the arrow shaft attached to Shelby's wrist.

Shelby winced as the vibrations ran through the metal and into her bones. "If you're going to hurt me, you may as well pull them out." She glanced over at Kale, feeling his relief at her safety as Theo leaned over him. "How does he look?"

"About the same as you, pin-cushiony with a side of cut up." He whispered something to his wisp, and Fizz began hovering over Kale. "No one can get through that wall while you both heal though."

Shelby gritted her teeth and had to close her eyes as Chelsea ripped an arrow out. "Some help would have been nice. Might have had fewer pins in my cushion."

Chelsea put her feet against Shelby's back as she yanked on an arrow that had lodged itself in a rib. "You be nice to the elf. He moved arrows away from you the whole fight. At least ten." She pulled the arrow free and toppled backward, landing hard. "Ouch."

Shelby swallowed her scream. "*So* sorry to hurt you."

"Oh, I'm okay." Chelsea brushed herself off.

Theo took a mound of metal from Fizz, the leftover of an arrow the wisp had removed. He tossed it into the pool. "She's as bad at reading sarcasm as most Fae. It was nine. I tried to help more, but she kept redirecting the arrows even after I'd shifted them away. Entropy magic as powerful as my own. I'm sorry I couldn't do more."

Shelby bit back a swear as Chelsea failed to pull an arrow from her thigh. "No, I apologize for assuming you just sat by and watched. You saved our lives with the door."

"A good DJ knows when to shut down a party." He smiled, but there was a hollowness in him she felt in her broken bones.

She knew the feeling well. "I'm so sorry about your mother. I lost mine too, years ago, but it still hurts."

Kale coughed and rolled her way. "And my father. But we're still here."

The hollowness inched further away. "That's my Alpha. Ow, ow, ow!" Chelsea tugged on a shaft that broke, leaving the arrowhead inside. "Maybe I'll let Fizz finish up, Chelsea," Shelby said as she winced.

"Okay." She threw the shaft into the pool. "Eat up, guys."

"And nice work on that net thing. It sounded painful as Athena went through it."

Chelsea laughed. "Oh, it would have been like being shot by arrows made of lightning. Not a barrier someone can typically go through, but someone kicks harder than most."

Kale sat up, Fizz done removing all the arrows and speeding his healing. "Good. Serves her right."

Shelby let Fizz buzz around her, the arrows dissolving out of her wounds. *Way better than Chelsea's approach.* "Thank you, sweet Fizz." Shelby slapped a hand over her mouth. "I'm not supposed to thank a

Fae."

Theo took another lump of metal from his wisp. "Fizz is not a Fae, and the more civilized of us have come to understand that the occasional thank you is heartfelt. We'll ask no proof of your gratitude."

Kale stood and stretched, his armor and his body whole once more. "Definitely grateful. We were not at our best." He stared at the door, rippling with light from the living fire. "Especially me. I'm so sorry, Kale." Shelby rubbed at her shoulder where the last bit of metal crawled out to Fizz.

He shrugged and flashed a smile that melted her insides. Helped that she could feel his forgiveness. "Not gonna say I had her . . . but I totally had her." His grin transformed into a frown. "She *was* at her best though."

Shelby couldn't help but agree. "She has the Fae key. I thought we'd beaten her to one this time."

"And she used it like she'd been handling Fae magic all her life," Theo said.

"We'll beat her to the next one, and the one after that." Kale held out his hand, the gauntlet melting away. "Together."

Shelby took it. Nearly dying yet again did not dampen the electricity of his touch. *Together.* She let him pull her close to him, their breath mingling in the chill air of Alvoira, though warmer and thicker inside the room with the flames. Her helm folded into the back of her breastplate and she kissed him hard.

Nothing could take away the magic of being rebonded.

"You may kiss the bride," Chelsea mumbled.

Shelby remembered she and Kale weren't alone. "What was that?"

Chelsea shrugged. "Means you two might really be married is all." She jerked a thumb over her shoulder toward the door. "That creeper was hiding while the light show happened."

Kale let go of Shelby slowly. "I don't understand the connection."

"Three witnesses," Theo nodded at the realization.

"Grant is gonna kill me," Shelby said.

Kale coughed. "You? I think I'll be the focus of his murderous intent."

Shelby sighed in mock relief. "You are totally right. Good luck with that."

She created a crossbow on her vambrace and willed her scythe into her other hand. She'd experimented for a few minutes with her new weapon, trying to push the boundaries. Seems she could only make bows, long, short, and cross. She'd been hoping for a magical bazooka, but the Fae magic had chosen its theme.

Kale drew back on his bow next to her. Chelsea pulled out her knives, extending them into miniature swords that glowed silver. Theo created a one-way illusion that the door was still closed. Even Fizz seemed to square itself up and prepare for battle.

I hope we're ready.

You are, Eira replied. *She surprised you last time. A second battle will not go her way so easily this time.*

I dig your confidence.

Eira smiled. *You have proven yourself worthy of my faith in you many times over. And you'll get better with the keys. The shield was new.*

Now you're just trying to pep me up, Shelby argued. *The shield barely helped and wasn't nearly as impressive as Athena's mastery of entropy magic or the bows. I wouldn't have even guessed I could make mine into mini-crossbows, if*

I hadn't seen her do it.

Amber eyes locked on her in her head and narrowed. *You are too hard on yourself.*

Maybe. Shelby nodded to Kale her preparedness.

"Go," Kale said, directing the Fae to open the doorway.

Theo slapped a hand on the wall. Stone ground against stone as it slid open.

Shelby tensed, pulling the string of her bow taut. Her eyes burned as she flared them amber to see into the darkness beyond for any hint of movement.

There was none, but Shelby knew that could easily be a trap.

Kale held up a fist. They waited. Still nothing happened.

Kale took several steps into the chamber of demon bones, his bow and notched arrow whipping from side to side as he scanned the room. "You feel anything?"

Shelby did not. "No, but Athena tends to block me out."

Chelsea muttered something at her side, fingers tracing designs in the air. A flash of light came from between her palms a moment later.

Kale and Shelby growled simultaneously as the sudden light blinded them and their sensitive wolf eyes.

"Warn us next time, Chels," Shelby snarled.

"Sorry, some of us can't see in the dark." The Wiccan wove her fingers in the air faster, and the light dimmed, pulsing. "Looks like your angry friend with the horns left though. Look." She pointed toward a pool of blood, her magic surrounding it with a gold outline. Flashes of golden light appeared farther into the tunnel, surrounding more droplets of blood and a bloody handprint on a pillar. "She went that way."

As Chelsea walked forward, her magic highlighted other

disturbances. Footprints in the ash, demon bones out of their piles, and more drops of blood all received golden outlines.

Kale bent down and touched a drop of blood. It cracked and shattered. "Ice. Looks like she didn't stick around long."

Shelby dipped her bow and relaxed the string. "She got what she needed, took advantage of our failure to notice her, and then retreated when her advantage was lost. She's getting smarter and wiser. I don't like it."

Kale absorbed his own bow back into his armor. "Me either. I was half-hoping she'd be stubborn enough to be waiting to be outnumbered when the door opened."

Shelby laughed, the bitter sound echoing down tunnels in all directions. "That's not our luck."

"I suppose not." Kale kicked at another drop of frozen blood. It slid across stone and shattered against a demon skull.

They picked their way out of Alvoira's Underhill slowly and on high alert, just in case Athena had doubled back or decided to try another ambush. They crossed the spells that kept the ash out without incident or any sign of Athena's departure.

It wasn't until they came to the base of the mountain that they found more evidence of the Lycan woman's retreat.

Kale picked up the sliver of obsidian. "How hard did you kick her to shatter demon bone?"

Shelby grinned. "Hard." She leaned over where ash and sand had been painted red with the blood of her foe. "The only rain Alsvoira has seen in a long time. Too bad nothing will grow. It would frustrate Athena so much to know she'd brought life to this world with her defeat."

Kale dropped the sharp piece of demon glass. "You could plant some of your Druid wheat."

Shelby opened her mouth and closed it. Stalks of wheat appeared in her hand. She studied them, eyeing the tufts of roots at their base. "Genius."

Kale cocked his head to the side. "I was kidding. There are still demons right over there." He gestured off to where the smoke billowed darker.

"I know." Shelby leaned forward and kissed him, their helms bumping awkwardly into one another. "That doesn't mean it isn't worth a shot. The demons are leaving it behind for our world anyway."

"That's not exactly better, love."

"Wait." Theo held out a hand. The dirt vibrated, blood mingling with sand that grew darker as minerals made their way to the surface from deep below. It also grew warmer near the plot, the air thicker and more humid. "That should help."

Shelby knelt down and held the stalks close to her mouth. "Grow, little friends," she whispered to the wheat. She dragged her free hand through the soil and pushed the stalks into the hole. "Make Alsvoira beautiful again."

"They'll need rain," Chelsea said. The Wiccan moved her fingers over the stalks, chanting to herself. A tiny cloud formed over the new garden. Drops of water fell as miniature lightning forked through the petite storm.

"Clever." Theo put his hands on opposite sides of the mini rain cloud. A shell formed around Chelsea's spell. The shell spiraled inward, collapsing the rain into nothing.

Chelsea pouted, crossing her arms. "Why would you do that?"

Theo frowned. "It's not gone. I just set a timer spell to recreate your magic every day for two minutes." He tapped the air where the storm had been. "See."

Chelsea's rain cloud grew from the spot and began raining again.

The Wiccan girl smiled. "That's so cool."

Shelby created new stalks and planted them, filling the space beneath the cloud. "It isn't much, and chances they survive are slim. Demons might find it and eat the magic tomorrow, but with a lot of luck, and a few hundred years, Alsvoira might just look like a planet worth visiting."

"Where's Chenoa when you need her?" Kale said.

Shelby looked up at him, still kneeling before her plants. "What? Why?"

Kale smiled down at her, his love bright as it burned its way across the bond. "She would have had some poignant bit of prophecy to quote about the Summer Omega reshaping worlds with blood and ash."

Shelby laughed. "No way would she paint it in a positive light though." But the thought of the old Lycan made Shelby miss her pack. She couldn't feel them since coming through the portal. "Let's go home. We have another key to find and a war to win." She pointed a finger at Theo and then Chelsea. "Not a word about the possibility of a Fae marriage to anyone, especially my dad."

Athena glowered at the desolation of Alsvoira as she limped toward the portal and the promise of warm, fresh air on the far side. *Your world sucks more than a little, Ptyas.*

I'm not arguing with you.

At least we're done with it. Goodbye, Alsvoira. I will not miss you. She speeded up, bracing herself for the numbing sensation of the portal, and bounced off it like a ping-pong thrown against a brick wall.

Athena landed on her back with a jolt and slid across sand and ash. She shifted from her wolf and stared up at the gray clouds, blinking at the ashfall. "What in the hells was that, Ptyas?"

My guess, the Fae spells that keep demons from easily using the portals.

Athena growled as she sat up. "I'm not a demon!"

Try it again, slower maybe? Let it see who and what you are.

Athena stood and made her way to the gate once more, glaring at her skid marks in the sand. She stood before the portal and held out a hand like she would to a dog. "I'm Lycan, stupid gate. Let me through."

She put her hand against the rippling surface of light. The tips of her fingers broke the surface, so she stepped closer, but her momentum stopped just millimeters into the portal. It felt like a wall of glass or ice. *What the?* She punched the rift, cracking armor and bones that healed just in time for a second punch. She then dug in her heels and pushed as hard as she could. The glass-like wall beyond the portal's edge flexed. A finger popped through. Fire tore through the digit.

Athena yelped, pulling her hand back. Her index finger was shredded to the bone, nearly eviscerated. It healed in front of her eyes—bones, tendons, muscle, skin, nail, and then armor. "That hurt." She could almost feel Ptyas's disappointment and disapproval. *Don't just sigh at me, you passive aggressive cricket. Spit it out. What is this?*

Keanie Meanie's last laugh, Ptyas replied. *You also know that makes you Pinocchio in this scenario, right?*

I'm tired, hurt, hungry, thirsty, angry, and not at my best. I also thought we agreed that nickname was juvenile. Athena leaned against the portal as what he'd said clicked within her fatigued mind. *You're saying she told the gate I was a demon?* She swore. *Probably used my blood from our fight to do it. And you think it serves me right for how I treated her, don't you?*

He nodded inside her. *Pretty much.*

That's fair. Keanierah of the Cereus family is one stone cold . . . flower. She sagged against the barrier.

Now you remember her name. Do we wait for the friends you just failed to kill to rescue you?

Ice ran up Athena's spine, and she straightened it. *Never. It means we find another demon gate, hopefully one without much traffic.*

Athena sprinted in the body of her Immortal Wolf over Alsvoira's decimated landscape, putting distance between her and the locked gate near Mount Estorathi. Her helm filtered the toxic air, but it still tasted acrid and sour. Ash and sand seemed to fill her mouth even as she resisted opening it.

She had failed. She had Shelby and Kale, *had them,* and she had failed. Then she had failed to return home. *So much failure in such a short time.*

But you succeeded in unlocking the third key of Ascension, Ptyas said.

She wasn't in the mood for his pitiable attempts to cheer her up. The wound on her back from the demon bone would heal faster in her wolf, but holy hell did it hurt as lupine muscles stretched and tore it open over and over. Still, the pain gave her something to focus her anger on.

The ground she ran over had an alien feel, a thin soft layer of a sandy-ash sediment with barren bedrock beneath. The world was truly dead, her father's doing, supposedly. His retribution could be terrible. She'd witnessed it firsthand. She shuddered.

What good does one more key do me here? Or anyone? How long can my helm's filter keep up with this rotten air?

Ptyas did not reply to her rhetorical questions, for which she was grateful, though she did not voice her gratitude.

She ran aimless at first, but a line of smoke in the distance drew her attention. *Demons, most likely, but that means escape . . . or a quick death. I'll take one or the other over slowly freezing, starving, and/or suffocating.*

That's the spirit! Yes, let's run toward the mountain on fire. Perfectly reasonable.

Athena saw he was correct. Liquid fire spilled from a peak some miles off. The mountain chuffed black smoke into the air, seeming to feed the thickening clouds above. The sun, a red one, of course, dipped below the horizon to her right. That meant she was running south. *If this place has a south. Might have a second sunrise right in front of me to prove me wrong out of spite.*

Above the mountain, flecks of fire danced in the billowing smoke, igniting for several seconds before winking out. Something within Ptyas stirred, making Athena slow her sprint. She ached in different places as her muscles ceased tearing open the wound.

What is it?

Reminded me of something that can't be, Ptyas said. *I don't like the sight of it.*

Yeah, it's a volcano. At least it's not spewing fire a mile in the sky. She could just make out individual orange rivulets of lava crawling down the sides.

Not the mountain. What's above it.

More flares of fire danced in the smoke. She had taken them to be fiery debris and embers, but that didn't fit the way they moved. No, they streaked through the smoke, leaving thin moats in their wake. Athena's heart jumped with disbelief. She leaped into a furious sprint toward the mountain, ignoring the pain completely.

Ptyas roared within her. *Athena, don't!*

She ignored him, pounding the barren ground with her large paws. After only a couple minutes, she had drawn to within a quarter mile, her muscles fueled by adrenaline and unbridled excitement. Dozens of *things* flew above the volcano, darting back and forth.

Are those what I think they are? Are they . . . dragons?

Ptyas sighed heavily within her. *Drakes, yes.*

I don't believe it! I thought Alsvoira was abandoned.

By anything sane, yes.

As Athena stared in amazement, what she saw came into full focus. *It's a battle, a battle of dragons!* Clearly, there were two divisions of the drakes going at it in an aerial skirmish of fire and fangs. A drake fell from the sky, engulfed in a ball of flames. It slammed into a stream of lava. Splashes of glowing red shot into the sky as the drake plunged beneath molten earth and stone. Athena ran toward where the fallen creature had disappeared, the ground growing uncomfortably warm beneath her paws.

Dead? Is it dead? she asked.

In answer, a form rose from the lava. Liquid fire dripped down the hardened bare chest and rippled abs of the sexiest body she had ever seen. Simmering steam ascended from the drake's square shoulders as dragon wings melted into his back. On the left side of his chest was a tattoo of a serpent wrapped in flame, and Athena immediately recognized the symbol from the *Isluxua*. Black hair framed a beautiful, lantern-jawed face. The eyes pierced her, smoldering with pale icy blue. The calf-deep lava he stood in seemed to not be a bother at all to him.

Athena's mouth went dry. She shifted, keeping her armor donned, Fae bow at the ready with a silver arrow nocked.

The godlike drake man cocked his head to the side, giving her a curious look. "You're new, aren't you?"

The sound of his voice made her lick her lips. *Five rivers!* His words sounded like silky fire, and the look in his eyes made her feel like prey. She decided she would allow him to hunt her. "You could say that."

"And who are you, then?" he asked.

"Athena. Your turn."

"Caden."

Another dragon swooped low, spewing fire. Chunks of igneous rock shot outward like shrapnel from a grenade as the pillar of fire hit the ground, trailing directly for them. Caden leaped on Athena, wrapping her in a cocoon of dragon wings just before the fire reached them. Athena closed her eyes. The heat came, but Caden's wings protected her from the brunt of the attack. As she opened her eyes tentatively, she stared into Caden's icy eyes only inches from hers as his bare chest rested against her armor.

"Does it hurt?" she asked.

"The fire? Yeah, but I've always kinda liked a bit of pain."

She didn't know how to respond to that, playfully biting her lower lip.

"Hey, I've got one question for you," Caden said. "You any good with that Fae bow of yours, or is it just for show?"

Athena felt the wicked grin split her face. *Oh, this is going to be fun.* "Nothing about me is just for show."

Shelby emerged from the gate to all but complete darkness, the flickering portal the only light. She shifted her eyes and released her helm, scanning the cavern for signs of life, ally or foe. A spear leaned against one wall. A handful of arrows dotted the floor. *Where are the guards?*

Shelby turned back to the gate. *And where's Kale? He was right behind me.* Minutes passed. The bond did not appear to work across dimensions, even though it remained intact, so she paced the small cave, her feelings alternating from concern to anger. When he finally stepped through, she ran forward and took his hand. His caution and tension mingled with her fear and relief.

She punched him in the chest with her other hand. "Took you long enough! I thought something happened to you. Not funny!"

He blinked at her, his own eyes shifting to see better in the dim room. "What are you talking about? It's been like five seconds."

Shelby's fear grew. "No, it's been like fifteen minutes, at least."

He shook his head. "What? No."

"Please tell me you're pranking me." Shelby took a step back, still holding his hand, to look at him fully. The bond told her he wasn't lying or joking with her. "You aren't, are you? That's bad."

"It's not really the time for pranks." Kale glanced over his shoulder. "Chelsea was right behind me. I should move."

Shelby leaned into him. "I think she's going to be awhile."

Chelsea appeared about nine minutes after Kale, and Theo emerged a good twenty minutes after her. He took one look at his traveling companions standing across from him with arms folded. "Something's wrong, isn't it?"

Kale nodded. "You could say that. It took us way longer to get through than we expected, and the guards are missing."

"Not to mention there's no flipping door," Chelsea added.

Fizz bumped into the back of Theo. The wisp buzzed up and added more light to the room, revealing the smooth stone wall where the door had been.

Theo rubbed at the back of his neck. "That's not a huge problem. I can get us out. It is a bad sign though. Means Underhill fragmented."

"What?" Chelsea asked.

"Underhill is mostly under Beverly Hills, but it also includes caverns from other parts of the world, including the demon gates." Theo stepped into the room. "You didn't think the demons just kept opening portals into Fae territory? We absorbed them into Underhill."

"Makes sense." Chelsea nodded. "Doesn't explain why they're all underground though. And what about the weird time dilation thing?"

Shelby and Kale stared at her.

"What? I took physics."

For all they had been through, Chelsea still had that valley girl attitude. Theo smiled and then frowned. "The reason they always show up in caves is easy enough. Alsvoira is smaller and denser than Earth." He rubbed the back of his neck again. "How long did it take everyone to come through?"

Shelby closed her eyes. "About ten to twenty minutes per person."

"What?" Theo turned back to the demon gate. "There's always been a slight time difference between worlds, but it was seconds per hour. Nothing you would notice. Nothing like this. We need to get back to Underhill. Now."

Shelby had been soothing the concern in her pack since they arrived and reconnected, but she and Kale had decided not to contact them until they knew they could get out of the sealed cavern. The link also felt weird, not synced up quite right. She nodded to her Alpha.

We are back. We have the key. We are coming. Kale used his Alpha voice to send the message.

It felt like a command to Shelby. Everything in that voice did. Relief rippled through the pack, but that relief felt far away. She spoke to Kale through their bond. *They've been really worried about us.*

Kale met her eyes. *If it took us minutes to get through, then it's been days for them. Days without the pack link. Days where they thought we might be dead. Do what you can to reassure them.*

Already on it.

Theo turned and raised his hands. A new, more stable portal appeared on the wall where the door had been.

Shelby stepped through, happy to feel Kale's hand in hers as he followed. Chelsea and Theo arrived seconds after each other. The relief didn't last long. Underhill was empty, dark, and dead. Theo led them down a winding path, their footsteps echoing.

Shelby felt the tension in Kale spike, his caution increase. Though she agreed the situation called for caution, she still sent forth reassurance through her bond. She kept her scythe at the ready, his presence a reassurance to her.

Theo pushed open the doors into the Unseely Court throne room, but it felt like a tomb. Fizz blazed brighter, revealing discarded possessions, stains of dried orange blood, and decaying demon bodies. It smelled of sulfur and rotten fruit.

"Where is everyone?" Shelby asked, her helm reappearing so she could breathe through the filter.

Theo didn't answer, he just walked slowly into the room, aimlessly. Fizz hovered over him, highlighting the disarray. Unseely Court had the distinct feeling of being abandoned, not just unoccupied.

Shelby dropped Kale's hand and went to Theo, taking his. She poured comfort into him. "Are you okay?"

He shook his head. "Where's the king? Where's my father?"

"I'm sorry, he's copulating dead." A familiar voice came from the far side of the room. "Thought I heard something in here. Thought I'd get to kill another demon, but I'm just as happy it's you all."

"Sadie!" Shelby forgot Theo and all her fear. She ran across the room and tackled the fiery redhead, hugging her and barely resisting a wolfish instinct to lick her face. "I've missed you."

"I can tell. Feculence, you're gonna break my ribs, Shelbs! What ya been eating?"

Shelby loosened her grip. "Demon blood." She laughed at Sadie's expression of disgust. "Not really."

"Good, that stuff is nasty." Sadie sat up. "Come on, everyone's waiting for you in the other throne room. Seely Court is no more. Actually, both courts are no more, but we liked the layout over there better."

Sadie guided them through a small conference room and into Seely Court. They stood on a dais of sorts next to the crystalline throne, staring out over a room brightly lit with wisps where hundreds of Lycans, Feral, Fae, and humans stood, lounged in chairs, sat on cots, and mingled in small groups. Gennesaret. Chenoa. Paul and Sophie. Shelby could smell a few Druids in the mix too. Her connection to the pack grew as she looked out on the crowd, her soul connecting and reconnecting with each one, and she still felt a void where Dakota had once been. If she were honest, she felt a void in her heart where each of her fallen packmates had once lived as their Omega. Oddly, she could even sense Bubba, Amanda, Bryanne, and many more non-Lycans as part of the pack. *How is that possible?*

She felt Kale's surprise too as he reconnected fully to his larger misfit pack. "So many." But he accepted the growth of his pack gracefully, standing stern and commanding, so much more than Elias ever had. That wasn't fair, of course. Elias had not had an Immortal Wolf. As if hearing her thoughts, Kale said through their bond, *The reason I stand tall is because I stand on his shoulders.*

Shelby nodded. *I know, and I love you for it.*

Sadie waved at the open doors at the far side. "There's more in the surrounding corridors. We're glad to have ya back, boss. Many mouths to feed and a lot to do. The cussing Fae weren't completely sold you'd bring their king back alive and well, but we promised them he was in the best company." Sadie cupped her mouth in her hands and shouted over the din. "Heya, fairies, I copulating told ya so!" She looked at Shelby. "They all owe me favors now. Small bet we had going."

Everyone stood and turned to face them. Several people ran out the back door to tell others of their arrival as a murmur rippled through the throng.

The Fae in the crowd bowed toward Theo.

Theo took a step back. "Whoa. I'm no king. I'm a freaking DJ."

Shelby soothed his fears and bolstered his confidence, dissolving her gauntlet to place a hand on his arm. "You're the son of both courts. You won't do it alone. We're here to help."

Theo looked at her and then Kale. Something clicked behind his eyes. He bowed toward them.

Shelby almost fell over as he and the rest of the Fae linked with her, connecting to her Omega powers in the strange, intimate way she still hadn't become accustomed to. Kale staggered next to her too as hundreds of Fae joined the pack. *His* pack.

The races of the Goddess are binding together under the Alpha Prime of Alsvoira, as they once did, Eira said within Shelby. *I pray we are not too late to resist the Advent.*

Isn't this the Advent? Shelby asked. *The union of the five races?*

No, Thyra. The Advent is not a prophecy that belongs to the Lycans, or any of the five races, but to the Goddess's brother, Tarloch.

Shelby felt bits of understanding begin to meld together in her mind. She again took in the sight of the expanded pack. "Sadie, you did all this?"

"What?" Sadie chuckled. "Did you think I was copulating sitting on my glutei like a flaming sack of feculence for the six weeks you were running around Alsvoira? Thanks for the invite, by the way. I didn't need to see another world or anything. I'm fine. *So* fine."

Shelby shrugged. "Sorry, I would have liked you there." She paused and stared hard at Sadie. "Wait? Did you say *six weeks?*"

EPILOGUE

Kale had told the pack they would stay in Seely Court that night since the pack had taken up residence there. Some of the Fae didn't love the intrusion of outsiders in their ranks. Shelby heard their mutters that their royal court had been turned into a dog pound, but she'd laughed. Kale, however, could not let resentment spread among such a mixed pack.

I prefer Lycan lair to dog pound, Kale had said, sending his words through the pack link. Though Shelby knew his words were playful, his tone was not, and all felt the command of their Alpha. The mutterings stopped after that.

Much had happened over the past six weeks, and Shelby did her best to pay attention as Gennesaret, Sadie, Chenoa, and Bryanne caught them up on recent history, but weariness pulled at her. Kale told the pack that tomorrow they would begin planning to take the fight to Mareus as well as the demons slicing up the world above. Underhill was at least safe for the time being, but being reactive to the Advent pack's advances apparently was at an end. But for now, Shelby wanted nothing more than to sleep.

She had been granted a room of her own as the pack's Omega. Naturally, that made her uncomfortable, as any special treatment always had, but the pack—even Sadie—had insisted. At least the Seely Court had hot showers. She felt Kale falling asleep in another room. He thought it would be good to sleep in the presence of the rest of the pack. Probably some macho Alpha thing she didn't completely understand . . . but she did, really. As much as she as the Omega could bring completeness to a pack, an Alpha gave confidence and direction, and they had lived without his focusing effect too long. He was right to be among them.

Good night, Wife, he said through the bond as she slipped into cool sheets. The Fae really knew how to live in comfort. The thread count on these sheets had to be like a thousand.

I thought I said to stop saying that.

You did. But I won't.

Shelby smiled into her pillow. *Okay then,* Husband, *good night.*

She slept fitfully, dreams assaulting her harrowed mind, dreams of losing those she loved.

"Dad?" she said in her dream. She saw him holding a sword, heard the flutter of large wings. That was odd. Shouldn't he have an M4 carbine rifle? Then, fire engulfed him, turning him to a pillar of cinders.

"No!" Shelby cried. "No! No!" Tears stung her eyes as she wailed. "Dad!" But she couldn't reach him, couldn't save him. Something held her back. A breeze took up the ashes of her father, cruelly ferrying them from her. And then she was there, no longer held back, trying to capture the embers of his body, futilely reaching for them as the wind intensified. She raged, swiping, clawing at the air. Then, another force restrained her, holding her down.

"Shelby."

A single ember landed on her tear stained cheek, burning through skin. She caught fire, screaming.

"Shelby!"

She thrashed, rolling to extinguish the flames but something held her down as the fire sunk deeper into her. She kicked and clawed, arched her back, and howled in abject pain.

She woke, Kale above her with a gash healing on his cheek, holding her down on torn sheets. Her heart raced. It was far into the night, and her fingers had claws sprouting from their tips. She had partial-shifted.

"Shhh," Kale whispered. "You're okay. I'm here." He slowly let go of her arms, his palms toward her in a placating gesture. "It's okay. It was just a dream. A really horrifying dream."

Shelby wiped at a tear. "It was my dad. There was fire and a sword and I think . . . I think something terrible is going to happen."

"I know. I saw it too."

"You did?"

"Bonded, remember? You sent your dream to me."

"That's kind of terrible. I'm sorry."

"And really rude."

"I said I'm sorry."

She felt Kale's mind working. He laid down beside her. "Nothing's going to happen. I promise."

She smiled a sad smile, turning on her side to face him and cupping his cheek with her hand. "You can't promise that."

"I do anyway. You might want to reassure the pack. You were projecting quite a bit. The Fae are twitching."

"Twitching?"

"Theo's pacing outside the door, Chelsea woke up weaving a spell that set a Feral's tail on fire—Sean put it out, don't worry—and Sadie's scratching like she has fleas."

"Oh. Does she?"

He gave her a look.

"What?" Shelby asked with mock innocence. "She was practically a Feral for a while."

His look turned sterner.

"Fine." Shelby calmed the pack, and she saw Kale deflate a bit.

"Thanks," he said. "They love you. All of them."

"Even the finnicky Fae?"

"It's an acquired kind of love."

Shelby punched his arm. "Are you saying I'm an acquired taste?"

Kale just smiled the goofy grin that still melted her.

"And you?" she asked. "Do you love me?"

"Do I have to say it for you to know it?"

The bond thrummed with his love for her. "You don't," she whispered.

"I'll stay with you until you fall asleep," Kale said.

Yeah, like she was going to be able to sleep with his dreamy voice echoing in her head.

"Kale?"

"Yeah, Shel?"

She bit her lip. "I don't want to sleep." She stared into those emerald eyes that had captured her from the first time she saw him and made her his.

He pushed a lock of her blonde-streaked hair behind her ear, then ran a finger over her lips. "Are you sure?"

"We're married, aren't we?"

"In a Fae ceremony on an abandoned world six weeks ago. Or

yesterday. Man, that's going to play havoc with anniversaries. Think it counts?"

In response, Shelby took his hand, kissed his palm, then his lips. Tenderly at first, but then hungrily.

Kale pulled back. "Hey, make sure you're—"

"I'm not projecting . . . to the pack, at least." She hit Kale with a powerful projection of her desire, of her wants. He pulled off his shirt, and Shelby's mouth went dry. He put his strong hand behind her neck, pulling her closer. She lifted her bare leg and wrapped it around his waist, pulling his pelvis to hers and digging into his chest with her nails. She found his lips again, those full lips that tasted of him. Her mate. Her Alpha. *My love.* She growled in pleasure as he deepened the kiss, and he ran his hand along her leg, sending electricity through her. Good thing she had shaved while showering. That could have been embarrassing.

But then his hand didn't stop. Slowly, it moved up the back of her thigh to the edge of her underwear. Through the bond, she felt Kale's burning desire for her but also his question, his hesitancy. And she loved him for it.

"Yes," she said, nodding. "I want you to." She traced her fingers down his chest, over his rippled abs, and then lower.

After their lovemaking, Shelby lay on her side, her back cuddled into Kale's hard body with his arm around her. His breathing came with the steady rhythm of sleep. A warmth she had never known played within her, a tingling, comforting fire. This was what it meant to have a mate, to truly be bonded, to be at peace despite a raging hurricane approaching.

Thyra?

Shelby smiled at the sound of her wolf's voice in her mind. *Yes, Eira.*

I do not wish to interrupt, but you should know.

Know what? Shelby asked. Then, she shot up, breathing deeply through her mouth, eyes wide. Bewilderment, utterly exquisite, terrifying, joyful, bewilderment ran through her. She brought a hand to her abdomen, protectively.

Yes, Thyra, Eira said. *Grant is going to be a grandfather.*

THE END OF ADVENT
BOOK 3 OF THE SUMMER OMEGA SERIES

ABOUT THE AUTHORS

JK Cooper is a husband and wife writing team. They write paranormal romance and romantic urban fantasy. After nearly two decades of marriage and four children, they have plenty to write about. When not writing about werewolves and the end of the world, they enjoy spending time with their family, traveling, reading, making fun of social media, and outdoor power sports (and watching Glimore Girls reruns … well, K does). They live in Utah with their four daughters and two massive Akitas.

JK Cooper loves hearing from their readers! For updates, sneak
peeks, and werewolf sightings, join our newsletter! Sign up here:
https://authorjkcooper.com/newsletter
Facebook: facebook.com/authorJKCooper/
Twitter: @authorJKCooper

Want to follow some of the characters in
The Summer Omega Series on Twitter?

Shelby Brooks @SummerOmega
Sadie Chandler @redhairbites
Bubba @Bubba_Tubba

www.ingramcontent.com/pod-product-compliance
Lightning Source LLC
Chambersburg PA
CBHW030902060726
47591CB00005B/1376